W9-BDO-053

"Time is running out."

Sarie woke to Vance's sharp whisper. She realized he was speaking into a telephone a few feet away. She pretended to be asleep.

"If anybody gets their hands on those records before I do it'll look bad. I need those records, damn it, and I intend to get them, court order or not."

This last was spoken with brutal determination. Did that cold-blooded voice belong to the same man she had spent the night loving passionately?

"Don't worry about her," Vance snapped into the phone. "I plan to take care of her in my own way."

Vance slammed the receiver down, and Sarie felt the bed shift as he rose. She turned on her side, buried her face in the pillow—and let the tears come....

ABOUT THE AUTHOR

Jill Bloom was born in New York and grew up in Miami. She attended college in Boston and never left. She now lives in Cambridge, Massachusetts, wih her husband and two children—Leana, seven, and Julia, one. Her work as a stringer on a prominent Boston newspaper led her to an actual arson case, which inspired *Playing with Fire*. However, the romance, Jill is quick to point out, was inspired by her husband. He's an ex-musician, but Jill says, "he's still playing my song." Jill has written two Temptations and has plans for a second Intrigue.

PLAYING WITH FIRE

JILL BLOOM

Harlequin Books

TORONTO • NEW YORK • LONDON
AMSTERDAM • PARIS • SYDNEY • HAMBURG
STOCKHOLM • ATHENS • TOKYO • MILAN

Harlequin Intrigue edition published January 1987

ISBN 0-373-22057-X

Copyright © 1987 Jill Bloom. All rights reserved.
Philippine copyright 1987. Australian copyright 1987.
Except for use in any review, the reproduction or utilization of
this work in whole or in part in any form by any electronic,
mechanical or other means, now known or hereafter invented,
including xerography, photocopying and recording, or in any
information storage or retrieval system, is forbidden without
the permission of the publisher, Harlequin Enterprises Limited,
225 Duncan Mill Road, Don Mills, Ontario, Canada M3B 3K9, or
Harlequin Books, P.O. Box 958, North Sydney, Australia 2060.

All the characters in this book have no existence outside the
imagination of the author and have no relation whatsoever to
anyone bearing the same name or names. They are not even
distantly inspired by any individual known or unknown to the
author, and all incidents are pure invention.

The Harlequin trademark, consisting of the words,
HARLEQUIN INTRIGUE with or without the portrayal of a
Harlequin, are trademarks of Harlequin Enterprises Limited;
the portrayal of a Harlequin is registered in the
United States Patent and Trademark Office and in the
Canada Trade Mark Office.

Printed in Canada

Prologue

Sarie Appleton coughed rackingly and surveyed the site of the fire with a sinking heart. The crystal-clear spring day was shrouded by the impenetrable cloud of soot, smoke and gloom left by the blaze. Even though she had been with the Boston Fire Department for four years, Sarie could not get used to the horror the sight of a burning building created in her. The Brewery condominium building had been unoccupied, but the terror lingered and her nerves were jangled as she waited for Sergeant Garrett to make his report.

"Things seem to be under control on the leeward side, Lieutenant," Garrett said, tramping up to her through the thick layer of ashes, mud and wet cement. "How's it going over here?"

Sarie sighed. "I think we've got it licked, Tom. For now, that is."

Tom Garrett's jowly features, streaked with soot and florid with the heat, seemed to sag as he looked at the smoldering brick building. He dropped his official tone and shook his head dismally. "I don't like the looks of this, Sarie. I'll tell you that. The blaze seemed almost too perfect, know what I mean?"

"Yeah." Unfortunately, she knew exactly what he meant. The pattern was all too familiar, even though they'd had three months to forget it. "Three small explosions and a quick blaze after each one. All very controlled, and all coming from the same corner of the building. I don't like the looks of it either, Tom." They exchanged wary glances, but neither wanted to admit that they had both reached the same grim conclusion.

"Well," Sarie said after a pause, "I guess we'd better take a look down in the basement and see what we can find."

"I guess we'd better." He sounded extremely reluctant.

"Tell the men to keep back while we take a peek, will you, Tom? I don't want them hanging around in case there's another explosion."

Tom nodded and shouted an order to the rest of the crew, who retreated to the two hook and ladders parked on the narrow cobbled street. Then he and Sarie made their way gingerly over the wet debris toward the basement.

A few wisps of smoke issued up through the opened bulkhead doors, and a dense gloom waited at the bottom of the cement steps. Sarie tried to make her heart stop pounding by taking regular deep breaths, but the sooty air made it impossible to breathe without choking. Under the thick patina of smoke, there was an odd acrid tang in the air that made her eyes tear and her mouth dry with terror. With an unsettling feeling of déjà vu, she signaled to Tom to put on his breathing mask and they descended into the darkness.

"Get down." She gestured to Tom behind her, and they both dropped to a crouch. "Smell it?"

"Yeah, I smell it," Tom replied. He muttered a coarse oath that was followed by a strangled cough. "Smells like hell itself."

Hell itself was a good description of the basement, dark and full of the hiss and crackle of burnt beams and plaster. Puddles of black water lay like lakes across their path as the two fire fighters cautiously circled the perimeter of the room. Their flashlights carved weak circles of yellow light into the palpable darkness, turning everything that crossed their beams into a hulking threat.

In the southeast corner of the building most of the exterior wall had crumbled under the combined forces of heat and water. The bricks lay crushed in smoldering heaps, and the smell of charred cement was rank, even through the masks. This had obviously been the source of the explosions, and Sarie and Tom made their way toward the corner with growing dread.

In a small ell created by the partially destroyed wall, their flashlight beams picked out the building's hot-water heater, looming eerily intact out of the wholesale destruction that surrounded it. The outer casing was charred and wet, but otherwise the heater was unharmed—except for a large chunk that appeared to have been bitten out of the bottom of it by the blasts.

Sarie and Tom saw it at the same time and knelt together in the dank puddle before the tank, training their flashlights on the hole near the floor. Sarie knew that Tom was as nervous as she was—both flashlight beams quivered uncontrollably on their target, and she could hear his breath coming through the mask in labored rasps.

She realized she was holding her breath, and she made herself exhale slowly through the mask, hoping to steady her nerves. Then she reached her gloved hand beneath the heater and began to grope around in the thick muck at its base. At first she felt nothing, but then her practiced fingers found a familiar long, rectangular shape attached to the bottom of the tank.

Sarie was aware of a bitter metallic taste in her mouth. "Witch's breath," the fire fighters called it. Even a protective mask could not filter out the sour taste of fiery destruction, a taste made bitter by fear. Her hand traveled along the length of the rectangle, feeling for the long wire and the small bulb protruding from it. She looked up at Tom.

"Is it?" His voice was ragged, and she could see his Adam's apple bob nervously in the dim reflected light.

Sarie nodded. Then, shutting her eyes in order to concentrate, she gingerly removed the rectangle and wire from beneath the tank. Holding her breath again, she slowly drew the device out into the yellow circle of her flashlight. It was small and deceptively fragile looking, and it vibrated in her trembling hand.

"A Jackson device." Tom's voice was full of dread relief. "I thought as much."

Sarie closed her fingers around the device. Her voice sounded unnaturally loud to her, even though they both spoke in whispers. "You know what this means, Tom, don't you?"

Tom shrugged. "What else could it mean?"

She looked at the object in her small fist and nodded. "Yup. It's arson for sure, Tom. Again."

Chapter One

"Arson."

"It was definitely arson."

"I hear they found a Jackson device."

"Another one? Omigod!"

"I thought that mess was finally done with."

"Arson. No question about it."

Sarie sat in the small officers' cubicle in the South End station house of the Boston Fire Department and listened glumly as the news spread like a chemical fire among the squad members. They were gathered in little groups of three and four, speaking in hushed tones as if they were at a funeral. Sarie looked out through the glass partition and sighed heavily. She and Tom Garrett had not made their preliminary report to the chief yet, but it had been impossible to keep the supposedly confidential information a secret in the tight little world of the squad room. The fire fighters who had been on the scene with her had only to look at her face, pale and drawn beneath layers of soot, to guess what she and Tom had found in the basement of the burning building that afternoon.

Sarie fiddled nervously with her pen and wondered why she was unable to make herself concentrate on filling out the triplicate forms Chief Wapshaw required. Given the circumstances, she reminded herself, her reluctance was not surprising. It was bad enough that it had been arson; there had been no arson-related fires since the Roxbury ring had terrorized the department—and the entire city—three months ago. Since then, Sarie and her colleagues had managed to lull themselves into a fairly comfortable state of forgetfulness, convincing one another that, now that the perpetrators of the Roxbury fires were behind bars, the horror had passed.

Of course it had been a false sense of security, a way to control the frightening memories of all those wintry blazes so that they could go on fighting the ordinary fires that sprang up around the city every day. And now, judging from the hushed, tense buzz of conversation that filled the squad room, that sense of security had been cruelly shattered. Yes, arson was bad enough. But to have found a Jackson device—the same inflammatory agent that had been responsible for the most serious of the Roxbury fires—was the most frightening part of all. No wonder they were acting like they were at a funeral—the next arson-caused fire could be just that for any one of them.

And the worst part was that Sarie knew that if one Jackson device had been planted in the city, there would probably be others. She wasn't sure how she knew this or why she was so dismally certain of it, but all her professional and intuitive skills told her she was right. Everything about the fire in the Brewery condominiums pointed to another rush of senseless, potentially fatal arsons. And everyone in the department, with the possible exception of Chief Wapshaw, who was a notable ostrich when it came to such matters, knew it, as well.

Sarie looked down at the thick sheets of triplicate forms in front of her and fought back a surge of helpless panic. *Blast the chief and his triplicate forms anyway!* she thought, angrily slapping the pen onto the desk. *This was no time for bland formalities! This was arson, and arson required action, not paperwork!* She picked up the pen, looked at it and put it down again.

I give up. She sighed bleakly. *It's no use trying to fill out forms—no form in the world is going to help me figure out who's starting these fires!* She would simply make an oral report to the chief first and let him wait for his interminable triplicate report. Sarie got up and began to pace the eight-by-eight cubicle. The paperwork and the waiting were the parts of her job that Sarie liked the least. She would much rather have been back at the Brewery building, sifting through the debris for clues, instead of cooling her heels at the station house, waiting to explain things to Chief Wapshaw, who generally required a lot of explanation, especially from her. The tiny office felt like a prison cell and the men milling around outside the glass partition did little to dispel the image. Sarie's nerves were strung taut, and she tugged at a lock of corn-colored hair in a characteristic gesture of impatience.

She was almost relieved when the dispatcher announced that she was wanted up in the chief's office right away. At least she could do something, even if that something was potentially frustrating. She and Chief Robert Wapshaw did not get along, and she knew it was not going to be an easy session. Before she left she checked her face in the small cracked mirror that hung outside her cubicle. She had showered and changed into clean chinos and a turquoise cotton sweater, but her hair still hung in damp strands around her face and she had not bothered to put on any makeup. Her toast-brown eyes looked back at her ruefully from under their heavy fringe of lash, and she wrinkled her nose at her youthful reflection.

"Well," she muttered, wiping a smudge of ink from her chin, "my looks never convinced the old boy that I was good enough before, so why worry about them now?" She made a wry face and stuck out her tongue. "Okay, Appleton. Here goes nothing. Let's just hope he listens."

Sarie knew she was one of Chief Wapshaw's pet peeves. He had not taken well to having a female fire fighter on his force, especially one who insisted on working hard enough to get several promotions, and *especially* an Appleton. The fact that she was about to deliver some very bad news was not going to endear her to him any further, but Sarie had never bothered with that ploy anyway. After four years of fighting with him for every inch of her career, she didn't consider the chief to be one of her favorite people, either.

His office was on the third floor of the station house, a much plusher setting than the Spartan squad room. The secretary looked up and nodded toward the inner doors with pursed lips. "You're expected," she said in an ominous voice.

Pulling herself together with a visible effort, Sarie opened the door and stepped into the inner sanctum.

Chief Wapshaw was a portly man with a shock of white hair and a bulbous nose that was always redder than his florid cheeks. These he puffed out importantly at Sarie as she entered the office. He did not bother to rise. "Ah, Appleton. There you are. It's about time."

Sarie let the door slam behind her, knowing it would irritate the chief. "I was trying to fill out my triplicates," she told him curtly.

"Never mind about that." The chief waved thick fingers in the direction of the visitor's chair on the other side of his desk. "Sit down. We have to talk."

This disregard for paperwork was sufficiently unlike the chief that Sarie stared at him as she made her way to the offered chair. The chief was big on protocol, too, and protocol did not usually permit a junior-grade lieutenant to sit and chat with a department chief, regardless of the circumstances. He must be really worried, she thought as she sat down across from him.

"Now look, Appleton," Chief Wapshaw began, adjusting the glasses beneath his bushy brows, "what's all this I hear about a Jackson device? Surely there must be some mistake."

So that was it. Chief Wapshaw was worried all right, but he was more concerned about his department's image than he was about the threat of another spate of arsons. "I'm afraid not, Chief," she reported crisply. "Sergeant Garrett and I found one attached to the water heater in the basement of the Brewery building."

"Are you *sure* it was a Jackson device, Appleton?"

Sarie bristled. "Of course I'm sure! I've seen them before, if you'll recall."

"Humph. You could be mistaken," he said without much conviction.

"I am *not* mistaken." Sarie went on coldly. "It was a Jackson device, made the same way as the incendiaries that Ira Jackson set in the Roxbury buildings. I'm quite positive of that, Chief Wapshaw." Then, in a softer voice, she added, "I'm sorry, but it's true."

"But Ira Jackson is in jail!" the chief exclaimed. "He and all his associates have been behind bars for months now. How can there be a Jackson device when Ira Jackson is in jail?" He spread his big hands helplessly. "How am I going to explain this to the city?" He bleated, making it sound as if the Brewery fire was a personal affront. Sarie knew that, given the chief's concern about positive public relations, this was indeed a personal setback.

Unfortunately, the chief had a point. After having lived through it once, the residents of Boston were not going to take kindly to the fact that the horrors created by the Roxbury arson ring had not been permanently laid to rest. "I'm afraid you're going to have to tell them the truth," she said in a gentle voice.

"Oh, really?" Chief Wapshaw's tone hardened in belligerent response to being challenged. "And what is that, in your humble opinion, Lieutenant Appleton?"

Sarie resisted the urge to roll her eyes impatiently. *Why does he insist on making everything so difficult?* "In my *informed* opinion," she replied tartly, "the Brewery fire was started in the same manner as some of the worst of the Roxbury arsons. The evidence is quite clear on that count. I found the Jackson device, Chief, and I saw the way it had been set up. It was the same as before." She took a deep breath before taking the plunge. "As far as I'm concerned, we can only assume that it means someone who was involved in the Roxbury arson ring is still at large.''

"Speculation is easy," huffed the chief, looking extremely put out by this information. "But how can you know for sure?"

Sarie took a deep breath to control her temper and opened her mouth to explain it again. Before she could speak, another voice, cool and controlled, sounded in the room.

"I think your lieutenant has made a fairly plausible case, Bob."

Sarie swung around in her chair. The speaker sat on the sofa against the far wall of Chief Wapshaw's office and had been so still that Sarie had not noticed him before.

Now she could not imagine how she had missed him. He was a tall, lanky man with dark hair and piercing blue-gray eyes. He lounged languidly against the pillows of the couch, but his elegance was unmistakable. He was dressed with superb understatement in a pale gray suit and light shirt and tie, and he gave off an air that was all too familiar to Sarie. Having grown up as a member of it herself, she could tell right away from his confident complacency that he belonged to that monied, privileged class known as the Boston Brahmin. Even the voice, with its measured drawl and obvious authority, was familiar enough to grate on Sarie's ear. She stiffened. Years of working to rid herself of her Brahmin-instilled attitudes made her automatically cautious in the presence of a man who personified them. She recognized the hauteur in his cool gaze, the automatic assumption of noblesse oblige in his very pose. Besides, what was he doing in the chief's office during a supposedly private session?

The man showed no signs of recognizing Sarie's discomfort or even of intending to acknowledge her presence. After that initial glance, during which he seemed to have assessed Sarie's assets and. liabilities right down to her scruffy Reeboks, he went on talking to the chief as if she were not in the room. "After all, Bob, you've got to admit that it sounds pretty much like the Roxbury affair."

His expression was impossibly bland and unconcerned—he might have been talking about the latest social event rather than a series of brutal fires. Sarie clamped her teeth together in distaste. She had no patience for that familiar narrow, self-centered, complacent worldview.

"It was not an *affair*," she snapped, addressing Chief Wapshaw as the stranger had. "It was arson. And I don't think it was an isolated incident, either. I think there will probably be more like it in the near future."

"Really?" the man drawled, addressing her directly for the first time. "And what makes you think that?"

Sarie threw him a furious glance before turning back to the chief. She was not about to answer to this man. Her business was with her employer. Besides, departmental business was supposed to be strictly confidential.

"Chief Wapshaw, you know this is classified information. Who is this man, and what is he doing here?"

Chief Wapshaw's eyes bulged out behind his glasses. "Appleton, for God's sake!" he hissed. "Do you know who you're talking to?"

"I thought I was talking to you," she reminded him. From behind her, she heard a soft laugh, either of appreciation or contempt. She did not acknowledge it.

The chief seemed to swell with indignation. "For your information, that man is Mr. Vance Leland!"

Sarie was angry. "I don't care if it's…" She stopped as the name registered. "Vance Leland?" Her voice went up a few notes.

"That's right," Chief Wapshaw said tightly. "Vance Leland. *The* Vance Leland."

Sarie swallowed. *The* Vance Leland. Of course! How could she have not recognized that broad, high-boned face, those remarkable slate eyes? She had seen his picture often enough in the newspapers and on television. Vance Leland, member of the board of regents for the Boston Fire Department and just about every other prestigious board in the city. Vance Leland, who always seemed to be accepting awards, squiring beautiful society women and donating scads of money to worthy charities. Vance Leland, privileged scion of a privileged clan, who had used his education and wealth to build a vast real estate empire and managed to make it seem like the easiest and least offensive thing in the world to do. Which it probably was, Sarie reflected, for someone like him. She swiveled her head slowly around to face him, expecting to encounter a haughty, arrogant stare.

Instead she found herself facing a broadly inviting grin. His eyes crinkled nicely in the corners, she could not help noting, and his lips curved generously as he cocked his head slightly to one side. His expression seemed to invite Sarie to try and meet it with contempt, which she did, and failed. The most she could manage was a rather stiff nod of acknowledgment.

He was not in the least put off by Sarie's discomfort. "Well, Bob," he said, turning at last to the chief with a mild, expectant shrug. "Aren't you going to introduce us properly?"

Chief Wapshaw coughed several times to give himself time to collect his thoughts. He obviously hadn't expected to be observing the social amenities, but he rose to the occasion with creaky decorum. "Uh, Vance, this is...uh, Sarie Appleton. Lieutenant Appleton." He barely glanced at Sarie. "Appleton, this is Vance Leland." After an awkward pause he fixed his beady stare on her and added with heavy emphasis, "You know about Mr. Leland, I'm sure."

Despite all her efforts to overcome what she saw as its handicaps, Sarie's breeding always stood her in good stead. "How do you do?" she said, automatically extending her hand and nodding pleasantly at the man. "I'm pleased to make your acquaintance."

Vance rose, unfolding what seemed to Sarie to be impossibly long limbs, and covered the distance between them in one stride. She scrambled to her feet so that he would not tower over her. "The pleasure is all mine, you can be sure," he said warmly, taking her hand in his and squeezing it. He cocked his head again and fixed her with his warm, inquisitive stare. "Sarie Appleton. You aren't by any chance one of the Beacon Hill Appletons? I know of a Sarah Jane Appleton, and a..."

"Sarah Jane's my grandmother," Sarie replied tersely, wishing she didn't have to go through the usual tiresome family-tree ritual. But there seemed no way to escape without being rude, and rudeness would never occur to her, despite her impatience with Vance Leland and his Brahmin social conventions. "I'm

Sarah Elizabeth. My family lives on Mount Vernon Street.'' She said this deliberately and without emphasis, hoping to avoid the usual spate of questions concerning her estrangement from her immediate family.

Vance looked at her more closely, and Sarie could almost see him confirming his assessment, taking in her modest clothes, her thick, unkempt hair and her too-young-for-its-age face. She tried to play the same game with him, but he was far too self-assured to be as put off by her stare as she was by his.

"I think I remember hearing something about an Appleton who made a rather unusual career choice," he said at last. Sarie was about to make a smart retort, but something in his expression stopped her. "Junior lieutenant, hmm? That's very good, isn't it?" Either he was genuinely impressed or he was doing an excellent job of mocking her.

"Not bad for a woman," Chief Wapshaw declared impatiently, and they both turned to look at him. "Now if you don't mind, Vance, I think we'd better get on with this mess."

Vance nodded. "Of course, Bob." He turned back to Sarie and gestured at the chair. "Won't you sit down again, Lieutenant?" He made it sound as if the office were his personal domain, and Sarie sat with an obedient nod of thanks.

"Now, maybe we can make some sense of this affair," he said, returning to his seat.

"I still don't..." Sarie began, but Vance overrode her objections with smooth authority.

"I think the best thing for you to do would be to start from the very beginning and tell us everything that happened this afternoon, from the moment you arrived at the Brewery fire.''

Sarie shook her head stubbornly. She was not about to let him get away without an explanation. ''I'm afraid I can't do that, Mr. Leland. What exactly is your position in this investigation?''

''Appleton!'' Chief Wapshaw was indignant. ''Mr. Leland asked you a question. Now answer it!'' He turned to Vance. ''I'm sorry, Vance. The lieutenant seems to have her own peculiar notions of protocol.'' He cast Sarie a dark glance. ''Comes from being a debutante, I expect.''

Sarie clenched her fists in irritation. If there was one thing she hated most about the chief, it was his churlish insistence on bringing up Sarie's privileged past. Like her parents, he seemed to think that a former debutante was constitutionally unfit for a career as a fire fighter.

But Vance seemed unconcerned by it all. ''Not at all, Bob. Sarie has every right to know why I'm here.''

That's Lieutenant Appleton to you, Sarie felt like saying, but she contented herself with repeating the question coldly. ''And just why *are* you here, Mr. Leland?''

Vance recrossed his legs languidly. ''As you might remember, I was involved in the investigation of the original Roxbury arson ring,'' he began.

''Involved! Practically solved the whole thing single-handed!'' the chief exclaimed. ''Why, if it hadn't been for your private investigation, Vance, we might never have figured out who was behind those crimes.'' He turned to Sarie and spoke as one might to a slow student. ''He managed to get information that none of our own investigative teams were able to get, blast them." Sarie knew the department's failure to solve the Roxbury case was a sore spot with the chief. Only the presence of someone as impressive as Vance Leland would force him to admit it. "I don't know how he did it," he added magnanimously, "but we are all eternally grateful, aren't we, Appleton?" He glared at Sarie. "Surely you can't have forgotten the great contribution Mr. Leland has made to our department and to the entire city!" He sounded as though he was making a speech, which he often did, and she knew she had better jump in before he really got going.

"I remember," Sarie said firmly. She ignored the chief's suggestion that she say something appropriately grateful and turned to look expectantly at Vance. *Well,* she thought rebelliously, *bully for you, Mr. Leland. But what does all that have to do with the Brewery fire?* "Go on, please, Mr. Leland," she demanded, as politely as she could.

Vance met her gaze steadily for a moment before speaking. "That's all there is to it, Lieutenant. I'm here because I'm interested in the fires. No big mystery, is there?"

"The Brewery fire happened a few hours ago, Mr. Leland," she said, wishing his eyes weren't so intriguing. "How did you come to find out about it so quickly?"

Vance paused, and she thought she saw his eyes narrow briefly before resuming their frank and pleasant regard. *He probably has that look down to a science,* she thought. It's the perfect public image.

"To tell you the truth," he confessed at last, "I'm actually here on some other business. I'm donating my collection of antique fire-fighting equipment to the Boston Fire Department so the chief here can open a museum and raise some much-needed funds," he said with a dismissive gesture that belied the generosity of the gift. He cocked his head and surveyed Sarie with bright eyes. "Are you by any chance interested in antique fire trucks, Ms Appleton?"

"Not really. Although I know someone who is," Sarie allowed grudgingly, thinking of her nine-year-old son, Taylor, who adored them.

Vance smiled. "At any rate, I came by to discuss the possibility of having someone in the department come and compile a catalog of the pieces for the museum. It's scheduled to open in a few weeks, in an old carriage house I own near Jamaica Plain—a lovely site. The fire trucks are already there. Perhaps your friend would be interested in the job?"

Sarie realized he thought *she* was the friend but that she was reluctant to admit her interest in his antique collection. "The friend is not qualified," she said, and added dryly, "But thanks anyway."

Vance continued. "Well, that's why I'm here, you see. And the chief thought that since I was so involved in the Roxbury investigation I might be interested in hearing what you had to say about the Brewery fire." Again, the eyes underwent some brief metamorphosis, as if a dark cloud had passed over them. "And he's right. I'm quite interested. I take a personal interest in the fire department—always have."

Sarie could not resist. "One of your pet charities, is it?"

Behind her, she could feel the chief stiffen, but Leland seemed to be pleasantly surprised by her impudence. "You might say that. I'm a bit of a fire-fighting buff—a sparkie, to tell you the truth. Always have loved the thrill of fire fighting. Of course, I never had the guts to join the force myself as you did, Ms Appleton.''

Once again, it was hard for Sarie to tell if he was genuinely impressed by her career choice or if he was mocking her. She decided to assume the latter. Very few people were impressed by the fact that she had turned her back on her privileged upbringing and joined the ranks of blue-collar civil service. Certainly nobody in her family or their acquaintances—with the notable exception of her grandmother and her nine-year-old son.

"It didn't take guts, Mr. Leland," she told him, meeting his gaze defiantly. "Just determination."

"I can see that you're determined about a lot of things," he observed, registering irony with the lift of an eyebrow.

"I'm determined to find out what's behind the Brewery fire and what connection it has to the Roxbury arsons," she retorted.

He pursed his lips and nodded. "I'd say that's a legitimate concern."

Sarie pounced. "So you do agree that there's a connection between the Roxbury arsons and the Brewery fire!"

"Of course he doesn't!" Chief Wapshaw exclaimed loudly, sounding disgusted. "You don't have proof of any such thing. How could he?"

Sarie was losing patience with the chief's determined avoidance. "Then how do you explain the presence of the Jackson device, Chief?" she inquired pointedly. It was time to get down to business, and she no longer cared who was there when she did it.

"You know, anybody could have duplicated the Jackson device, Lieutenant," Vance interjected gently. "After all, it was practically diagramed in all the papers during the Roxbury arson trials. And unfortunately copycat crimes are all too common these days."

"Damn media," grumbled Wapshaw. "But Vance is right, Sarie. You have no proof of any connection except what you say is a Jackson device. And I'm afraid that's not enough." He sounded pleased about it.

Sarie let out her breath in a heavy sigh of frustration. How could she explain to Chief Wapshaw and to this...this society boy, what she knew intuitively to be true. Neither of them had participated in battling the Roxbury blazes, and neither of them had been at the Brewery. Vance Leland may have attended a few fires as an interested spectator and sparkie; the chief made it a habit not to show up at any fire until the danger was well past and the work done. But she had been on duty at many of the Roxbury fires, and she knew the pattern too well to be fooled.

"Whoever started the Brewery fire knew what he was doing," she declared flatly. "It was not a copycat crime, I'm sure. Someone wants the BFD to know that the Roxbury arson ring is not all behind bars. Or else to throw a good scare into someone else." She knew they were both staring at her, and she chose to face the chief rather than Vance Leland's discomfiting gaze. At least with the chief she knew what to expect.

"Look, Appleton," he began with predictable impatience, but Vance interrupted him.

"I think we had better stick to our original plan and hear the lieutenant's story from the beginning before we draw any conclusions. Don't you agree, Ms Appleton?'' That smooth, cajoling voice seemed to appear from nowhere and float across the room with a silken insistence. Sarie understood why he was such a successful businessman. Aside from his impeccable background and impressive credentials, the man had the persuasive powers of a born-again preacher. There was no mistaking the powerful command behind the soft tones, and Sarie knew better than to turn to Chief Wapshaw for help. She had no choice but to comply.

With a meaningful sigh of resignation, she collected herself and began. ''At first we thought it was just a regular two-alarm fire,'' she said, looking out the window over the chief's head. ''After all, the building has just been renovated—it wasn't even finished. There was no obvious reason to suspect foul play in a building that was newly completed and uninhabited. We thought it was most likely that an improperly installed electrical circuit had triggered the blaze.'' She paused. ''But as soon as we got there the explosions began. Three of them, in quick succession, all coming from the same area of the building— the southeast corner of the basement. They were clearly not spontaneous combustions, because they occurred at regular intervals and erupted into easily controlled blazes. As soon as we got one under control another would break out. It's a classic pattern for arson.'' She took a deep breath as the memory of those awful muffled sounds filled her ears. ''That's how we first connected it to the Roxbury fires. The combustions were so regular.''

''What did it smell like?'' Vance asked.

''Smell like?'' Sarie was surprised by the question.

''That's right. Did you smell anything unusual?''

In spite of herself, Sarie grinned. "It smelled like old beer."

"What?" Chief Wapshaw was dumbfounded by this remark.

Vance smiled back at her as he said to the chief, "The building is a converted brewery, Bob. It must have been quite an aroma, all that forty-year-old beer roasting along with the bricks and wood. But I was thinking of something else, Sarie. Some other smell."

Sarie nodded. Even the memory of it made her nostrils flare with distaste. "Yes. There was another smell. An acrid, chemical smell." She shuddered and saw that he had noticed. "That's how I knew to look for the Jackson device. The chemical that triggers the explosions always smells like that. Like burning rubber or...burning flesh." She wished Vance wasn't watching her so intently. She didn't want him to know how frightened she was. It seemed important that she maintain her professional detachment in front of him.

Vance nodded knowingly, "Carbon tetrachloride. Cleaning fluid." He turned to the chief to explain. "It always smells like that when it comes into contact with the insulating material on the furnaces or burners."

"That's right," Sarie agreed, noting that the chief wasn't spared his patronizing tone. Then a thought occurred to her. "How did you know where we found the device? I didn't tell you that."

"Is that where you found it?" he asked immediately. "Under the furnace?"

"It was underneath the water heater," Sarie replied slowly, her voice full of puzzlement. "In the same position that we found it in several of the Roxbury fires. But you couldn't have known that, Mr. Leland."

Vance shrugged lightly. "You've already told us that the scenario duplicated that of several of the Roxbury fires, Lieutenant," he reminded her blandly. "And, as I recall, the Jackson device was usually planted under the furnace, wasn't it?" He turned and smiled briefly at Chief Wapshaw. "Of course, that is one difference between this and the Roxbury fires. This Jackson device was under the water heater, not the furnace."

"This building was electrically heated," Sarie said. "There was no furnace, so the arsonist chose the next-best thing—the water heater. In the Roxbury buildings, which were old tenements, the furnaces were a more logical target than the water heaters. It was winter, and even a slum landlord keeps the furnace working. They gave off steady heat that made it easier to control the explosions."

"And those buildings were all torched so that the owners could collect the insurance and build new high-rent condos on the property, isn't that so, Miss Appleton?" There was an edge in his voice as he became precise, and Sarie began to feel uneasy again. His disarming gentleness was rapidly disappearing.

"That's right," she replied. "Scores of people were left homeless by those blazes."

"Whereas the Brewery had stood empty and unused for ten years before its conversion into condominiums. There was nothing to be gained by torching it, was there?"

Sarie realized she had been trapped. "That doesn't mean there isn't a connection."

Vance's tone was sharp now, and tipped with poison. "Doesn't it? All the members of the arson ring have allegedly been rounded up and are in jail. I myself was responsible for providing the list of landlords to your chief, as well as uncovering the identity of Ira Jackson. The Roxbury arsons were set up as an insurance scam, so that those landlords could collect the money and rebuild to turn their real estate into more lucrative high-income housing. I fail to see how a smallish fire in an already converted building could serve such a purpose."

Sarie felt her pulse accelerate, and her breathing become rapid and shallow. Vance Leland was destroying her argument with cold, hard logic, and there was little she could do to stop him, despite the fact that she was still firmly convinced that her intuition was right.

"That may not have been the purpose," she said, trying to shore up her failing command of the situation.

"And what other possible connection could there be?" Vance inquired pointedly.

Sarie searched wildly for an answer. "I don't know," she admitted. "Maybe it was . . . a warning. Maybe the perpetrator wanted to let us know that he's still at large. Maybe he wants to warn somebody else that he's still at large."

"But Ira Jackson is most certainly not at large," Vance reminded her.

"There could have been someone else." Sarie's conviction was faltering. "Someone who was not caught and convicted." She was grabbing at straws and she knew it. "Maybe the real perpetrator was never caught."

"Lieutenant Appleton!" roared the chief, half rising in his seat. "I'll remind you that you are talking to the man who was responsible for seeing to it that the

Roxbury arson ring was apprehended. That *all* of them were apprehended!''

But Vance Leland seemed to be interested in her remark. ''Is that what you think, Lieutenant Appleton? That there's someone involved in the Roxbury fires who's still at large?''

Sarie quailed under the diamondlike brilliance of his gaze. ''It's a possibility,'' she said defensively.

''And what would the purpose of such a fire be, may I ask?''

Sarie hated his imperious tone. She had grown up with that tone, surrounded by voices that made it clear in no uncertain terms that she was out of line, out of order and hopelessly inappropriate. Those voices had told her not to get married before finishing college—they had been right about that—not to have a child—her charming son was a point for her side—and, most vociferously, that Appletons were not meant to be fire fighters, especially not Appleton women—to date, that was a draw. She reacted, more to the tone of voice than to the words, with impetuous anger.

''I'm not sure yet, Mr. Leland,'' she snapped. ''Perhaps the owner of the Brewery is in some way connected to the Roxbury fires. Perhaps this fire was a warning to that person—and to all of us—that the horror is not over yet. The owner could be another victim, or he could be the perpetrator himself. I really don't know, but I can assure you I won't rest until I find out.''

Once again, Vance Leland's reaction was surprising and unsettling. Instead of bristling with indignation at her impudence, he sat back with an almost satisfied smile. ''Is that so?'' he mused, mostly to himself. "Is that what you really think, Ms Appleton?"

For some reason his response fanned her anger. "Yes, that's what I think," she retorted, although the conjecture had come to her as she voiced it. "But I'd still like to know what this all has to do with you, Mr. Leland. You haven't explained, to my satisfaction, what you're doing here, and I don't think I have to explain myself to you until you do so."

Behind her, she heard Chief Wapshaw's scandalized intake of breath. She knew she was being rude and was out of line, but she was responding to that patronizing tone, to those coolly assessing slate eyes. She pulled herself up defiantly in her chair and watched Mr. Leland's face, waiting for it to explode into righteous indignation.

He was silent for a full minute—long enough for Sarie's courage to fail her, although she did not lower her eyes. Inside she could feel herself wilting beneath his penetrating gaze. She wished he would huff and puff and make a scene—anything to break the spell of that potent stillness.

At last he lifted one hand and drew it slowly across his face. He seemed suddenly weary, although Sarie thought she detected a faint gleam of amusement on the face behind the long fingers. "If you must know," he said finally, "I have a perfect right to know what's going on with the Brewery fire. The building belongs to me."

Chapter Two

"I'm telling you, Tom, you can't imagine what a patronizing prig he was!"

Sarie was sitting in the kitchen of the station house with Tom Garrett, ignoring the cup of coffee he had poured her while she ranted about her recent meeting.

"That's funny," Tom remarked placidly. "He sure doesn't come across like a patronizing prig in public." He was used to Sarie's sudden outbreaks of temper, and he endured them with the same good-natured patience that had seen him through eighteen years on the force.

"Oh, I know, I know!" Sarie gesticulated dismissively with one hand. "I know all about his public image. People like Vance Leland have made image presentation a fine art. It comes from spending your life in fancy drawing rooms and private schools where nobody says anything real to anybody else. All you *have* is a public image when you grow up like that."

Tom cast a sardonic glance at the small figure before him. Her elbows were propped glumly on the table, her legs wrapped around the legs of the chair. He knew all about her struggle to free herself from her

Brahmin bloodline and had always observed her efforts with a bemused interest, having come from a strictly working-class background himself. "You grew up like that," he pointed out calmly. "And look how you turned out."

Sarie threw him a wan smile. "Yeah, but I'm the black sheep of the Appleton clan, remember? And Vance Leland is the apple of old Horace Leland's eye." She had heard about Vance's great-uncle Horace Leland from her grandmother, Sarah Jane. He was the patriarch of the Leland empire, and Vance the heir apparent. Sarie glared moodily into her coffee cup. "He's the apple of everybody's eye, as a matter of fact."

"Except yours, of course," Tom added dryly.

Sarie ignored him. "People like that are all the same. They think they can run the world, polite as you please, but when anybody gives them a hard time about it, boy, can they get nasty!"

"I hope you didn't give him too hard a time, Sarie," murmured Tom. "You've got to be careful, you know. The chief has a hard enough time with you being a female and all, without your giving trouble to his biggest public supporter."

Sarie scowled. "Believe me, I know. According to the chief, affirmative action for women is a bad dream in general, and I'm the starring monster in his personal nightmare. But Vance Leland is the answer to his prayers. I mean, you should have seen the way the chief played up to him. It was sickening. And Leland just lapped it up, like he deserved every bit of it."

"He has played an important role in the department, Sarie," Tom reminded her. "After all, he's not just another name on the board of regents. He takes an active interest in the goings-on of the BFD.''

"He's a sparkie. Of course he's interested. He has a thing about fires."

Tom sat down heavily in front of her. "First of all, sparkies don't necessarily just have a thing about fires. A lot of them—most of them, really—are pretty serious about their hobby, and they're a big help to us, too. You know that."

"I know," Sarie admitted grudgingly.

"And second of all," said Tom more severely, "you know perfectly well that Vance Leland went beyond the call of duty during the Roxbury arson investigations. If it hadn't been for him, and for the information he was able to obtain, Ira Jackson and those criminal landlords might still be plying their dirty trade."

Sarie looked up, her eyes suddenly bright again. "And it looks to me like one of them still is," she confided breathlessly.

"What?" Tom looked dumbfounded.

"Well, think about it, Tom. What other explanation is there for the Brewery fire? It was an exact duplicate of the Roxbury arsons, and you know it."

Tom shifted heavily in his chair. "Yes, but . . ."

"But what? I know how hard it is to face, but someone around here has got to acknowledge the fact that there has to be a connection between those arsons and this new one."

He shook his head. "But why? What possible reason would anybody have for torching the Brewery?"

Sarie grimaced. "I'm not sure. Maybe to warn us that the case is not closed. Maybe to make a point to whoever owns the building." She leaned across the table and lowered her voice. "Or maybe the person who owns it was involved himself. And you'll never guess who owns the Brewery, Tom!"

"Who?"

Sarie's eyes glittered. "None other than our dear Vance Leland, prince of the city."

Tom's jaw dropped. "You're kidding! Do you mean to say..."

"I don't mean to say anything, Tom. But those are the facts. There *is* a connection between the Roxbury and the Brewery fires, and Leland is connected to them both."

Tom narrowed his eyes. "And did you happen to mention to Leland and the chief this theory of yours about the connection between the fires?"

"Of course I did."

"Even though you knew he owned the building?" Tom gaped. "Sarie, do you realize what you're saying here?"

Sarie swallowed hard at the memory of that awkward moment. "Well, actually, I said it before I knew he owned the Brewery. Not that it matters," she added somewhat defensively. "It really doesn't change a thing, as far as I'm concerned. After all, Vance Leland's not a saint, you know."

Tom shook his head and sighed. "Sarie, you're not honestly thinking that Vance Leland is in some way connected with those fires, are you?"

"Well of course I'm not!" Sarie sat back resentfully. "I never really said..."

But Tom looked doubtful. "Because that's just about the most..."

"Actually," came a voice from the doorway, "the lieutenant was well within her rights to make the conjecture."

Sarie and Tom spun around to see Vance Leland leaning against the open door. His hands were thrust casually into the pockets of his pants, and one foot was crossed over the other. There was no telling how long he had been standing there or what he had overheard.

Sarie tried to disengage her feet from the legs of the chair and only succeeded in getting them more entangled. It was Tom who rose first and went over to Vance, his hand outstretched.

"Mr. Leland, it's a pleasure to make your acquaintance," he said with a gruff but genuine welcome. "Please come in. Care for a cup of coffee? I make the station's best."

Vance smiled and shook his head, but his eyes were on Sarie. "Thank you, Sergeant, but I'm afraid I can't stay." He approached the table where Sarie still sat, awkwardly trying to look at ease. She did not blush easily, but she knew that if she sat too long under that gaze the freckles across her cheeks and nose would stand out against the pinkness of her acute embarrassment.

"I just came down to apologize to the lieutenant," he said, using that blandly pleasant public voice that was so soothing to the ear.

Sarie looked nervously at Tom, who was making himself very busy at the sink. "Apologize for what?" she asked, wishing she could sound more haughty and look less disconcerted by his presence.

He shrugged disarmingly. "For making it tough for you up there. I should have known you and Bob aren't exactly bosom buddies."

In spite of herself a dry laugh escaped from Sarie. She saw Tom's back tense and made an effort to control herself. "We manage," she said evenly, and then couldn't resist adding, "Although we don't always see eye to eye." Tom turned his head and cast her a black look that she chose to ignore.

"About things like gender equality?" inquired Vance with an amused lift of one eyebrow. "I imagine Bob's something of a dinosaur on that score." The smile suddenly hardened. "But I suppose you're not seeing eye to eye on the issue of this arson investigation either, are you?"

Sarie recognized the cool warning cloud that passed across his face and chose her words more carefully this time. "I'm sure the chief will do everything possible to investigate the Brewery fire," she said evenly.

Vance watched her face closely for several seconds, seeming to look for something in her expression. Sarie hoped he wouldn't find it. Then he smiled again. "At any rate," he went on brightly, "I really do feel bad. I had you at a disadvantage in there, and I shouldn't have allowed it to happen. Please accept my apologies."

He extended his hand, and Sarie had no choice but to take it. His fingers were long and cool, and there was no pressure in his grip. But he did not let go of her hand, and his eyes never left her face. "Of course," she said, wondering why she felt so confused. "I accept." She managed a fake, nervous little laugh. "You're forgiven."

"Can I offer you dinner tonight?" He went on as if she hadn't spoken, still holding her hand in his impersonal grasp. "By way of sealing a truce?"

The invitation was so unexpected that Sarie nearly jerked her hand out of his. It was then that she realized how tenacious that seemingly casual grip was. Without giving any evidence of increased pressure, he made it impossible for her to pull away.

"Oh, there's absolutely no need..." she began, casting an imploring look at Tom's resolute back.

"Oh, but I think there is," he pursued. "I really hate to make mistakes without making amends for them. That's no way to do business, is it?" His smile was briefly dazzling. "And besides, it wouldn't do for an Appleton and a Leland to be quarreling, now would it? Why, all of Beacon Hill would be agog."

"I'm sure they wouldn't give a..."

"But I couldn't live with myself," he went on with relentless politeness. "I would hate to think of a schism between our families arising from such a petty incident as this."

It was such a patently ridiculous statement that Sarie couldn't summon up a response. If he knew anything at all about the Appletons—and she was sure he knew plenty—Beacon Hill society was very insular—he knew that there was no love lost between the "good" branch of the family and Sarie. But he seemed perfectly serious and waited with apparent eagerness for her to reply.

"Oh, I don't think it's necessary," she began, and stopped when she could not think of a valid objection. His gaze was politely attentive and betrayed nothing more.

"Please," he went on, taking advantage of her disorientation, "I insist on making amends. Come out to dinner with me. Please." For the first time Sarie heard a note of real entreaty, which intrigued and confused her even more. A man like Vance Leland probably dined with socialites seven nights a week. Why on earth was he so intent on taking her out to dinner?

At last Tom turned from the sink. "Go ahead, Sarie," he said heartily, but with a meaningful glance in her direction. "You're through for the day anyway, and I happen to know you didn't get any lunch."

Vance cocked his head. "No lunch? Well, we can't have you starve because you were working too hard for the department, can we?" He looked brightly at Tom, who shook his head vehemently. "Then it's settled. You'll come with me and I'll feed you well at my favorite spot in town. It's the least I can do."

At last he exerted the tiniest pressure on her hand. It was enough to disengage Sarie nearly from her chair and pull her toward him. She managed to cast a silent plea for help in Tom's direction before Vance tucked her arm neatly under his elbow and began to promenade her out of the kitchen. "This will give us an excellent chance to catch up on our mutual acquaintances," he remarked jovially as he squired her out. "And," he added with casual aplomb, "while we're at it, we can talk about the Brewery arson."

THE RESTAURANT TURNED OUT to be little more than a hole in the wall along the main street of the North End, Boston's Italian neighborhood. Inside there were only eight tables and a big stove, behind which stood a stocky man in a white apron and hat who greeted Vance by name when he came in.

Sarie was extremely uneasy, despite the casual ambience. She couldn't figure out why Vance had insisted on this dinner. Did he want to press her for more information about the Brewery, find out how much she knew? If so, why? As the owner, he was more likely to have some of the answers than she was. Or did he have another reason—a more personal one? This thought made Sarie even more uncomfortable. She hated mysteries, especially one as intriguing as Vance Leland.

"*This* is your favorite place in town?" She couldn't hide her astonishment as they sat down at a table covered with a plastic red-checkered tablecloth. His choice of restaurants was a mystery in itself.

"That's right." He looked at her with amusement. "What's wrong? Did you expect something posher? More Beacon Hill, perhaps?"

That was exactly what she had been expecting. "Frankly, yes," she replied, returning his amused smile. "This doesn't look like your style."

"Appearances can be deceiving, you know, Sarie. Look at you, for instance." He leaned forward and poured her a glass of wine from the bottle that had been placed on their table unordered. "To look at you, who would think..."

"That I come from a fine Boston family?" Sarie finished for him sarcastically. "I know. People are always surprised and dismayed to find out that I've ruined myself this way."

"Ruined yourself?" Vance's eyebrows arched. "Actually, I was going to say I wouldn't expect you to be a fire fighter." He shook his head and smiled. "Good bones and gorgeous skin don't lie, Ms Apple-

ton. You're a Brahmin through and through, like it or
not.''

Sarie took a sip of her wine, trying to digest this
surprising statement. She wasn't sure she liked being
reminded of her patrician past, but she could tell
Vance meant it as a compliment. The slightly fruity
aftertaste of the wine was unexpectedly refreshing, and
she glanced at the bottle for the first time. "And so are
you, Mr. Leland," she replied with a knowing smile.
"I doubt many customers in this place get Château
d'Yquiem served to them automatically."

Vance laughed delightedly. "Touché." He reached
out and clinked his glass against hers. "Here's to rising above our class," he said, and smiled into her eyes
as they drank. "Now then," he went on, putting his
glass down, "tell me about yourself. How did you
manage to turn out such a rebel with parents like
Georgina and Foster Appleton?"

Sarie grinned. "With parents like them, I had no
choice. Fortunately I have Sarah Jane on my side and,
of course, Taylor."

"Taylor?"

She took another sip of her wine before continu-
ing. Sarie had learned from long experience that it was
best to bring the subject of her son into the open at
once. People's reaction to it was usually a good indication of their general character. "Yes, Taylor is my
nine-year-old son. I was married briefly while I was at
college."

"Ah, yes, I think I heard something about the affair from Uncle Horace."

Sarie watched him over her wineglass. It looked like
he was going to be as disapproving as the rest of Boston's society had been. "I'm sure you did," she said

dryly. "Everybody was talking about it, much to my parents' dismay."

Vance cocked his head meditatively. "I think Horace said it was about time someone shook the complacency out of an old stuffed shirt like Foster Appleton."

Sarie sputtered and nearly choked on her wine. "And what do *you* think?" she inquired cautiously when she had recovered.

"I don't think you should give a damn what I think," he retorted promptly. Then he grinned, and it was as if a light had gone on inside his eyes. "But if he takes after his mother's side of the family, I'll bet your Taylor is as cute as a button and twice as hard to pin down."

Taylor was Sarie's favorite topic, and she warmed to it immediately, regaling Vance with tales of his unbridled enthusiasm for baseball, soccer and anything that had to do with his mother's unusual career. From Taylor, the conversation seemed to proceed easily to other members of their families, and dinner passed in an enjoyable blur. Vance seemed to share Sarie's unconventional view of their common social circle, and she found herself enjoying his offbeat perceptions of mutual acquaintances and his witty stories about their foibles.

It wasn't until they had finished the wine and two tiny cups of bitter espresso that she realized she was actually enjoying herself because she was with Vance Leland. At the same moment she realized that, in spite of the delicious food and their easy conversation, there was an air of expectancy, almost of apprehension, about the meal. She felt as if Vance was waiting for something, and she knew that she, too, felt as if something needed to be said but hadn't.

Sarie realized that she hadn't felt this comfortable with a man in a long time but reminded herself rather severely, while he was paying the bill, that she really had no reason to trust Vance Leland. Despite their common backgrounds and mutual interests, they were really impossibly different people, and they were on different sides of a very dangerous issue—arson. She knew instinctively that he had asked her out for a reason and not just to settle a score with his conscience. He wanted something from her—but what?

It was the Brewery, of course. Both of them wanted desperately to talk about it, but neither was willing to break the enjoyable spell that had bound them together during the meal. Still, she could think of no reason to refuse his gentle chivalry as he took her arm when they left the restaurant, and she found herself enjoying the closeness much more than she thought she should. Anyway, she reminded herself defensively, she wanted something from Vance, too. She wanted information.

"Shall we walk awhile?" he asked, and without waiting for her to say yes, he started off in the direction of the darkened waterfront.

The night was balmy, with a hint of summery fragrance already in the air. Boston's waterfront was always an exciting place to walk; the salty dilapidation of the piers was a fascinating background for the posh stylishness of some of the city's most desirable real estate. Sarie and Vance strolled aimlessly, both occupied with their own thoughts. The elegantly renovated buildings reminded Sarie all too clearly of the Brewery condominiums, and the awful surprise she had found in the basement. She also remembered that she was walking with the owner of that building. *Well, kiddo,* she encouraged herself, *you're supposed to be the professional investigator here. Who says he has to make the first move?*

"These are lovely buildings," she remarked, trying to make her voice sound casual.

"Yes, they are. The old facades have been preserved, which is a good thing."

"They're worth preserving," Sarie said, and then, with a quick sidelong glance at her companion, added, "Unlike the Roxbury buildings, of course."

Vance did not miss a beat. "Of course. Those buildings had absolutely no architectural value whatsoever."

"But they had a lot of value to the people who lived in them," Sarie pointed out. She had the feeling she wasn't getting anywhere with this talk—Vance's expression, seen in profile, looked pleasantly unconcerned about the topic of conversation.

"Absolutely," he said cheerfully. "Which is why it is such a crime that they were torched."

"It's a crime that your building was torched, too, don't you think?" she said, too quickly.

Vance stopped so suddenly that Sarie's arm was tugged in the knot of his elbow. He was still smiling, but his eyes had narrowed slightly. "That's assuming, of course, that it was arson."

"Of course it was. I found the Jackson device!"

"Sarie," he said slowly, as if speaking to a child, "there's arson, and then there's malicious arson. Arson with intent to hurt people, arson with intent to make personal gains. There are degrees of arson, you know."

His patronizing attitude annoyed her. "Arson is arson, Vance, whatever the motive. Your building was torched this afternoon. Aren't you interested in knowing why?"

He did not answer her right away but continued to stand very still, watching her face closely, as if he expected her soon to be done with this childish outburst and resume her grown-up composure. It only made Sarie angrier.

"Or perhaps," she insisted defiantly, "you already know why it was burned."

Vance's mouth clamped shut with a small clicking sound. Sarie could see his jaw tighten, as if he was struggling to get himself under control. When he finally spoke, his normally genteel voice was edged with a frightening passion. "I think we should let the arson investigation unit handle the matter, don't you, Sarie? That's what Chief Wapshaw plans to do, and for once I have to agree with him." His expression was still mild, except for the menace in his voice and the shadow of tension in his jaw. Sarie was more taken aback by this controlled fury than she would have been by an outright display of violence.

And she suddenly became aware of the futility of their conversation. Vance was not going to tell her a thing about the Brewery or about his connection with the Roxbury arson investigation. He didn't have to. He held all the cards. But at that moment Sarie vowed to herself that she was going to find out more about both fires and find out why everybody seemed so eager to ignore the possible connection between the two. And she knew that Vance Leland was one of the connections she was going to have to look into—with his permission or without it.

"Whatever you say, Vance," she agreed politely, and slipped her arm back into his. At any rate, there was no reason to terminate the evening. Sarie reminded herself that she would have to cultivate some sort of relationship with the man, if only to be able to figure him out. And, since being with him happened to be so pleasant, she might as well enjoy herself at the same time.

There was a hint of amusement in his smile as Vance tucked her hand back under his arm. Once again silent, they resumed their promenade around the convex curve of the harbor to the shipping yards that looked across the channel to the Charlestown Navy Yard. Each of them walked and waited, and continuously reminded themselves that things weren't necessarily as delightful as they seemed. Sarie's suspicions about Vance were growing in direct proportion to her attraction to him.

It was when they neared the municipal skating rink that sat at the mouth to the channel that Sarie's skin began to prickle with apprehension. The dark-domed rink offered glimpses of black water beyond its open-air roof. Staring out at the pale lights of the Navy Yard, Sarie saw something else, as well. She saw a man.

At first she didn't think anything of it. She assumed her skin had prickled because of a sudden sea breeze or because she was tired. Besides, there was no reason why another human being shouldn't be taking advantage of this pleasant spring evening for a stroll. But then she realized that the man had been there for some time, perhaps for the past fifteen minutes, riding like a shadow in the corner of her eye. Now he was keeping pace with them from the far side of the rink;

his head was not turned to gaze out across the harbor, but toward them. He was watching them, very closely.

Sarie felt chill fingers of fear drum up her spine. Somehow, despite all rational evidence to the contrary, she *knew* that the man was there for a purpose; he was not out for a solitary stroll, not out to perpetrate some random urban crime. He was following them. She was certain of it without knowing why—perhaps it was the way he moved when they moved and stopped when they did, always keeping the same distance and making no attempt to get any closer. Her intuitions weren't always right, but they were right often enough to make her feel uneasy and anxious now.

"Let's turn back," she said, suddenly, stopping in her tracks.

Vance looked at her in some surprise, as if he had been startled out of a private reverie. "Turn back? Why? Are you cold?"

Sarie looked over his shoulder. The man had stopped and turned away to face the water. "No, of course not. I just . . . I should be thinking about getting home. Taylor's been with his father all week, and he's being dropped off at nine."

"It's only seven-thirty," Vance said, looking at her more closely.

Sarie hitched her shoulders and managed a careless-looking smile. "Well, anyway, I'd like to mosey back through the North End," she said brightly. "I love those narrow little streets and all those delicious smells coming from the Italian bakeries."

Vance watched her for a moment longer and then, without a word, wheeled around and led her across the street. They climbed Salem Street in silence and headed back through the maze of crooked winding thoroughfares that were barely wide enough for a car. The silence between them was now fraught with tension, and Sarie knew that Vance was looking at her from time to time, trying to figure out what had caused her sudden change of mood. She kept her gaze resolutely ahead of her, but she could not help flicking her head skittishly every time a shadow crossed her field of vision. She was sure the man was still nearby.

"What is it, for God's sake?" Vance inquired testily at last. "You're acting like you saw a ghost."

"I am not!" Sarie retorted guiltily.

"You're acting like you saw *something*. You're unusually jumpy all of a sudden."

Sarie's nerves were frayed by the long day and the eventful evening. "Vance, you haven't even known me for eight hours," she snapped. "How can you tell if I'm acting unusually anything?"

He stopped suddenly and wheeled her around by the arm. "Stop acting like an Appleton, Sarie," he said in a low, impatient voice. "You and I don't have to observe the social amenities. What does it matter how long ago we met? I know you well enough to tell that you wouldn't be nervous like this unless there's a good reason for it."

His eyes bored into hers with drill-like precision. "That's ridiculous," she said, her voice rising with unaccustomed shrillness. "You don't know the first thing about me!" Vance's scrutiny only added to her nervousness. She wished they could keep on walking toward the brighter lights of Hanover Street.

A mocking gleam appeared in Vance's eyes. "That's what you think. Or that's what you'd like to think. In either case, you're quite wrong, my dear, and you know it. You and I are bound together by some very deep ties, Sarah Elizabeth Appleton, and I'm not just talking about our Mayflower heritage.'' Despite his direct stare and forceful manner, there was something bemused in his expression. ''There was something fateful about our meeting this afternoon, whatever the reason—something almost preordained.''

''I...I don't know what you're talking about.'' Sarie felt suddenly cold, and a shiver passed down her spine. She wasn't sure if she was apprehensive about the man or if she was unsettled by his uncanny ability to read her. In spite of herself, her eyes kept darting over Vance's shoulder, drawn to a dark alley that seemed unusually menacing.

''I think you do,'' he said. ''I think you know exactly what I'm talking about. Sarie!'' He took her shoulders and shook her briefly. ''For God's sake, what is it!''

But Sarie had stopped listening to Vance's voice. Her eyes widened, and she found it suddenly hard to breathe. ''I think...I think there's a man there, Vance,'' she whispered through chattering teeth. ''I think he's been following us.''

Vance's reaction to this news puzzled Sarie. Rather than laughing it off or getting annoyed, the first thing he did was to pull her into the relative obscurity of a narrow doorway. He wrenched her arm so suddenly that her head snapped back, and as it did she saw the shadow of a small and stocky man disappearing down the narrow alley. He seemed to have a shock of thick, electric hair that stood up like a halo around his face-less head, like an apparition out of some horror movie, and Sarie barely resisted the urge to scream.

Once they were hidden by the doorway, she turned and looked at Vance. He had definitely moved to hide from the man, but, although he was breathing rather hard, he spoke with his usual bland confidence. His eyes, however, darted nervously from Sarie to the alley. "This is ridiculous, Sarie, and you know it. Why on earth would anyone be following you?"

Sarie was taken aback by the discrepancy between his actions and his words. She stared as his statement sank in. Of course, there was no reason why anyone would follow her. But, even as she realized that, she recognized that she had not assumed that she was the target. It was Vance who was being followed, and, from the way he had reacted, she was sure that he knew it.

"Not me, Vance," she said breathlessly. "I didn't say he was following me."

They looked at each other for a full minute, their eyes locked in the dim reflected light of an old-fashioned streetlamp. Sarie thought she saw Vance's expression change to the same calculating look she had seen in Chief Wapshaw's office. He glanced once more toward the alley, but since there was no movement from that direction he turned back to her.

"Sarie," he said at last with a forced laugh, "I can see now how you managed to free yourself from the narrow restrictions of an Appleton life. You have the most fantastically vivid imagination I've ever come across."

"If that's a compliment, thank you," she said primly, "but I know what I saw, Vance. I saw a man, and, since he was surely not following me, I think he must have been following you."

Vance was still smiling, but he made no move to pull her out of the doorway and walk on. "Now why on earth," he asked with a brittle smile, "would anyone want to be following me?"

Because of the Brewery, Sarie wanted to say, but she knew it was too outrageous to suggest such a connection. Still, the fact remained that there *had* been a man—she was sure of that now. "I don't know," Sarie said evenly. "After all, I don't know you as well as you think you know me. Why *would* someone be following you, Vance?"

"No reason at all," said Vance lightly, but he swallowed as he spoke.

"Then why are we still hiding in this doorway?"

Again the flinty cloud passed across his face, replaced at once with a generous smile. Clearly, he had regained his famous composure. "Because," he said with sudden and surprising gentleness, "it provides me with an excellent opportunity to do what I've been wanting to do all evening."

Without warning he placed his lips on hers. Even given the unusual circumstances and the unexpectedness of the gesture, it was an extraordinary kiss. Vance was not tentative; he skipped the preliminaries and moved right into the kiss, taking possession of her mouth as if it was his by right. His lips pressed full against hers so that she could feel the hardness of his teeth behind them. His tongue explored hungrily, tasting the perimeter of her mouth before plunging inside with hungry abandon. It was not an intrusive gesture, but it was an overwhelming one, and Sarie felt hot and winded and excited all at once. She knew now that this was what she had been expecting all evening—the subject of the Brewery fire had only been a pretense, an excuse to keep them together until they could arrive at this moment of physical passion. Vance wrapped his arm around her neck and pulled her closer, so that their bodies melted together. Leaning back so that her head rested in the crook of his arm, Sarie felt the gorgeous lassitude of early arousal stealing over her, making her limbs pliant against his and her spine molten against his forearm. All other thoughts but one were wiped from her mind. She was enjoying this kiss more than she had ever dreamed possible. Vance had been right—this moment had been preordained since their first meeting, and they had both known it.

They remained entwined for a long time, reluctant to break the spell of the kiss. But by the time they separated, Sarie was breathless and weak with passion. Vance, too, seemed shaken. "My God," he muttered with a rough laugh, "I haven't done any necking in doorways since I was a very young man."

"Me, either," Sarie said, laughing nervously. Her eyes did not leave his face, but she was sure that the danger in the alley, whatever it had been, had passed. In fact, now she was not even sure it had been real to begin with. Everything had been blotted out by the power of that hotly chaste embrace.

"And I certainly never necked like that," he added huskily. He reached up and trailed one finger languidly across her cheekbones and over her narrow chin. "Sarah Elizabeth Appleton," he mused, shaking his head slowly. "This has certainly been an eventful day."

Sarie swallowed, nodded and made an unsuccessful attempt at a laugh. "All very unexpected," she agreed shakily.

"No, I don't think so," he replied thoughtfully. "Not unexpected at all." He turned and leaned out of the doorway, looking in both directions. "Well," he said with forced joviality, "what do you say we get going? Whatever or whoever you think you saw is certainly gone by now. And I'd hate for you to miss that son of yours."

Sarie looked at her watch and was surprised to find that it was nearly a quarter to nine—she seemed to have entered a time warp and had lost the last hour. But as soon as they left the narrow confines of the North End and headed in Vance's car toward her apartment, reality pressed back in on her in the oppressive brightness of the sodium lamps that lit the city streets. In spite of that mesmeric kiss, there *had* been a man, and he *had* been following Vance. What's more, Sarie was certain that Vance knew why.

But there was no way to bring the subject up again—the kiss had effectively destroyed any possibility of discussing either the man or the Brewery. Sarie was annoyed with herself for having let the situation get away from her. There was a lot of information she wanted to get from Vance Leland and falling into his arms at the first opportunity was not the way to get it.

Following her directions, Vance drove to Brookline, where Sarie lived in an apartment on a modest tree-lined street. He pulled up in front of the brick-fronted building. "Shall I see you in?" he asked with his customary politeness.

"That won't be necessary," she said stiffly. All of a sudden she felt that they were like two youngsters on their first date, awkward and ill at ease. Vance fiddled with the dashboard of his BMW and then turned to Sarie, his features lit by the pale yellow glow of the sedan's interior lights. His expression was unreadable, but a small smile toyed on his lips.

"Well," she said, acutely aware of how inadequate the words would sound. "Thank you for dinner." She smiled lamely.

He seemed amused. "Dinner," he repeated. "And everything else. It was a very…intriguing evening. I'd like to do it again sometime—mystery man and all."

Although she suspected that he was using it to hide his uneasiness, Sarie found his sardonic tone offensive. "You still don't believe me, do you, Vance?"

The pause was eloquent. "I'm not sure what to believe about you, Sarie. You throw up a lot of smoke screens, you know."

"*I* do? What about you?"

"I have nothing to hide. I am what I am, and I'm not trying to deny it."

This implied criticism stung Sarie. "You're the owner of the Brewery building," she blurted, "and there's no denying that, Vance."

"Ah, so that's where we end up! Right back at the beginning." He leaned forward and took her shoulder, and Sarie, thinking that he was about to stop the discussion with another kiss, resisted. But this time he did not pull her toward him. Instead his grip was hard and viselike and so was his expression. "Now you listen to me, Lieutenant Appleton. I'm sure you have the best interests of the city and the fire department at heart in your eagerness to pursue this investigation. But take a hint from me—leave it alone. Keep your busy little nose out of the whole mess, and it'll stay pretty and clean, just the way it looks now." He reached out and flicked his thumb across the tip of her nose and Sarie winced. "And don't be so skittish," he added, his voice softening. "You didn't get to where you are in your life by jumping at every bogeyman, did you? Just relax, and everything will take care of itself."

The hand on her shoulder relaxed, and his thumb wandered to her lips. "Trust me," he added gently, while his thumb traced the full outline of her mouth with tender precision. "I know what I'm talking about, Sarie."

Sarie could only stare at him, a thousand thoughts racing through her mind, gone before she could catch them and put them into words. There was such an odd blend of menace and tenderness in Vance's manner that she was thrown completely off balance. Part of her wanted to accuse him of withholding information from her and demand to know why. Part of her wanted to kiss him again.

Her indecision was interrupted by a bright voice from the sidewalk. "Hey, Ma!"

It was Taylor, and his voice released her from Vance's spell. "Oh, Tay," she breathed in a voice so full of relief that Vance smiled. "It's Taylor, my son." She had already opened the door of the car, and now she scrambled out. "Hello, darling," she called to the gangly boy who waited on the steps. And then, to insure that Vance did not get out, as well, she leaned back into the car. "Thanks again," she said abruptly, and closed the door with a firm slam.

Still, she was disappointed to see the alacrity with which Vance sped away from the curb and off into the night. He raised his hand in a brief farewell salute, but he did not say goodbye.

"Some wheels," whistled Taylor, coming to stand beside her, his shining eyes fixed in admiration on the retreating silhouette of the BMW. "Who's the big wheel driving 'em, Ma?"

"No big wheel, darling," Sarie said absently, watching the red taillights disappear. "Just someone from the department giving me a ride home."

"Hah!" snorted her son, who fancied himself an authority on anything that had to do with the BFD. "No chance of a fireman making enough money to cruise around in that machine unless he's got a little deal going on the side."

"What are you talking about?" Sarie asked sharply. "What do you mean, a deal on the side?"

Taylor lifted his shoulders in an exaggerated shrug of innocence. "Nothing! Nothing! I was just kidding around." He tugged on her hand and was suddenly a little boy again. "Now can we go inside? I'm *starving*!"

Sarie's expression softened into a smile. "So what else is new?" she inquired, ruffling his thick hair. "Let's go, sport, I'll treat you to some milk and cookies."

As they turned to go in, her attention was caught by another car pulling slowly away from the curb. It was a small nondescript car of foreign make, and it moved at a measured slow pace down the street. But it wasn't the car itself that caught her eye. It was the man in it.

She was sure it was the same man she had seen following Vance in the North End. The shock of upstanding hair was unmistakable, even at this distance and without light.

Except the man wasn't following Vance. Rather than taking off after the BMW, he was obviously watching her.

Chapter Three

"Ya see, Ma, there's this neat 1930 Hercules Master Engine—that's the biggest hook-and-ladder setup they had back then—and you had to crank it up to get it going, and all that stuff, ya know?"

"Uh-hmm." Sarie sat with Taylor at breakfast the next morning, listening to him with half an ear while he downed three bowls of cereal and talked nonstop through them all.

"So anyway, it was a real pain to get the truck started, but they had this terrific system for getting the water pressure going! Because they couldn't be waiting for the water while some old building was burning down, could they?"

"No, I suppose not," Sarie replied absently. She was staring out the kitchen window at the street and thinking about the car she had seen parked below last night. In the clear light of day it seemed outlandish for her to have imagined that the man was following her. There was no reason in the world for anyone to be following her. Come to think of it, there was no really good reason for anyone to be following Vance Leland, either. Her suspicions that his involvement with the Roxbury arsons and the Brewery fire was in some way mysterious seemed pretty farfetched too, this morning. After all, the only connections were perfectly legitimate—he owned the Brewery, and he had been instrumental in uncovering the Roxbury scandal. Nothing untoward about that, was there?

"Mom? Are you paying attention? Mom!"

Sarie blinked and focused on her son, who was glaring at her over the Cheerios box. "I'm sorry, honey." She smiled apologetically. "What were you saying?"

Taylor pushed a large picture book toward her.

"I was talking about the Hercules," he said reproachfully. "I was telling you about the water-pressure system they had." He pointed to the color photograph of an impressively ornate antique hook-and-ladder truck. "Ya see, there was this neat-looking brass lever, and you just pressed it down and then flipped this little toggle-deal here, and then—" he threw himself back against his chair, flinging his arms out and splattering milk off his spoon "—wooosh! Out it came! Isn't that absolutely wizard, Ma?"

Sarie looked at the photo with interest for a moment and then slowly raised her eyes to the trail of milk. "Real wizard," she said dryly. "But who cleaned up after the fire fighters?"

Taylor followed her gaze to the milk trail and, sighing heavily, got out of his chair and went to get a paper towel. "Firemen, Ma. In the old days they didn't have fire fighters. They had firemen."

The phone rang and she went to answer it. Probably Sarah Jane, calling to say hello. Sarah Jane was the only Appleton who continued to take an active interest in Sarie's career, and the only member of the family for whom Sarie still felt a deep affection. She called almost daily to check on her granddaughter and great-grandson.

But it was not Sarah Jane. It was the dispatcher from department headquarters. "Lieutenant Appleton?" he inquired. "Sergeant Foley here. I have a message for you from the chief's office." He rustled a piece of paper and then read stiffly. "'Lieutenant Junior-grade Sarah Elizabeth Appleton is temporarily reassigned to the curatorship of the antique fire-fighting museum in Jamaica Plain, at number 22 Pond Road, for the purposes of cataloging the antique fire equipment located there prior to the public opening of said museum.'"

"What!"

"That's what it says, Lieutenant," the sergeant told her apologetically. "'Effective immediately,' it says. I think that means you're supposed to go over there today and get started listing the machines right away." He paused. "I never even knew we had an antique fire-fighting museum out there."

Sarie was so angry that she had to fight not to snap at the innocent sergeant. "We didn't," she said through clenched lips. "This is a new development. Thank you, Sergeant Foley." She hung up before she lost her temper entirely.

"Hey, Ma, what's the matter?" Taylor saw her trembling and paused in his cleanup.

"That...that..." Sarie was trembling all over, and she began to pace the room. The idea of being taken off active duty for any reason was unbearable to Sarie. But to have been removed for some frivolous little task at the request of some privileged snob for some specious reason... "I could just... He is such a..."

"Who? Who? Is it Wapshaw again? What'd he do this time?" Chief Wapshaw was a man Taylor loved to hate.

"It wasn't the chief's fault this time," Sarie told him, spinning into action as she pulled her shoes on, grabbed her purse and threw Taylor his lunch. "It was a friend of his. A certain Mr. Vance Leland."

"Who's he?" asked Taylor as she shepherded him out the door. "Who is he and what'd he do?"

"He tried to give me a job," she said, her eyes snapping with anger. "Working on his damned antique fire-engine collection!"

"His antique—" Taylor skidded to a halt and his jaw dropped "—Mom, are you kidding? That's... that's..."

"No, Tay," she remonstrated severely. "It may seem like paradise to you, but it is definitely *not* wizard in my book. And he's not going to get away with it, either."

SARIE DROPPED TAYLOR OFF at school and went straight downtown. She stopped at the fire department headquarters to make some inquiries, and what she found only confirmed her worst fears. The chief had decided that the Brewery fire was an accidental arson and had ordered only a preliminary investigation. That meant, Sarie knew, that her triplicate report would receive a routine and cursory glance and that would be all. Someone had managed to convince the chief that there was nothing worth investigating, and Sarie had an idea who that someone was.

The offices of Leland Enterprises were located on the forty-second floor of a new high-rise complex that towered above the city's financial district. The glass elevator that took her up offered a spectacular view, but Sarie was too angry to notice. So Vance Leland had thought he could pull rank and have her transferred to some obscure outpost in Jamaica Plain, did he? Did he think he was doing her a favor because she really had been interested in antique fire-fighting equipment? No, he was too perceptive to have made that mistake. Maybe it was just his idea of a cute little joke, having the chief yank her off active duty to sit on her hands and make lists of outdated fire equipment for a week.

What was Vance's motive? Perhaps he really *did* want her out of the way. Off active duty she couldn't pry into the Brewery arson investigation. After all, he had warned her to keep her nose clean, hadn't he?

But why? Once again, Sarie tried to make sense of Vance's involvement in the matter. He had plenty of sound reasons for being involved, but she still felt that there was something more to it than that. The man in the shadows last night had added fuel to the fires of her suspicions, and Vance's latest move only intensified the blaze.

In any case, she was not going to take it lying down. That was definitely not her style. Ignoring the impressively sleek reception area and the breathtaking view, she strode purposefully over to the wedge of mahogany desk, where the receptionist presided in crisp expectancy.

"May I help you?" the woman asked sweetly.

"Where can I find Vance Leland?" Sarie demanded.

"He's in conference at the moment," the receptionist replied, indicating the double oak doors behind her with a manicured hand. "Do you have an appointment?"

"I do," Sarie muttered, "but I don't like it." She whipped around the big desk, heading for the double doors.

"You can't go in there!" the receptionist warned shrilly.

"Oh yes I can," Sarie retorted. "I just open the doors, like...this!"

After the ruckus she had caused in the reception area, the conference room seemed unnaturally quiet. Sarie, her hands still on the two ornate brass doorknobs, found herself facing a long conference table in a room that was predominantly gray and blue. Twenty-four chairs in pale blue suede surrounded the sea of polished cherry, but only five of them were occupied down at the far end. Framed by the strong morning light pouring in through the floor-to-ceiling windows, the five men formed a tableau, their actions arrested in midgesture by the sudden interruption. The six occupants of the room stared at each other for a long moment.

Then the receptionist scurried in behind Sarie and broke the silence. "I tried to stop her, Mr. Leland," she quavered, "but she just wouldn't listen!"

"You bet I wouldn't listen," Sarie said, raising her voice so that it could be heard across the thick expanse of muted gray carpet. "I didn't come here to listen. I came here to talk—to you, Mr. Leland."

She could barely make out the figure at the head of the table silhouetted against the light, but she could tell it was Vance by the elegant inclination of his head. "Which Mr. Leland did you want, Miss Appleton?" came his unmistakable voice, as genteel and urbane as if he had been inquiring after her health. "There are two of us here this morning."

"Don't play any more games with me," Sarie retorted. "I just want to know where you get your nerve."

Now that she had moved closer, she could make out the individual figures. Aside from Vance, four men sat around the table, and all of them, except Vance and an extremely old gentleman in a wheelchair, looked at her with shocked disapproval. The old man was nodding rapidly, and Vance seemed to be genuinely pleased to see her. "My nerve?" he repeated. "Oh, I guess I get that from my Uncle Horace here." He turned to the old man. "Horace, I'd like you to meet Miss Sarah Elizabeth Appleton. Of the Beacon Hill and Beverly Farms Appletons, naturally."

The old man peered at her from under bushy white brows and grinned. "Are you the one who put it to your old man and joined the firemen?" he inquired.

"I . . ."

"Well, I say good for you, little girl!" He hooted delightedly. "Glad to see someone in that family's got some backbone. Your father's a stuffed shirt and your mother's a snob. Hasn't been an interesting Appleton since Sarah Jane, if you ask me."

Sarie couldn't think of an appropriate response to this outrageous remark, so she ignored it and did what came naturally to her. "I'm pleased to make your acquaintance, Mr. Leland," she said politely, and extended her hand for him to shake.

Vance introduced her to the other men at the table. "That's Mr. Parkman, the insurance commissioner for the city of Boston, Mr. Edward T. Crane of Crane Paper, and Fred Hapgood of the Beverly Hapgoods," he went on blithely. "These gentlemen are some of the partners in the Brahmin Trust. You've heard of the Brahmin Trust, I presume?"

"No, I . . ." Sarie tried helplessly to regain control of the situation.

"We're a real estate holding concern. Nothing to do with Leland Enterprises, you understand. It's more sort of a . . . a private institution, a hobby, if you will. Of course, not all the members take the same active interest. But we've been together for years, haven't we, gentlemen?" He laughed and the other men smiled nervously. "Actually, being a blind trust, we don't do much except oversee other people's real estate investments and turn the profits back into the Trust. I don't think any of these gentlemen could even tell you what buildings we own, could you, gentlemen?" He smiled brightly, but nobody said a word. Sarie wondered why he was taking such pains to make them uncomfortable. "To tell you the truth, none of us really seems to know what the others are doing, but we do gather for these meetings every six months or so and gossip like old ladies. Helps keep up the illusion of interest, you see."

He spoke with a mild condescension and a cheerful tone, as if it was the most normal thing in the world to interrupt a private business meeting and explain things to a stranger. But Sarie was struck by the definite tinge of sarcasm behind the instructional tone. She looked at Vance more closely, but he returned her gaze without a trace of irony. "Gentlemen," he said, turning to the uneasy assemblage with a graceful gesture of his hand, "this is Miss Sarie Appleton, a good friend of mine."

Sarie was utterly taken aback by this turn of events. She had stormed in with the intent of throwing Vance off balance, and here she was shaking hands as if she was paying a social call. The men seemed equally confused—only Vance and his uncle seemed to be having a good time. She had to make a real effort to maintain her anger, especially before this unexpected audience.

"A good friend of yours? Is that how you treat your friends, Mr. Leland, by going behind their backs?"

His eyes widened. "Behind their...I don't know what you mean, Sarie."

"Don't tell me you don't know what I mean," she snapped impatiently. "Of course you do."

He shrugged his shoulders. "No, honestly, I don't. If it was something I did last night..." He looked genuinely puzzled, and ignored the pointed throat clearing from his colleagues while he regarded Sarie with concern.

"Last night was bad enough," huffed Sarie, trying not to think about their kiss, which had not been bad at all. "It's this morning I'm talking about."

"This morning?"

"This morning. When you called Chief Wapshaw and had him assign me to that ridiculous museum job of yours just to get me off the Brewery case. That's what I mean, and I want to know why you did it."

For the first time Vance seemed to be really concerned. He looked at Sarie for a moment and then at the other men, who seemed more and more scandalized at this public airing of private linen.

"If you'll excuse me, gentlemen," he said at last. "I think this matter needs my immediate attention." He rose with a courtly bow and swiftly squired Sarie into his private office.

Once there, his demeanor changed at once. "Now do you mind telling me what that ridiculous performance was all about?" he demanded.

"I want to know why you had me reassigned, Vance," she replied curtly. It was even harder to maintain her angry stance confronted by those eyes. Suddenly she was not as certain of Vance's perfidy as she had been before.

"I don't have the slightest idea what you're talking about," he said with a trace of impatience in his voice.

The fissure in Sarie's certainty was rapidly widening. "I just found out from headquarters that Chief Wapshaw has decided to declare the Brewery fire an accidental arson, and he's only authorizing a minimal investigation."

"So? You have a problem with that?"

Sarie's anger flared up again. "Of *course* I have a problem with it! That fire was not just some kid playing copycat arsonist, Vance, it was the real thing! Chief Wapshaw may want to cover it up to protect the department's sacred image, but it's not going to stay covered. I intend to find out who started that fire, and I intend to find out why."

He looked at her with such coldness that Sarie bit her lip. But when he spoke his tone betrayed nothing of his mood. "I thought I told you not to get involved with this, Sarie," he said quietly.

"So you *are* trying to get me out of the way!" she exclaimed triumphantly.

"Don't be a fool," he snapped. "There's nothing to get in the way of. It's nothing, don't you understand?"

"Then why the warning last night?"

He smiled wearily. "That was to protect you from yourself. You tend to get a little overzealous once you've got your sights set on something, don't you agree?"

Sarie ignored this. "Is that why you got the chief to reassign me to your project? To protect me from myself?"

Vance looked at her as if she was crazy. "What are you talking about, for God's sake? *What* reassignment?"

Sarie had to admit that he seemed really mystified by her accusation. "To your museum, of course. To write up that ridiculous catalog or something. I don't know." She felt flustered and confused, and the look on Vance's face was not helping. She couldn't tell if he was angry or disgusted with her, and neither alternative was a pleasant one.

Then he burst out laughing, which was even worse. "Oh, this is rich," he said, chuckling. "This is really rich. You mean to tell me that Bob Wapshaw shunted you off to J.P. to catalog that old collection of mine? And you think I got him to do it?"

That had been exactly what she thought, but Vance made it sound so ridiculous that Sarie felt her stomach drop, taking her resolve with it. Could she have been totally wrong in her assumptions? She tried to remind herself that a man like Vance made it his job to get people to see things his way, but she knew she had made a mistake.

"It seemed to be a sensible explanation," she muttered.

"It's a ridiculous explanation, and you know it," Vance snapped. They had been standing face-to-face, and now he wheeled away from her and began to pace over the huge Oriental rug. "If I really wanted you out of the way, I'd see to it that you were out of the way, not off in Jamaica Plain, for God's sake."

Sarie swallowed. "Why would you want me out of the way, Vance?" she inquired tightly.

"I said *if*," he reminded her. "*If* I did, it would be for your own good. But I certainly didn't arrange this…this travesty. Although I think I know who did."

Sarie knew too. "The chief," she muttered, nodding resignedly.

"Obviously Bob Wapshaw has a thing about women fire fighters, and you in particular. And you certainly don't do anything to win him over, I must say. I left it up to him to find someone for the museum, and he probably figured he could kill two birds with one stone—get someone to do the job and twist the knife in your back a little bit." He snorted impatiently. "He's an idiot, that man, he really is." Then he swung around suddenly to face Sarie. "But for you to have thought that I was responsible—why, that's even more idiotic than Bob Wapshaw!"

"I don't think it's so idiotic," she said defensively.

"You don't?" There was a mocking twist to his lips that Sarie didn't like. "I'll bet you don't."

"After all, you do seem pretty interested in keeping me away from the Brewery investigation," she pointed out accusingly.

"I am," he said curtly. "But that's no reason why I would want you taken off active duty, even for a week. You're too good a fire fighter, Sarie, and God knows the city needs you now."

"Why? Why do they need me now?" she asked sharply.

His eyes glittered. "They always need you. I didn't mean they need you now more than usual. You're a fire fighter, and you should be fighting fires, not making lists in some musty museum."

"I couldn't agree more," she said hotly.

Vance took a few steps so that they were standing nose to nose. "But that doesn't mean I want you messing around with this arson investigation."

"There *is* no arson investigation, if you'll recall," she said, meeting his stare boldly. "Nobody seems to think it's necessary."

Vance paused. "Right. Well, it's not."

"Then why are you so anxious to keep me away, if there's nothing to keep away from?"

He clamped his jaw together and searched her face, his slate eyes raking over her features with relentless intensity. Sarie resisted the urge to step back.

"Things are not always what they seem, Sarie. You of all people should know that."

Sarie thought suddenly of the man who she thought had been following them and of the car parked on her quiet street. "That's not an answer, Vance, and you of all people should know that."

"I'm afraid it'll have to do for the moment, Sarie. Let's just say I don't like to mix business with pleasure," he said in his most measured voice. "For instance, I have a business relationship with those men out there, Sarie, but I never mix with them personally. Other than my uncle, I have no idea what any of them do with their lives, and they don't know what I do with mine. It makes trust a harder game to play, but those are the rules, and I have to play by those rules. I like to play by those rules."

"And what am I?" she murmured breathlessly. "Business or pleasure?" Sarie knew she had been set up to ask the question, but she couldn't keep from uttering the words.

The slow smile that spread over his face stripped away his control revealing a sensual heat that made Sarie suck in her lower lip. "Take a guess, Miss Appleton," he said, his lips tantalizingly close to hers. "Just take a guess."

She was so sure he was going to kiss her that she actually closed her eyes and swayed slightly toward him. But when she opened them, he was already halfway across the room. "Right now is business time," he said over his shoulder, giving no evidence in his tone or manner of the lush desire he had just displayed so clearly. "The Brahmin Trust is waiting," he added dryly. "And you have a job to do." He paused at the door, and for a moment Sarie thought he was going to change his mind and come back to her. He looked at her with an almost beseeching expression and opened his mouth to say something. But then he seemed to think better of it. And, turning once again without a word of farewell, he was gone.

Sarie glared at the heavy oak doors for a moment, trying to sort out what had just happened. She was torn between annoyance and dissatisfaction, and decided that, in all, it had been a pretty useless encounter. She left the office quickly, ignoring the imperious stare of the receptionist and grumbling acridly to herself about what she would do to Chief Robert Wapshaw if only she had the chance. She knew better than to try to get him to put her back on active duty. Vance had been right about one thing—this assignment was her punishment for giving the chief a hard time and refusing to play the departmental game according to his rules. He enjoyed making life difficult for her, just as she got a certain satisfaction out of the discomfort her female presence caused him. She would just have to concede this round to the chief and let it go at that.

But she would not let Vance Leland off the hook as easily. It was clear to Sarie that, even if he hadn't had a hand in her reassignment, he wanted her to stay away from the Brewery investigation. She could think of no other reason than Vance knew more about the fire than he was letting on; more than he wanted her to find out. He knew that Chief Wapshaw, following Vance's suggestion, no doubt, would not let the investigation go any further than it already had. Obviously he wanted to keep Sarie from asking too many questions of her own. But why? What was he trying to hide?

The obvious explanation was difficult for Sarie to accept. Was it possible that Vance was not merely involved, but actually implicated in some way in either the Roxbury fires or the Brewery fire? There was no reason in the world for him to start a fire in his own building, she reminded herself—unless he was deliberately throwing up a smoke screen to cover his tracks. But, if he had been involved in the Roxbury fires, someone might have started the Brewery fire to scare him.

Sarie chided herself for thinking in circles. All the supposition in the world was no good at all without facts, and she knew of only one way to get the facts. She went back to the station and, carefully avoiding anyone who might report her presence to the chief, went to the records library on the second floor. Tobey

Witt, the man in charge, was a genial older man who ran his department like a fiefdom.

"Hey, Tobey," she greeted him with a smile. "I need a little favor."

"I've heard that before," Tobey remarked. "What is it this time? A copy of all your commendations? A list of your promotions to show the chief that a woman can do a man's job?"

Sarie grinned. "Not quite. I want to look at the records from the Roxbury investigation."

"What on earth for, Sarie? That case has been closed for months, thank the Lord."

"I know, but . . ." Sarie thought quickly. Those reports were not supposed to be circulated. "My son, Taylor, is doing a report on arson in school. And he wanted to use some of the cases I worked on to impress the kids."

Tobey nodded sagely. "I understand. I've got kids myself, and they'll never forgive me for going off active duty. They love to impress their friends with their daddy, the fireman. Your boy can say 'my mommy, the fireman,' though, can't he?" Tobey chuckled. "Okay, I'll let them out this time. It's for a worthy cause." He went into the locked records room and returned with a thick sheaf of papers. "This is everything—the police reports, the arson team reports, the court records, even the newspaper accounts."

"Thanks, Tobe." Sarie took the file from him, trying to suppress her excitement. *At last,* she thought to herself, *some answers.*

"Only thing not here is Mr. Leland's private notes."

Sarie stopped in her tracks. "Why not? Aren't they part of the public records?"

Tobey shrugged. "Guess not. He made some kind of deal with the chief—kept the records of his private investigation to himself. They're not even in the court records. Too bad—I'll bet there's some juicy stuff in his notes."

"That's pretty unusual, isn't it?" Sarie asked cautiously. "I mean, his evidence was supposedly what put the guilty men behind bars."

"Yup. But then Leland's an unusual guy," Tobey said. "He can pretty much get away with whatever he wants in this city, and if he wanted his notes kept private for some reason, you can bet no one batted an eye."

Sarie looked at the folder. There was only one reason he might have for not wanting his notes made public. There was something in them he didn't want anyone else to see. *Well,* she thought, *I guess this means I'll have to try and get my hands on those notes.*

"Now, you get that stuff back to me," Toby called after her as she started out of the office. "The chief'll have my hide and yours if he finds out that file has been taken out of here."

Tucking the papers into her bag, Sarie thanked him and left. She wanted to study the reports at her leisure, and she couldn't think of a better place to do it than somewhere deserted and silent—an antique firefighting equipment museum in Jamaica Plain.

THE CARRIAGE HOUSE was set back off the Jamaicaway on a small plot of land that offered a glimpse of Jamaica Pond and the Fen beside it. The scene was pastoral for a spot so close to the city, and Sarie took a moment to appreciate the elegant grace of the building in its sylvan setting before going in.

Trust Vance Leland to do everything up right. Not only was the carriage house a small architectural gem, but its contents were impressive and displayed with a fine eye for detail and a lavish disregard for expense. Set up in a large central room with a high beamed ceiling were several dozen old fire engines, ranging from a century-old wooden wagon to a sleek, art deco locomotive coupe. Track lighting displayed each one to advantage and enormous photo murals and etchings were mounted as backdrops for each one. Waist-high glass-enclosed cases nearby included smaller paraphernalia as well as information on the machines and their uses. Despite the extensive renovations, the carriage house still retained a faint leathery odor of horses and saddlery that Sarie thought only added to the nostalgic air of the place.

In a smaller room, which must have once served as the tack room, stood two more engines—one of them the Hercules engine that Taylor had been raving about just a few hours ago. Sarie reminded herself that there was one bonus to this dreary task—Taylor would have a field day exploring his favorite vehicles close up. She ran her hands over the sleek chrome finish on the Hercules. Taylor was right—it was a gorgeous piece of machinery.

In the back of the room there was a small desk, where Sarie found the information she was to use for the catalog neatly laid out in towering piles. Vance—or whoever he got to do the job for him—had left nothing to chance, she thought dryly. But she had other things to do first, and she pushed the books aside in order to make room for the notes on the Roxbury fires.

The records were incredibly detailed, and it took Sarie hours to sift through them for any information that she did not already know. What had happened in Roxbury was not unusual in a city where arson was a common and frequent crime. What set the Roxbury fires apart was the subtlety with which the arson had been carried out.

The police reports revealed that the pattern of the fires had been specific and complex, indicating that a master plan had been in place right from the start. In hindsight, it was hard to believe that the pattern hadn't been apparent to the investigators. It was a tribute to whomever had masterminded the plan that it had escaped the detection of so many trained people.

The buildings had all been low-rent, low-income tenements in an area that was rapidly turning into an upscale urban haven. The landlords of the buildings had hired an arsonist to systematically burn only those buildings that would garner them the highest insurance payoffs. They had planned to use the money to build high-rent condos on the burnt-out sites, thus collecting twice on their scheme—once when the insurance company paid off and again when they reaped the long-term profits from the new buildings.

It had been an audacious and heartless plan, and it had been carried out with chilling efficiency. The idea of the landlords all working together had apparently appealed to the men because it would make it harder to trace those who would benefit directly from arson. The buildings were not owned outright by the individuals, but were held for the landlords in a complicated financial arrangement that even the insurance investigators had had a hard time untangling.

The method of destruction had been Machiavellian, too. Certain buildings in the targeted area had been left standing and others were chosen for burning seemingly at random in order to divert suspicion. Various incendiary methods had been used, but the Jackson device had started most of the major fires. Even the decision to hire Ira Jackson, the technical man who had been called in from Detroit to oversee the mechanical aspects of the blazes, had been brilliant. All the known local arsonists had been able to come up with airtight alibis for the times in question, and Jackson's diabolical invention had led investigators hopelessly astray as they tried to figure out where and how the device had been made.

There was nothing new in the reports, but as she read Sarie began to see the old information in a new light. She became more and more convinced that there was a connection between the Brewery fire and the Roxbury arsons. Still, before she could find out what that link was, she needed to know more. It seemed obvious to her that there was some piece missing from all the detailed minutiae of the reports, and Sarie knew there was only one place she was going to find it.

"It all comes back to Vance Leland," she said aloud, her voice echoing in the silent room. She would have to figure him out before she could come up with any answers. The problem was that he was the biggest puzzle of all. Why did he seem so unconcerned about the Brewery fire, and then so adamant about her not looking into it? Why had he pretended he didn't know he was being followed when it was so clear to her that he did? Why had he insisted that his private notes on the investigation be kept out of the records? And why was he having such a disquieting effect on her?

"Persistence," she announced to the Hercules engine. "Persistence and objectivity, and I'll get to the bottom of this thing sooner or later." She squinted up at the dusty sunlight filtering in from a small high window and frowned. She just hoped it would be sooner rather than later.

BY THE TIME Sarie was finished reading, it was early afternoon, and she was starving. She decided to get a sandwich and eat it as she worked. If she didn't get something done on the catalog, she would have a lot of explaining to do, and she wasn't ready to do any explaining yet. Fortunately there was a small sub shop around the corner from the carriage house. She ordered a turkey sub with extra pickles and took it back with her.

She ate quickly and then, with a sigh of resignation, she turned to her assigned task at last. Her instructions were to condense the information on each engine into one or two paragraphs using the stacks of books and computer printouts for reference. These instructions were neatly printed out for her on another computer sheet, and they were exhaustive to the point of being ridiculous. "Whoever went to all the trouble to set this up might as well have done the job himself," she said in exasperation. Included in the instructions was information that Sarie was to write an introduction to the catalog, which would describe Vance's generosity and public spiritedness. "Great," she muttered as she surveyed the pile before her with a grim resignation. "Not only am I stuck here writing précis like a superannuated high school student, but I'm supposed to write a song of praise for a guy who may not be as clean and upstanding as he looks." She scowled at her reflection in the chrome exterior of the Hercules. "Chief Wapshaw, you'll pay for this."

Suddenly a piece of paper stuck into the corner of one of the books caught her eye. It was a small piece of yellow foolscap, which had obviously been crumpled up and then smoothed out and folded several times. There was something written on it in dull pencil, and it attracted her attention only because it stood out so sharply from the crisp efficiency of everything else on the desk.

"What's this, someone's shopping list?" Sarie pulled it out. "I guess a computer didn't put this mountain of busywork together without some human assistance after all." She uncreased the note in front of her.

"'You're right about the Brewery,'" she read aloud. "'If you want to know the truth about Vance Leland, you'd better keep your eyes and ears open. Someone else is doing the same.'" It was unsigned.

Sarie read the note three times before its meaning sank in. Then she sat for a long time holding it in her trembling hands. Someone else had been keeping eyes and ears open—and obviously for quite a while. As she looked around the room, she wondered if her heart could possibly leap out of her chest as it threatened to. All her fears and doubts had telescoped into a single terrifying focus. She had not been imagining any of it. There *had* been someone following her, and there *was* something more than met the eye about Vance's involvement in the fires.

And there was someone still out there, watching her every move. Sarie forced herself to stand up. Was the author of the note still in the carriage house? Obviously someone had gotten in while she was at lunch—but had he (or she) left again? Sarie felt danger in the air, smothering her like a hot towel, robbing her of breath. She forced herself to walk across the small tack room and into the large central display area. There was no one in either room. She tiptoed over to the corridor that connected a series of smaller rooms off the other side of the central hall and opened the doors one by one. A closet, a storage area, two bathrooms—but no other living human being. Just herself and the huge old fire engines, outlined in what now seemed like frightening clarity in the dim interior of the carriage house.

Suddenly Sarie felt an uncontrollable urge to bolt outside. Her labored breathing and the thudding of her heart were too much to bear in that uncanny silence. Abandoning what was left of her control, she raced for the front door. Once outside, she slammed it behind her and leaned weakly against it.

The sun shone brightly, and there was a pleasant sea breeze lifting the spring air. Sarie drank it in in great gulps. She felt as if she had left the horror—nameless and unidentifiable—locked inside the carriage house. But she knew, even as she struggled to slow her racing pulse, that she had done no such thing. The terror was still with her; it lay in the tiny kernel of certainty she carried within and would not be tamed until she found the truth.

Think, she told herself sternly. *You've got to think clearly about this. Someone else knows something about Vance Leland, and whoever it is thinks that you know, too. But you don't know anything—not for certain. So how can you find out for sure? And do you want to? What are you getting yourself into?* Sarie closed and opened her eyes several times, trying to find perspective, to get a fix on the situation.

It was then that she saw the car—the car she had seen the night before on her street. It was parked halfway down the road, pulled off onto a grassy shoulder and away from the heavy traffic on the Jamaicaway. Whoever was in the car was hidden behind an open newspaper and probably hadn't seen her come out of the carriage house. Sarie blinked again, hoping the car and its occupant were a hallucination that would fade from her vision. They weren't.

Well, old girl, she told herself in a voice she scarcely recognized. *You have several choices. You could call the police. You could quit your job. You could take Taylor and move to Brazil. You could do the smart thing and get the hell out of here before this whole thing gets out of control.* She paused and took three slow, steadying breaths. *Or you could go over there and find out who that guy is and what he wants with you.*

Steeling herself by digging her nails into her palms— a trick that always worked when she was fighting a dangerous fire, but had no effect now—she walked boldly over to the green Toyota.

The man saw her coming when she was only a few yards away. He crumpled the paper and looked wildly about, apparently for some way to escape. Seeing his state gave Sarie the necessary boost of courage required to carry her to the car window.

"I think," she said, putting a trembling hand on the car door, "that it's time we had a talk."

Chapter Four

"Um, um, I don't think...uh..." The man gaped at Sarie, his eyes darting from side to side as he tried to recover his wits. "Uh... Do I know you?"

"You probably do," Sarie said, wondering how she was managing to sound so composed. "But I'm afraid I haven't had the pleasure yet—unless you count last night, that is."

"Last night?"

Now that she had begun to talk, it was clear she was controlling things. She even began to feel a bit annoyed at the man. "That's right—last night. When you were following me, remember?"

The man blanched. "I never—"

"I saw your car," she interrupted him sternly, and watched as he gave up all pretense of innocence with a heavy sigh.

"Okay," he said resignedly, "you win. Let's talk." He indicated that Sarie should go around to the other side of the car and get in.

"Not on your life," she told him crisply. "I'm not getting in there with you." She pulled on the handle of the driver's side. "I want to keep this as public as possible. You get out."

After peering nervously up and down the road, the man did as she demanded. He was tall and lanky but had a potbelly and receding hairline. Still, Sarie figured that he was not as old as he looked—and possibly not as out of shape, either. She shifted, into vigilant alert—her fire fighter's stance—as he fell into step beside her.

"I can't believe you found me," the man muttered, shuffling along beside her as they headed up the road toward the carriage house.

"You didn't make it very hard," she remarked more gently. She had a sudden image of the man as the cowardly lion in *The Wizard of Oz*, a favorite movie. He had seemed so menacing until she got up close. Now, he seemed more of a bumbler than a threat.

"I thought I was being pretty cool," he said defensively. Then he cast her a look of grudging admiration. "I never thought you'd have the . . . the nerve to come up to me, even if you did notice."

"Who are you?" she asked.

"John Smith," he replied promptly, and then, seeing the look of disbelief on her face, began again. "Oh, what the hell. The whole thing is blown to bits anyway. I'm Doug Eldridge." Sheepishly he extended his hand. "Pleased to meet you, Miss Appleton."

With a chuckle, Sarie gave his hand a single shake. "Now, Mr. Eldridge, do you mind telling me what this is all about?"

He sighed and shook his head morosely. "It's a little hard to explain," he began.

"Give it a shot."

Doug seemed at a loss. "I wanted . . . I need to talk to someone," he said plaintively. "Things have just gotten so far out of control that I..." He looked at her beseechingly. "I was following you because I was trying to figure out if you could help me."

"Me, help you?" That was the last thing she had expected to hear, and Sarie took this explanation with a grain of salt.

But Doug's dismay seemed genuine. "Yeah. Ya' see, I've gotten myself into this mess, and now I think I'd better get out. But I don't know how. Everywhere I turn I... It's..." He raised his shoulders and dropped them helplessly. "I'm really in over my head."

Despite Sarie's skepticism, she was intrigued. If Doug's dismay was an act, it was a very good one. Besides, whatever he had to tell her would be more than she already knew. "Why don't you start from the beginning?" she said, and had a sudden memory of Vance Leland's cultured voice prompting her gently to do the same thing. Doug seemed to be having second thoughts and said nothing. "It has to do with Vance Leland, doesn't it?" she prodded.

He flashed her a wary look that made Sarie certain he was not as befuddled as he appeared. But he sounded relieved. "Yeah, of course it has to do with Leland. I used to work for him, ya' see. Not officially but..." He looked guilty. "I'm a sparkie, and I used to see him around at fires. I mean, we don't exactly travel in the same circles, and we never really talked much. He's such a big deal with the bigwigs, I never even really got close to him, if you wanna know the truth. But I knew who he was, all right, and apparently he knew who I was, too—knew that I had certain...valuable street connections." He stole a glance at Sarie to see if she caught his meaning, and Sarie nodded sagely, even though she was not quite sure what sort of street connections Doug was referring to.

"Well, you know, Leland's very hoity-toity and all, but when he needed help he knew where to come." He sounded proud of himself. "He came to me."

"Help for what?"

"To find out about the Roxbury arsons, of course," he said, as if surprised that she hadn't known. "I did a lot of legwork for him on that investigation."

Sarie's heart rate accelerated with a lurch. She couldn't believe her luck. Now perhaps she wouldn't have to get those private notes from Vance. That would have been a formidable task, and this man did not seem nearly so daunting, despite his shady act. "So you helped Vance collar the Roxbury arson ring, did you?"

"You bet I did." Doug was warming to his tale now, and Sarie knew the best thing to do would be to keep quiet and let him talk. "Leland could never have done it without my help. I knew the guys on the street, see, and I heard rumors—rumors about who had done it, and why, and everything."

"It was pretty clear who had done it," Sarie couldn't help pointing out.

He shook his head. "Nah, I don't mean the guys who owned the buildings. That was obvious. But Ira Jackson, the chief torch man. He was hard to pin down, being from out of town and all. Nobody on the street was willing to give the cops any information on a guy like Jackson—too scared, I guess." He actually swaggered a bit. "But I wasn't afraid of Jackson. I kept my ears close to the sidewalk and I heard plenty. Leland knew I heard it too. I don't know how, but he did. So he contacted me. Believe me, Leland couldn't have tracked Jackson down without my help, that's for sure." He paused and became reflective. "And then there were the others. That was his department."

Sarie felt her throat seize up. "What others?"

"*You* know," he said in a low voice. "The others."

Sarie didn't want to shake Doug's confidence in her. She had to recover quickly. "There were twelve men indicted for those arsons," she said carefully. "The eight landlords, Ira Jackson and three of his associates. All of them are behind bars. What others are you talking about, Mr. Eldridge?"

Doug stopped walking. "Didn't Leland tell you?"

"Tell me what?" Sarie realized their voices had dropped to a whisper, even though they were standing beside a busy major thoroughfare.

Doug slapped his hand to his forehead. "Omigod, I thought you knew! I thought that was why..." He peered at her from beneath his palm. "You mean he never told you anything?"

Sarie took a deep breath. "Mr. Eldridge, I've been trying to investigate Vance Leland's connection to the Brewery fire. He's been pretty uncooperative—and so have you. Now, would you mind explaining what you're talking about?"

Doug looked nervous. "I don't think..."

"I thought you needed help," Sarie reminded him pointedly. "I can't help if you don't tell me what's going on." She saw how miserable he looked and decided to change tacks. "Okay, let's take this one step at a time. Who started the Brewery fire, Doug?" she asked more gently.

"That's what I'm trying to figure out," he replied morosely. "That's why I came to you. If it's who I think it is, then I'm in deep trouble."

Sarie fought to keep her patience. "And who is that?"

But Doug shook his head. "I'm in enough trouble already. I can't tell you who."

"Why not?" she asked, exasperated.

He looked like he was about to cry. "Because I work for him, that's why!"

Sarie felt a momentary stab of panic. "I thought you said you worked for Vance," she said softly. Doug did not seem to notice the impact his rambling tale was having on her.

"I did. I used to. But he took all the glory, and he didn't seem to have any use for me after the trials were over, even though I knew . . . even though he knew the whole thing wasn't really finished. It was like I had ceased to exist in his mind." Sarie could hear the bitterness in Doug's voice, and she could imagine how easily Vance had dismissed Doug when he was finished with him. It was a typical move for a man like Vance. But it didn't sound as if Doug was accusing his former boss of arson.

"I was pretty miffed," Doug went on. "See, I'd been out of work for a while, and I thought he would at least give me a job, or something, in return for my good work. But no. Nothing."

"Didn't he pay you?" Sarie inquired.

"Oh, yeah, he paid. But I thought…" Doug's voice trailed off disconsolately. "Anyway when the…when these other guys approached me, I agreed to help them out. Besides, I thought they had a pretty convincing argument, not to mention a hefty financial offer, if ya' know what I mean."

"Help them do what?"

"Well, that was the funny part. They wanted me to do the same thing I was doing for Leland. Find out who else was behind the Roxbury arsons. Or, rather, they wanted me to find out what Leland knew about them."

"But I thought you knew that already."

"I didn't. At least, I didn't know anything for sure. I knew that Leland thought there was someone else involved—someone really big, so big he had managed to escape notice completely. But I didn't know who, and he never told me." He pursed his lips. "I figured hooking the big guys wasn't really my area of expertise anyway, it was Leland's. If anything was going to come down after the trials, Leland was gonna handle that part himself." He paused and squinted at the road. "But nothing happened. I thought Leland probably hadn't gotten anywhere with it, and I pretty much forgot about it. But then, when this other guy approached me, he said he thought he knew who it was. Naturally, I was interested."

Sarie forced herself to ask the question as casually as possible. "Who did your...your new employer think it was?"

He looked at her slyly again and spoke with ponderous effect. "He said he thought it was Leland himself. That's why he wanted me to look into Leland's investigation—in case he was covering his own tracks for some reason."

"Vance Leland?" Sarie's voice rose in shock and confusion. "But I thought..."

"Shh!" Doug looked around worriedly. "Don't talk so loud!"

The conversation seemed to be getting out of control. Who did this man work for and why did they suspect Vance? "But how could it possibly have been Vance?" she asked in a lower voice.

Doug shrugged. "I didn't see how either at first. But this guy...he pointed out how it could have been. That's why he wanted those notes. After all, how else did Leland know so much about the whole thing? How else did he find out about the landlords and that blind trust thing?"

"Blind trust?" Sarie stumbled over the suddenly familiar words. "What on earth does a blind trust have to do with this?"

"I don't know. I don't even really know what they are, except they make a lot of quiet money for people who like to keep their money quiet. You know anything about 'em?"

A very clear picture of the conference room at Leland Enterprises came into Sarie's mind. The Brahmin Trust. "I think I do," she said slowly. "I... recently ran into one."

"Well, there are tons of them in this city. Everybody who's anybody is part of one. I guess it's supposed to be another good way for the rich to make money off the poor." He snorted derisively. "According to...to my source, the landlords in the Roxbury buildings didn't even know they were partly owned by a blind trust. That's why it never came out at the trial."

"So I figured, hey, yeah, that's right—how else did Leland know all that stuff? And I started thinking—it could have been Leland behind it all the time. He could 'a been playing me for a fool along with the rest of the city. And that made me mad. So I agreed to work for this fellow for a while, just to see where it would get me."

Sarie felt a pit opening in the bottom of her stomach and her lunch sliding slowly into it. She swallowed hard. "But it…it *couldn't* have been him." She wasn't sure what she thought of Vance just yet, but she hadn't seriously considered that he was directly involved in the arsons.

"Ya' never know," Doug said darkly.

"But why would Vance go to all that effort to expose the arson ring in the first place if he was really behind the whole thing?"

"He didn't expose the whole thing," Doug reminded her, "just the parts that didn't touch him. Makes him come out smelling like a rose, of course."

Sarie was barely listening. "And why torch the Brewery—his own building?" She was working desperately to come up with an explanation that would dispel her rising sense of panic. "What would that prove?"

Doug let his breath out in a loud flutter. "Yeah," he said miserably, "that's when I began to have my doubts too. Why would he torch his own building? Someone must'a done it to warn him…and I think…I have a sneaking suspicion I know who it is."

Sarie's head snapped up. "Your new boss, right?"

Doug nodded miserably. "Maybe."

But now it was her turn to play devil's advocate. "You know," she mused, half to herself, "Vance could have done it to draw attention away from himself."

He glanced at her sharply. "Hey, whose side are you on, anyway?"

"Nobody's at the moment," Sarie told him. "I'm just trying to figure it all out." She was silent for a few moments, sorting out the nightmarish possibilities.

The information was coming in too fast for her to process it. She looked appraisingly at Doug. "Why come to me with this tale?"

"Because I knew you were at the Brewery fire and that you suspected arson. And I knew you were a friend of Vance's."

"How did you know that?" she asked too quickly.

Doug grinned briefly. "I saw you kissing last night, remember? You gotta be friends to kiss like that, right?"

Sarie chose to ignore this truism. "But if you thought I was Vance's friend and you suspected him, why come to me?"

"I said I *used* to suspect him," Doug muttered darkly. "Now I don't know who to trust. That's why I came to you. I figured..." He looked sheepish. "You just looked honest," he finished lamely.

"Thanks," she said dryly. "But why not go straight to the authorities with what you know? Or even to Vance himself, if you don't think he's responsible anymore?"

"I can't go to the authorities. They'd never believe me." He avoided her gaze. "I've had... I've been in a little trouble in my day. Spent a little time in jail for a minor problem. They'd never take my word in something like this. And I don't think Mr. Leland would, either, especially if he knew who I was... that I was working for someone else on this matter. Besides," he added in a hushed voice, "I'm still not sure he didn't do it, y'know what I mean?"

Sarie looked across the Jamaicaway at Jamaica Pond, gleaming blue and deceptively clean in the strong afternoon sunlight. Was it true? Was it possible that Vance Leland was himself at the bottom of the biggest arson scandal in the city's history? The facts that she had and the information from Doug's patchy story seemed to confirm her intuitive suspicion that someone had escaped capture in the Roxbury case. But could it really have been Vance himself? On the surface, it seemed that Vance had the essentials required to engineer such a scheme—he had the power, the money and the cunning to make it work without drawing attention to himself. And, as Doug said, he might have had a lot to gain monetarily, through his blind trust, if he could get away with it.

But still she found it hard to imagine him actually executing such a demonic plan. Despite what she saw on the surface, she had seen something of the heart of Vance Leland, as well—the man who had kissed her was not the kind of man who could commit cold-blooded arson.

Or was her own impulsively sensual reaction clouding her vision? Sarie shivered. Maybe it *was* possible. Lately the word had gone so topsy-turvy that anything seemed possible.

Sarie forced herself back to the present. Doug Eldridge had contacted her for a reason, not just to pour his heart out. If he wasn't going to tell her who he worked for, she was going to have to weigh his information carefully. Before she gave any credence to his story, she had to know more. "If you won't go to Vance, and you won't go to the authorities, what do you think I can do for you?"

Doug wrung his hands and looked at her pleadingly. "I told you. I'm scared. I need help."

"What kind of help?"

"These guys—the ones I'm working for—they've got me very nervous. They will stop at nothing to get what they want—believe me, nothing." He shuddered, and Sarie felt a chill of fear herself. What kind of people had she gotten herself involved with? "Leland's got me nervous, too, to tell you the truth," Doug confessed.

"Oh, terrific," Sarie muttered. It was clear to her that Doug, though confused, really did feel himself to be in danger—and, if he was in danger, so was she. "This is just what I need in my life. Look, Doug, what can we do to get out of this mess?"

Doug's pale eyes brightened. "What I need is something to give me a little leverage—a little bargaining power, in case I get caught in the middle. I thought if I could just get my hands on Leland's notes before..."

Suddenly he stopped talking and turned so pale that Sarie thought he was going to faint.

"What is it?" she asked.

Doug's eyes were fixed over her shoulder, and he was moving his mouth in a vain attempt to talk. Sarie turned and followed his frightened gaze. A long gray limousine was moving slowly along the road in the opposite direction. Its windows were tinted, so she could not see inside. But she didn't have to. Clearly Doug's employer had seen them together.

Sarie looked farther down the road to the carriage house. What she saw there made the gray limousine fade into immediate insignificance. A black BMW was pulled up on the grass, right in front of the door. A tall, slim man in a crisp gray suit had gotten out and was holding open the door on the passenger side.

Sarie knew who it was before Doug spoke. "Jesus," he breathed, "They're both on my trail! Now I'm really in for it! I'd better get out of here, pronto!"

He shot off in the opposite direction before Sarie could stop him.

It wasn't until she had turned back to the carriage house that she recognized the person getting out of the passenger's side.

It was Taylor.

SARIE STRODE PURPOSEFULLY OVER the fifty yards separating her from her son. She grabbed him and hugged him against her with such force that Taylor grunted in pain.

"Hey, Ma, quit it!" he complained, struggling to get out of her grasp. When she reluctantly pulled away, she saw that his freckled face was red with embarrassment. "Jeez, you're acting like you haven't seen me in a hundred years."

Keep calm, Sarie told herself over and over. *There is probably a logical explanation for them to be here together.* Her heart hammering, she held Taylor at arm's length and tried to read the situation in his face. "I'm just surprised to see you here, honey, that's all." Surprised, suspicious and scared to death.

"Well, it was *supposed* to be a surprise," he said, exasperated. "That was the whole idea, Ma." He rolled his eyes expressively at Vance, who stood quietly near the door, but Sarie refused to look up, not trusting herself to look at him.

"How did you... What are you doing with Mr. Leland?"

"I went down to the station house after school to see if you were still as mad as you were this morning, and I asked Tom where the museum was so I could come and see you." He stopped and looked longingly at the door. "I also wanted to see those antique engines real bad. Anyway, Vance happened to be there at the time and . . ."

"It's Mr. Leland to you, young man," Sarie interjected automatically.

Vance spoke for the first time. "So, the rebel Appleton has a strong sense of etiquette, does she?"

Sarie steeled herself and looked up at him. His eyebrows were arched sardonically over his usual winning smile, his arms were folded across his chest and he seemed to be enjoying the scene between mother and son. But when he caught Sarie's eye, she thought she saw a flash of some stronger emotion cross his features. Was it a private look of warmth that flashed between them, or was it a warning? In her current state of mind, it was too easy to assume the latter. *Keep calm,* she reminded herself once more. *You have absolutely no proof that this man is guilty of anything worse than a kiss.*

"There are certain fundamentals of polite behavior that can't be ignored," she said aloud, hoping her tone of voice didn't belie the authority in her words. "Taylor hardly knows you, and he is aware that adults should be addressed with respect."

Vance unfolded his arms and opened the door of the carriage house. "That's a crock of old Appleton nonsense. Friendship has nothing to do with how long you've been acquainted. Taylor and I have already become good buddies, thanks to our mutual interest in antique fire-fighting equipment, isn't that right, Tay?"

"You bet!" Taylor replied eagerly, and headed for the museum.

"Besides," Vance went on as he stepped aside to allow them to enter, "his mother and I are good friends, too, which is another reason to do away with ridiculous social conventions." He stopped her with a small gesture as she attempted to sidle past him after Tay. "At least," he added with a soft, inquiring look, "I *thought* we were good friends."

The gesture was brief and hesitant—a mere lifting of the hand—and Sarie could easily have ignored it. But she could not ignore the entreaty she saw in his expression or the commanding potency of those eyes. "We *are* friends, aren't we, Sarie?"

Was this, too, a warning, or was Vance as eager to verify their odd intimacy as he seemed? Sarie had no idea whether he had seen her standing with Doug Eldridge on the shoulder of the road—the Jamaica-way curved just enough that she might have been hidden from his view. Given what she had learned about Vance in the past few hours, she had been prepared to accept the worst about the man, although she still had a lot of questions to be answered—by Vance himself, if possible.

Still, she could not deny the physical and emotional attraction that bound their gazes together. She recalled what he had said to her the previous night—*"There was something fateful about our meeting... You and I are bound together by some very deep ties."* And she remembered the kiss, as clearly as if the taste and warm pressure of his mouth still lingered on hers. Despite all her fears about his possible involvement in a serious crime, she knew that he was right. She was bound to Vance Leland in some mysterious way, whether by fate or by his own design. "What brings you here, Vance?" she managed to ask, hoping to break the spell. "Aside from my son?"

"I wanted to see you," he said simply. "All day long I thought about you stuck in this mausoleum against your will." He smiled. "Even the machinations of the Brahmin Trust meeting couldn't keep you out of my mind."

"How did the meeting go?" Sarie wondered if she could bring the subject around to the Trust's specific holdings without letting Vance know the reason for her interest.

"As boring as usual. Nothing ever happens with that group. We just hold on to old properties that none of us has ever seen."

"You mean you don't even know which buildings you own?"

"Not really. I haven't looked at the portfolio in years, if you want to know the truth."

"Why bother meeting, then?" she asked.

"Protocol. Those gentlemen wouldn't know what to do with themselves on the first Friday of October and April without the Trust. Sometimes eight or nine of the old codgers show up. Sometimes only two or three. But they have to know it's there."

"You don't need those meetings to feel useful. You're hardly an old codger," Sarie pointed out.

"Thanks." He grinned. "I'm sort of a de facto member. I'm the only one with legitimate real estate experience, so Uncle Horace insisted that I be brought in a few years ago to deal with . . . certain internal irregularities. Since then there hasn't been a thing for me to do, but the old boys like to have me around in case one of them should decide to find out what the others are up to." He laughed. "Besides, they like my office."

Vance led her into the carriage house, where Taylor could be heard exclaiming excitedly over the displays. "Actually, as Trust meetings go, this one was pretty eventful. One of our members is trying to buy out the other members, although he won't get very far with Uncle Horace. He never lets go of anything." He touched her shoulder lightly. "And then, of course, there was your little interruption."

"I'm sorry if I disturbed your meeting," Sarie said. The memory of her impulsive intrusion embarrassed her now.

"Don't be silly. You had every right to be annoyed about your reassignment." He looked around at the engines. "This is not exactly the most exciting spot in the city. Especially for someone like you."

Taylor let out a particularly high-pitched whoop, and Sarie knew he had found the Hercules. "It is for someone like Tay," she said, grinning in spite of herself.

They entered the tack room and found Taylor astride the Hercules, his eyes shining and a grin splitting his face from ear to ear. "Ma, look! It's exactly like the picture I showed you this morning. Isn't it absolutely excellent beyond belief?"

"Wizard," agreed Sarie. Taylor's delight went a long way toward quelling her anxiety.

"Vance—Mr. Leland, I mean—can you show me how the pumping system works?"

"Be glad to." Vance approached the gleaming machine and activated a brass release lever. Instantly the room was filled with a low-pitched hum. "That's the gear valve getting right to work," he told Taylor.

"Yeah, yeah, I know! That's so the firemen could use the water without waiting to crank up the motor.

It creates instant water pressure, right?'' Taylor's words tumbled over each other in his excitement.

"You're absolutely right. Then all they had to do was depress this lever and throw that switch." His slim fingers worked expertly, and Sarie found herself watching as closely as her son did.

"And the water would come out like a tidal wave, right?"

Vance reached up and ruffled Taylor's corn-silk hair. "You sure do know your stuff," he complimented him, and Taylor beamed.

"Does it really work, Vance? I mean, is there really water in it and everything?"

"You bet. I bought this machine from a collector who kept it in mint condition, and insisted I do the same. As a matter of fact, all these machines are in perfect working condition, once you know how to use them. Why, if we wanted to, we could fight a six-alarm fire with this machinery this very minute."

An expression that his mother knew all too well lit up Taylor's face. "No, Tay, that does *not* mean we will. After all, this is a museum, not a blazing building." She shook her head. "You'll just have to take Mr. Leland's word for it."

Taylor shrugged off his disappointment. "I'm going to check out the Cyclorama wagon in the other room," he said, and disappeared down the short hall.

Left alone with Vance again, Sarie was suddenly at a loss. Here she was with the man who had probably suppressed important information about arson—a man who might just have been involved in arson himself—and all she could think about was how nice he looked in his custom-tailored suit. She felt hopelessly unsophisticated in her jeans and oversize button-down shirt, and wished she had worn something that didn't make her look quite so much like an overripe teen-ager.

I should be scared to death of this man, she told herself. *I should be trying to get him to tell me what he knows about the Brewery. I should be demanding to see his private notes on the Roxbury fires.* But she could not convince herself to bring up the subject, and it appeared that Vance, too, was uncharacteristically at a loss for words. The two of them watched each other warily for a long time, each trying to fathom the other's thoughts.

"Well," said Vance at last, with a little laugh, "this doesn't look like such a bad job to me."

"It's not, really," Sarie said quickly.

"Of course, for a woman of action like yourself, I can see where it could be a little confining." He be-gan to stroll around the room, and Sarie was aware of the compressed energy in his movements. He made the little room seem even more confining than it really was.

"I would prefer to be back on active duty," she confessed, trying not to dwell on the powerful move-ment of his thighs beneath his expensive trousers as he walked. "Not," she added quickly, "that I want you to intercede on my behalf."

"Why not? I could very easily, you know. It is my museum, after all. Besides, Bob Wapshaw would do anything for me—even if it meant recalling his favor-ite female fire fighter from Little Siberia here. Don't worry about it. He'll just send someone else out to do the job." Sounding blithely unconcerned, he bent to examine the running board of the Hercules.

"I'd rather you didn't," said Sarie stiffly. "I don't believe in patronage."

Vance kept his eyes on the machine, running his hands back and forth along the smooth surface. "Ah, yes, I forgot. The rebel Appleton has to keep her political integrity, even if it means not doing what she wants to do." He straightened up suddenly. "Like investigating the Brewery fire."

Sarie felt the tension explode outward into the room. So this was it. Time to face-off. She tried to collect her thoughts for the onslaught. "I do want to find out what really happened," she said evenly.

"I can see you do," he replied. "I can tell you're not the type to listen to warnings, even when they're given in good faith."

Sarie thought about Doug Eldridge. It was on the tip of her tongue to tell Vance about her meeting with his former employee, but she thought better of it. If he already knew, there was no sense in bringing it up. And if he didn't, she might as well keep it to herself. "I don't listen to warnings when I don't understand the reason for them, Vance. And I can't understand why you don't want the Brewery fire investigated."

"I didn't say I didn't want it investigated," he replied, moving closer to the desk where she stood. "I said I didn't want *you* to undertake the job."

"Why not?"

He smiled at her and then laid his fingertips on a pile of papers. Sarie looked down and realized that it was the court records he was touching. She stared into his eyes, willing him not to look down. If he did, he would know that she had been going on with her investigation behind his back. If he didn't already know. "Let's just call it my old-fashioned sense of chivalry,'' he said, still smiling. "I can't bear the idea of a damsel in distress."

"Why should I be in distress?" she persisted. "What's so dangerous about looking into the case, if it's just a chance of accidental arson, as you and the chief seem to believe?"

His eyes narrowed briefly, and he took another step toward her. "And you don't, of course."

"That's right." Sarie could feel her heart rate accelerate.

"You think I know more than I'm telling you, and you're wondering why, aren't you, Sarie?"

"That's right," she said again.

He took another step, and Sarie squared her shoulders to control her response. Her body seemed to have become a geiger counter that measured his nearness. "You're thinking that if Vance Leland knows so much and he isn't telling, then he must have a reason—like maybe he has something to hide. Isn't that right, Sarie?"

Another step closer, and now Sarie could not even manage a reply. She felt trapped and helpless before his relentlessly cool gaze. He had a strange facility for echoing her thoughts aloud and exposing her feelings just when she was trying hardest to hide them. Now he tapped his fingers on the pile of papers beneath them. "You're thinking that if you could just get to the bottom of the whole case, read all this information, find out everything there is to know about the Roxbury fires, then you'll be able to figure out what my deep dark secret is. Am I right again, Sarie?"

His face was just inches from hers, and Sarie felt a strange sense of vertigo overtaking her. The only way to keep her balance was to keep her gaze locked onto his, but doing that made the world spin even more. She fought against the growing sense of disorientation. She broke her gaze, hoping to end the hypnotic control of those eyes, of that soft, persuasive voice. "I don't know what to think," she confessed weakly. "I don't know what to believe." At the moment she spoke the truth.

"Why don't you just believe in me?" he whispered.

Sarie knew that he was no longer referring to the arson investigation, that he had taken her to the brink of another, even deeper trap. She backtracked to avoid it. "I can't," she said, surprised to find that she, too, was speaking in a hushed, expectant whisper. "You won't tell me anything."

Now his face was so close that she could feel his warm breath moving her hair. She could no longer focus on his eyes. "I didn't think I had to tell you," he said softly against her cheek. "I thought you understood without being told."

Sarie felt her equilibrium tilt, and she closed her eyes in an effort to regain control of body and mind. "Understood what?" she asked hoarsely.

"Understood about you and me," he said, his lips coming closer until they brushed against the soft hairs at the side of her neck. "Understood that we belong together. If there's a master plan at work here, it has more to do with the fire between you and me than with any other blaze."

Sarie was acutely aware of a vein in her neck throbbing and of the dazzling red light behind her tightly shut eyelids. She opened her eyes just in time to focus on Vance's lips approaching hers with agonizing slowness and his bottomless blue-gray eyes beneath half-closed lids compelling her forward to meet them halfway.

The first touch was tender and tentative, and contact was made only with their mouths. Sarie felt Vance probing, nibbling at the corners of and underside of her lips. She could hear the prolonged, ragged expiration of his breath, and she realized that he must have been wanting to kiss her for a very long time—as long as she had, him. With a small sound of release, she reached her arms up and wrapped them tightly around his neck, pressing her mouth harder against his in silent hungry acquiescence.

Vance responded immediately by pressing his hands against the small of her back and welding her to him along the length of his torso. She felt as if he could gather her up and envelop her completely with his passion. Her thick straight hair flowed down from her arched neck over his fingers like a rich waterfall, and her pounding heart beneath her small breasts beckoned him to her core.

His tongue pressed harder and her mouth opened to allow him entry. Tentative nibbles became hungry attacks on her mouth, chin and cheeks. She felt a rain of kisses across her eyelids and down behind the tender hollows of her ear. Sarie found herself reaching eagerly for any portion of Vance's face that she could find with her lips. His hands encircled her back so completely that his fingertips wrapped around to touch the undersides of her breasts, and she could feel her nipples hardening against her soft, old cotton shirt. Beneath her probing hands his back felt carved and solid, its power traceable through his jacket. She slipped more deeply into his arms, losing consciousness of anything but the tender power of his touch.

Suddenly there was a loud crash and the sound of rushing water. Sarie and Vance leaped apart, their pupils still dilated with desire.

"What on earth..." gasped Vance.

"Ma!" Taylor's voice came from the main room, high-pitched with fright. "Help me!"

"Taylor!" Sarie was out of Vance's arms in a flash. She rushed into the central hall, scarcely aware that Vance was a few steps behind her.

They reached the room at the same time, and stopped short at the sight. There stood Taylor beside the Cyclorama wagon, dripping wet, with a growing puddle of water at his feet. He still held the hose in his hand, and the water geysered forth with surprising energy, belying the age of the pump. Tay looked like a water rat, and, in a release of tension and concern, Sarie and Vance burst into laughter.

"You were right, Mr. Leland," sputtered Taylor, sounding very young. "They all work pretty good."

Chapter Five

"Ma, I'm really sorry. Really I am."

Taylor was flat on his back in bed in his usual manner—without a pillow or a blanket—but his face was unusually solemn. "I really blew it, didn't I?"

Sarie sat by his side, absently stroking his hair back from his high forehead. "Darling, you didn't blow it. It was a mistake. Mr. Leland told you it was all right, didn't he?" She smiled encouragingly, thinking how young and vulnerable Tay looked tonight, with his damp hair and wide-eyed concern. "And don't worry about the cleanup. There was no real damage, and Mr. Leland was planning to have the place professionally cleaned before the opening anyway." She shrugged lightheartedly. "Just think. You saved him the expense of getting the floors washed."

Taylor made a face. "Don't joke, Ma. This is no laughing matter."

Sarie tried to look more serious, even though she was not particularly concerned about the aftereffects of Taylor's watery mishap. After all, the worst thing that could happen would be that Vance would ask the chief to pull her off that museum assignment before she destroyed the place, which was exactly what she had wanted all along. And it would not be patronage, she reflected, merely common sense.

But Taylor was not nearly as sanguine. "Come on, darling," she chided, "It's not that bad. Mr. Leland was very nice about the whole thing." Almost too nice, she reflected, but she put the thought aside for later.

Taylor was still morose. "Yeah, but now he thinks I'm an idiot."

"What should you care what he thinks?"

"I do care. I want him to like us."

Sarie stopped stroking and looked more closely at her son. "Why on earth should you want him to like us, Tay?"

He rolled his eyes at her. "You know, Ma."

She did, but would have preferred not to. "What are you getting at, Taylor? As if I didn't know."

Taylor sat up and prepared to give her one of his famous lectures. "Look Ma, you've got to meet a nice guy sometime, don't you? And as far as I can see, Vance is a pretty nice guy. I mean, he's got a lot of money and an excellent car..."

"A prime consideration of yours, I'm sure," she murmured.

"And besides, he's a Leland. You know the Leland family, don't you, Ma? Gram does, and she says they're very nice people."

"Taylor Frayne Colton, don't be such a snob. You know perfectly well I have no use at all for that kind of nonsense." She looked at him narrowly. "Where on earth have you been picking up this snobbery? I know Sarah Jane isn't to blame, and you certainly didn't get it from me."

Taylor sighed patiently. "Oh, Ma, I didn't mean it's just because he's a Leland. But he *is* a nice guy, you have to admit."

"I'll admit nothing of the sort," she said defensively, wondering how a nine-year-old boy could so easily turn the tables and make her feel like the child. "You don't know the first thing about him, Taylor," she added. "And neither do I."

A familiar look of firmness came into Taylor's amber eyes, so like her own. "I know what I like," he said, crossing his skinny arms over his pajama top. Then he cocked his head slyly. "I know what you like, too. And if you want to know the truth I think he likes you, Ma."

Sarie pushed gently on the top of her son's head so that he was forced back onto the bed. "That's quite enough from you, young man," she said firmly. "Lights out—now."

She switched off the light, but Tay would not be silenced by the dark. "Jeez, Ma, you gotta get married again sometime. After all, a kid like me needs a father, doesn't he?"

Sarie chuckled and bent down again to her son. "I swear, Taylor, you are just too much." She kissed him. "But I adore you. Now go to sleep and stop playing Cupid for your old mom."

"All right. Night, Ma." Taylor obediently closed his eyes. But as Sarie shut the door to his room she heard him murmur cajolingly, "But he does like you. I know he does."

Sarie was still grinning as she went into her bedroom. Matchmaking on her behalf was an old game of Taylor's, and although it amused her, the idea of his forming an attachment to Vance Leland was a little disturbing. After all, she had no proof yet, but at this point he was a more likely candidate for a jail term than for matrimony.

Still, Taylor had been right about one thing. There was a strong mutual attraction between Vance and herself—a bond that even her worst suspicions could not destroy. He had a way of looking at her and talking to her that was eerily intimate and familiar. Although she didn't know much about him, she felt as if she had known him for a very long time.

It was late, and it had been a very tiring day. Sarie decided she needed to sleep more than she needed to think. She undressed and washed and, crawling under the comforter on her old brass bed, tried to push all thoughts of Vance Leland out of her mind. But she had no success. As soon as she closed her eyes, memories of the afternoon's events came flooding in with Technicolor clarity.

All right, she told herself resignedly. *If you want to stay up all night going over the whole mess again and again, be my guest.* Crossing her hands over her breasts, she stared up at the high ceiling of her bedroom and waited for the disturbing thoughts to begin churning through her consciousness.

Instead, all she saw was Vance's laughing face as he waded through the water to turn off the hose. His head was thrown back, his eyes glinted with little sparks of delight and it was clear he was really enjoying the mess. "I swear," he had said to her as they tried vainly to mop up the water and Taylor, "I haven't had this much fun in weeks."

And Sarie had to admit that, despite her initial embarrassment and annoyance at Taylor's disobedience, she hadn't, either. Every few minutes she or Vance would recall the picture of a sopping Taylor and burst into new gales of helpless laughter. Even Taylor, although he was at first confused by the adults' odd reaction, had joined in the fun. They had begun splashing one another, stomping in the puddles and sending sprays of slightly musty-smelling water all over the room.

In the end, wet and still giggling, Vance had decided that there could be no more work done in the carriage house until the cleaning crew arrived. He had made the call from his car phone and assured Sarie that it would all be taken care of by morning.

"I insist on paying for it," Sarie had said, trying to regain some dignity and inject some gravity into the situation.

"Don't be silly," Vance had told her. "I won't permit it. After all, it wasn't your fault. And I'm certainly not going to allow Taylor to be penalized for his enthusiasm about my machines."

Sarie had tried in vain to insist, but Vance had only become more adamant. "Don't you go getting all equality minded on me about this issue, Lieutenant Appleton. I can out-chauvinist Bob Wapshaw with one hand tied behind my back when I want to. You're not going to pay for it, and that's final. Now come on and let me take you both home before you catch pneumonia. I insist on bearing the cost of the cleanup, but I will not be responsible for your hospital bills."

So they had all driven home in Vance's BMW, and Sarie had taken the back seat so that Vance could give Taylor a guided tour of the car's instrument panel, which Sarie thought looked more like it belonged in a jet cockpit than in a car. He was right about being able to out-chauvinist the chief, she reflected. Any man who told her to keep her pretty nose clean and out of trouble had definite chauvinist tendencies. But then, just as she was getting out of the car, he had reached out and put his hand on her arm. "I know you're going to do what you're going to do, Sarie," he had told her, his voice suddenly serious. "I can tell I won't be able to stop you."

Sarie looked out at Taylor, who was already halfway up the apartment steps. "That's right, Vance," she said in a low voice. "If you won't insist on a departmental investigation, I'll have to do it myself. But I'm not going to stop until I find out who's responsible for...for the Brewery fire." *And the Roxbury arsons,* she added silently.

He looked at her so closely that she was certain he had read her thoughts. "But I don't think," he said slowly, "that you really know what you're getting yourself into."

"I think I do," she replied, her heart hammering. *He means to frighten me,* she thought, and added in a stronger voice, "And I think I can deal with the truth, whatever it turns out to be."

She had started to get out again, but he still held her arm. "Listen to me, Sarie. What you're getting into is dangerous. More dangerous than you know. If you won't let me protect you from it, then you must remember something." His eyes bored deeply into hers. "Will you remember this?"

"Remember what?" Sarie's voice came out in a high whisper.

"Remember that I am not the enemy. Remember that you can trust me. If you find out anything important, please come to me with it before you go anywhere else. We owe each other that much, don't you think?''

"Owe? Why?" She had been genuinely confused.

Vance had dipped his head deprecatingly. "A lot of reasons. Because we have common interests. Because we're a lot alike in many ways. Because you're an Appleton and I'm a Leland, I suppose."

"That's ridiculous," she had said, but he still had not released her arm.

"It may seem that way to you now. But someday you'll understand. And that's when I expect you to be honest with yourself—and with me." He paused. "And, for God's sake if you're going to go through with it, remember not to be afraid." Despite the seriousness of his words, he managed a small smile. "It doesn't suit you at all." Then, he had let her go.

And now, in the darkness of her small bedroom, Sarie tried to make sense of those last words and of the glittering promise in his eyes as he spoke them. *Surely,* she thought, *he doesn't expect me to actually trust him. Surely he doesn't think I'd be likely to confide in him if I suspect him of being involved in this scandal in any way.* But she could think of no other meaning behind his warning. He wasn't trying to scare her even more than she already was. In fact, she had the impression that he was truly concerned about her.

But she could not leave it at that. She had to wonder why he was suddenly so interested in Sarie Appleton. Although she was strongly attracted to him, she was not blinded to the possibility that it might not really be mutual. A man like Vance Leland, so well schooled in the powers of persuasion that came with his class, might easily affect an interest in order to further his own cause. But what could he possibly want from Sarie?

Except cooperation.

The shrill sound of the telephone made Sarie jump. She looked at her clock. After twelve. Who would be calling her after midnight? Her palms were sweaty, and her fingers shook as she reached out for the phone.

"Hello?"

"Sarie?" The voice was instantly familiar, but it took her a moment to place it.

"Who is this?"

"It's me." There was a nervous pause, and then the name was muttered, almost indistinctly. "Doug Eldridge. Remember?"

Remember? How could she forget. "Don't be silly. Of course I do." Something in his voice brought a sharp taste of fear into her mouth. "Why are you calling me at this hour?"

"I'm in trouble, Sarie. I really need your help."

"You told me that this afternoon, Doug," she replied, trying to keep calm in the face of his obvious panic.

"But this is different. Something's happened."

"What's happened?"

"They know something. They know about me." Doug's voice faded in and out, as if he was constantly moving his head to look around.

"Who? Who knows?"

"They will stop at nothing to get what they want, and they know I'm getting scared. They'll want me out of the way, I'm sure of it."

"For God's sake, who?"

"I can't tell you. Not on the phone."

Sarie tried to control herself. It would do no good if both of them were panicking. "Where are you calling from, Doug?"

"From a phone booth. Downtown. It doesn't matter. They know—they're on to me."

"On to you about what, dammit!" She was beginning to get annoyed with Doug's evasions. "Doug, I can't help you unless you tell me what's going on."

"They might know about you, too," said Doug as if he hadn't heard her.

Sarie drew in her breath sharply. The peaceful silence of her street seemed suddenly ominous. She found herself wondering whether she had remembered to double-lock the front door. "How do you know this, Doug?" she asked in a low, urgent voice. "What's happened to make you so scared? Has someone threatened you?"

"Never mind how. I just know. I've got to get out of this fast, and you can help. You can help me convince the authorities that I'm telling the truth. That I made a mistake getting involved with these guys, that I want to come clean. I don't care if I . . . I don't care if they put me in jail—maybe I'd be safer in jail!"

Sarie knew he was babbling now, and the important thing was to calm him down. "Doug," she said in her firmest voice. "Doug, listen to me. You have got to calm down so that you can think clearly. So that we both can think clearly."

"No time for that," he rushed on. "Listen. I've got an errand to do for them tomorrow morning. It's the last thing I'm gonna do for these creeps, but I've gotta do it." His voice dropped so low she could barely hear him. "I think there might be something of interest to us both there."

"What? Where?" These cloak-and-dagger antics were driving Sarie crazy.

"That's what I'm trying to tell you. You have to meet me. Then we can find out together. If I'm right..."

Sarie felt as if she was in the middle of an absurdist melodrama. This conversation was getting nowhere and making no sense. "Right about what? For God's sake, would you please..."

"Never mind about that, just listen. There's a big warehouse on South Tremond Street, right on the corner of St. Paul Street. You know where that is?"

"Of course I do, but..."

"Meet me there tomorrow morning at nine. Don't be late." Doug hung up.

Sarie sat up in bed for a long time holding the receiver in her hand, as it buzzed insistently its off-the-hook warning. Still she sat without moving, staring out her window at the mild spring night.

Things had begun to get really serious. If Doug's nameless employers knew that he was trying to blow the whistle on them and that she had been talking to him, then she was in real danger, too. She remembered Vance's warning. Had it been genuine after all?

Slowly replacing the receiver on the hook, Sarie forced herself to review what she knew. Vance knew that the fire in his Brewery building was not accidental, even though he didn't want to admit it to her. And he had also known more than he cared to admit about the Roxbury fires—why else would he insist on keeping his notes confidential? Clearly, he understood that there was a connection between the two fires. But he was holding something back—from her, from Chief Wapshaw, from everyone. But according to Doug

Eldridge, someone else knew, too. Someone who was out to prove that Vance was involved—or to make sure he didn't prove that they were.

Then there was the matter of the blind trust. If there was still someone at large who had masterminded the Roxbury arsons, it was someone whose identity had been hidden behind a blind trust. Why shouldn't it be Vance or one of his privileged colleagues in the Brahmin Trust? Sarie remembered the four well-dressed, well-fed men sitting around the polished table in the conference room. Could one of them have been the brains behind the devilish arson scheme? Or one of the other members who never bothered to attend? If so, was Vance just trying to protect one of his own?

Or himself?

Now, more than ever, it was important that she get her hands on those private notes of Vance's. They seemed to be the only hard evidence, the only missing piece of the puzzle. And Sarie knew she was not the only one interested in them. Clearly Vance had taken pains to see to it that they did not surface, and clearly Doug's employer—whoever he was—wanted to get his hands on them, as well.

She lay back on her pillow with a heavy sigh of frustration. Here she was, a simple fire fighter trying to find out who had started a simple arson, and now she was mixed up with an ex-con, a mysterious, sinister figure in a gray limousine and a surprisingly eccentric Boston Brahmin who may or may not be involved in mayhem. It was absurd. If she had an ounce of sense, she would wash her hands of the whole thing at once. She would go to the chief in the morning and insist that she be transferred to the records library or to some other obscure place where no one could find her, no one could bother her...

But on some level she knew that no matter where she was, where she tried to hide, Vance Leland would find her if he wanted her. With that thought in mind, she fell asleep, unaware that she was smiling.

THE PHONE RANG early the next morning, but Sarie let it ring. She was deeply asleep, and she was dreaming that it was Doug calling again to shout gibberish in her ear. "I'm not going to listen to this anymore," she told the dream Doug in a polite but firm voice. "I've decided this whole thing is no fun at all, and I don't want to play anymore."

"Ma!" Somehow Taylor's voice penetrated at last. "Ma, it's for you!"

She opened her eyes and looked at him groggily. "For me?" she repeated stupidly.

"Yeah. It's Tom Garrett, from the station house." He held out the phone.

Still half-asleep, Sarie took the phone and fumbled it up to her ear. *Oh, no,* she thought. *Vance decided to complain about yesterday's flood after all, and it was Tom calling to tell her she'd been fired.* "Tom?"

"Sarie, you awake?" Tom sounded excited.

"Sort of. Has it happened?"

"Yes, it's happened. Just like you said it would."

"I knew it," said Sarie with a sigh. So, she *had* been fired. "I knew he wouldn't keep his word."

"Who? What word?"

"Vance Leland. I knew he wouldn't keep his word and not tell the chief."

"Not tell the chief what?"

"About the flood."

"What flood?" Tom sounded exasperated. "Sarie, what the hell are you talking about?"

"I'm talking about getting fired. Vance Leland told the chief about..." She stopped and blinked. "Aren't you calling to tell me I'm fired?"

"For God's sake, of course not! Why should I be telling you that?"

"Because... Oh, it's a long story." She rubbed some of the sleep out of her eyes. "Why *are* you calling, then?"

"I'm calling to tell you to get your butt down to the station house quick. You're back on active duty, as of this minute."

Her first thought was that Vance had spoken to the chief after all, not to complain but to see to it that she was reassigned to active duty. But then she realized that Tom wouldn't sound so urgent if that was the case.

"Why? Has something happened?"

"You bet something's happened. We just got a four-alarm call. A building's been torched, Sarie."

Sarie swallowed. "Are you sure?"

"We're sure." Tom paused ominously. "It looks like it might be a Jackson device, Sarie."

She was fully awake at last. "My God," she muttered. "Where is it?"

"In the South End. I'm not sure exactly about any of the particulars yet. Just come down and grab your gear and number ten'll bring you over. I'm going right now in one of the other trucks. See you as soon as you can get here."

In the rush to get dressed and get Taylor hustled out of the house early, Sarie didn't have time to think of the consequences of Tom's words. Even when she got to the station house she wasn't really thinking—just reacting to the situation with her well-practised professional efficiency. She was in command of one of the four trucks called to the scene, and it was her job to see to it that hook-and-ladder number ten went out fully equipped and ready for any emergency. She barked commands and checked rosters and double-checked equipment and then, in a matter of moments, they were on their way.

It wasn't until they actually pulled up in front of the burning building that Sarie realized where she was. An empty warehouse on the corner of South Tremond and St. Paul streets. A warehouse with gilt lettering over the door that was now unreadable because of the flames that licked upward toward the sky. The warehouse where Doug Eldridge had told her to meet him.

"My God, someone's in there!" she shouted as she scrambled down from the truck.

"There's no one inside," said Tom, hurrying up to her. "We've already checked. The blaze is confined to the front of the building, and there's no one inside."

"But there is, I know there is!" She checked her watch. Eight-thirty. "Someone's in there, Tom. That fire was set to trap someone."

"What are you talking about?"

Sarie looked at him wildly. How to explain in twenty seconds all she had been through in the past twenty-four hours? She could scarcely believe it herself. But she knew that Doug was in there somewhere, trapped by a diabolical plot to make sure that he never got a chance to tell the truth. Doug must have known the risks he took in carrying out his employer's instructions—he must have thought that whatever was in the warehouse was very important and worth the risk. The notes, perhaps? Had Doug's boss sent him in after the notes because he thought Vance had hidden them there? Or had it merely been a ruse to get Doug into the abandoned building?

In either case, she had to act fast. "Where was the device?" she demanded.

"Just inside the door," Tom told her. "Apparently the door was wired to go off as soon as it was moved."

"Then it *was* opened!"

"If it was, whoever opened it got out somehow. There was no one in there, Sarie, believe me."

Sarie sized up the building with a trained eye. "Where's the blaze confined to?"

"Just to the front half, it looks like. There's a brick retaining wall halfway back. The blast was too small to get past it, although I suspect we'll find some damage in the rear room, as well."

"Has anyone been back there yet?"

"Sarie, we only just got here. The fire's still at the acute stage. I'm telling you, there's no one in there!"

"And I'm telling you there is!" Sarie faced him with blazing eyes. "I'm going around back," she told him. "I've got to find that man."

She tramped away, leaving Tom stunned and silent.

There was a narrow alley leading to the back of the building, and Sarie made her way down it. The height of the warehouse and the neighboring structure blocked out most of the sun, but she could see that there were no side entrances, and that the alley was rarely used, if ever. The back of the building was in even worse shape—full of refuse and overgrown weeds that came up to Sarie's waist.

Using her flashlight, she beat her way to the rusted metal doors that faced out onto the back lot. They

looked as if they hadn't been used in years. Sarie tried
the handle on one, and it came off in her hand in a
cloud of rust. Pushing the handle of her flashlight
through the rust-ringed hole, she tried to lever the
door open.

It was a heavy door, and the ground in front of it
was so overgrown that she could not get it to budge.
She looked around until she found a length of a rusted
mattress spring, which she wedged between the two
metal doors. Slowly the door gave inward a little bit.
Using all her weight, Sarie leaned until they gave way
just enough for her to slip between them. The small
opening sent a sliver of light into the vast room ahead
of her. It was dim and dusty and filled with the cav-
ernous silence peculiar to large empty spaces. Cob-
webs hung like sheeting from the timbers, and the
floor was carpeted with some unnameable filth. The
ceiling was too high to be seen in the weak dirty light.
This portion of the warehouse had not been directly
affected by the explosion out front, but there had been
considerable damage, particularly up near the brick
wall that separated this room from the front of the
building. Sarie moved toward the wall cautiously,
thrusting her torch beam among the fallen timbers and
old storage partitions that lay in damaged heaps
around her. The terrifyingly familiar smell of carbon
tetrachloride filled the air.

"Doug?" Sarie called his name as loudly as she
dared, and heard her voice echo and ricochet off the
high-beamed ceiling. There was no reply, but she was
sure that Doug Eldridge was in there somewhere. She
stood still for a moment, listening breathlessly. The
silence was deafening, and her own rapid heartbeat
was all she could hear.

Perhaps Doug wasn't here after all, she reasoned with herself. Perhaps he had gotten out in time. While Sarie hoped that was the case, her intuition told her it was not. She stopped and opened her mouth to call his name one more time and then quickly shut it. For no reason that she could name, Sarie was suddenly aware that she was not the only person in the room. Either Doug was lying somewhere, injured and unable to respond to her, or there was someone else in here, waiting in silence for her to approach. Sarie switched off her torch.

Dry-mouthed with terror, Sarie forced herself onward through the utter blackness. The brick wall was giving off heat now, and she squinted against the curtain of smoke that hung in front of it. That wall was not solid, she knew. The explosion in the front room had done more damage than she had thought. If Doug was over there somewhere, she had better get to him quickly.

Then she heard a soft moan. It came from the corner of the room nearest the brick dividing wall. She could not make out its source in the vast darkness.

"Doug! Is that you?" She made her way cautiously toward the sound. The rotten floorboards groaned threateningly beneath her feet and slowed her progress, as did the tangle of debris through which she had to thread her way. This time the moan was a little louder.

"Sarie."

"My God," she exclaimed, and inched forward, feeling in the large pocket of her oilskin coat for her torch. By the time she got it out and flicked it on again, she was standing directly above her target. Another footstep and she would have landed on him. It was Doug, lying prostrate amid a pile of lumber and wire. Sarie could vaguely make out a connecting door between the front and back portions of the warehouse. The door hung crazily on its hinges. Doug must have managed to pull himself through it before collapsing.

He moaned again. "Help me out," he said.

"Are you hurt?" she asked, feeling his bones quickly for any breaks.

The man shook his head. "I'm okay," he whispered. "I'm okay, aren't I?" He lay very still and looked up at her imploringly. Sarie put her hand on his neck and felt his pulse. It was rapid and shallow, a sure sign of shock.

"Yes," she said, mustering a confident smile, "you're all right." Sarie had enough first-aid skill to see that he was not in immediate danger, but she knew that Doug would need medical attention soon. He was badly bruised and had obviously suffered a mild concussion. Still, she had to know what had happened before she led him out and handed him over to the emergency medical team. She had to find out about the notes.

"Do you know what happened, Doug?" she asked urgently.

Doug nodded and then shook his head. "Yes. No." He closed his eyes and spoke with a great effort. "An explosion." He seemed confused. "I came in here to get away."

Sarie nodded. She had to get him to talk now, before shock clouded his memory of the events.

"Yes, we know. The front door of the warehouse was wired."

"Jackson device," he said faintly.

"I know. Now, can you tell me what happened?"

"I came to get . . . to get the notes."

So she was right! Sarie found herself wishing he would speak more clearly and quickly, and had to force herself to be patient. "Which notes are you talking about, Doug? Tell me which notes."

"Leland...notes." Doug tried to move and fell back with a heavy sigh.

Sarie swallowed hard before asking the next question. "And did you find Mr. Leland's notes, Doug? Do you have them?"

In answer, Doug shuddered with a sudden racking sob. "Oh, I should never have listened," he moaned. "I should have known they wouldn't be in here."

Sarie's heart sank. There had been no notes after all. It had merely been a ploy to get Doug to the warehouse, to make him think that he could retrieve Vance's notes and get away with them. And poor Doug had underestimated the vengeful power of his employers. "Never mind that now," Sarie said soothingly. "The immediate problem is how to get you out of this warehouse."

"Crane's warehouse . . ."

"Yes, and then—" Sarie's jaw dropped. "Did you say Crane's warehouse?"

Doug gestured weakly upward and Sarie, glancing into the penumbra near the ceiling, saw a sign hanging across a heavy beam. E.T. Crane Paper Goods, she read. Although she was already terrified, a sudden chill stole over her body, making her feel clammy beneath the heavy oilskin. She passed a hand across her face to steady herself. "Doug, do you know who E. T. Crane is?"

"He's a friend of . . . a friend of . . ."

Vance Leland. He did not have to finish the sentence for her to know what he meant. A friend, and a fellow member of the Brahmin Trust. Once again, the possibility of Vance's involvement loomed like a specter. A terrible thought occurred to her. "Doug, who told you to come here and get the papers? Could it have been Vance?"

"No, no, not Leland." Doug's voice was getting weaker, but Sarie could not stop now. She had to get the information from him before anybody else did.

"Then was it the man you've been working for? The man in the gray limousine? Was it Edward Crane?"

He shook his head wildly.

She was becoming exasperated. "Is that a no, or are you still afraid? Doug, who have you been working for?"

Doug rolled his eyes feverishly. "Kelly sent me," he said at last. "He had Joe Kelly send me out here."

Despite her fear, Sarie felt a flush of satisfaction—at last, a name! Something to go on! "Joe Kelly was the man in the limousine?"

Doug shook his head impatiently. "Not Kelly. Kelly works for..." Doug's eyes were beginning to roll back in his head.

"Who?" Sarie resisted the urge to shake him. The man was obviously in shock and needed medical attention. But she could not stop now. "Who does Joe Kelly work for? Doug, you've got to tell me!"

But Doug had passed out. "Damn," Sarie muttered. She knew she should have gotten him out sooner. Now she would have to get him all the way back to the rear exit. She could not trust the door in the brick dividing wall. Even now, the brick was sending down showers of dust that covered them both in a fine, gritty powder. She thought about leaving him there and going for assistance, or even of shouting for reinforcements. But the wall could give out at any moment, and no one would hear her calls from outside.

"I've got to get you out of here, Doug," she told him in a firm voice. "I need you to try and help as much as possible, okay?" Squatting beside him, she positioned her shoulder below his rib cage, pushed up with her legs and adjusted her center of gravity to permit her to perform the traditional fire fighter's carry. It was a painful and laborious procedure for both of them. Their progress was dismally slow, impeded by the unsafe condition of the floor and by Doug's weight. He slipped in and out of consciousness, sometimes muttering, sometimes groaning in pain.

"Steady now," she kept crooning, knowing that the sound of her voice was the only sedative she could offer at the moment. She knew better than to ask him any more questions or to try to make sense of what he said. She needed him to devote what little energy he had to staying partially upright. She would not be able to carry him otherwise. "Just a few more minutes. Don't panic. I've got you," she said soothingly. "That's good. That's right."

After what seemed to her an eternity, they approached the rear door—near enough, Sarie decided, to call out for help. She yelled, and in a moment she could hear the sounds of running feet. Two fire fighters appeared in the partially opened doorway.

"What on earth!"

Sarie nearly fainted with relief when she heard Tom's voice. "Tom! Thank God! Pull the door open wider. I've got a victim here."

Tom stepped forward and tried to pull the other half of the double doors open so that they could get in and help Sarie. She could just make out his thick fingers yanking on the heavy metal. But the door seemed to be jammed shut. The side Sarie had slipped in through would not budge any farther and the other half seemed to be locked.

"Come on," she heard Tom say to his companion. "One big tug and this side ought to give." Sarie saw another pair of hands grasp the door.

Suddenly Doug seemed to come to his senses. "Don't!" he mumbled weakly. "Door is wired, don't!"

"What?" It took a moment to decipher his slurred words, and another moment to understand what they meant. But Tom and the other man had not even heard him. Together they gave a strong pull and the door started to bend open.

"Wait!" Sarie shouted, but it was too late.

The door swung inward, and, as it did, there was a flash of light from inside. The events seemed to register in Sarie's brain in stop-action slow motion. A wall of powerful heat and light surged forward like a tidal wave, flattening everything in its path. Sarie had time to think how strange it was, the way the room tipped up and away from her, as if the horizon had suddenly shifted. She tried to hold on tighter to Doug, but he was not in her grasp anymore. Then she realized it was she who was tilting forward, pitching down toward the floor. That was the last thing she remembered.

Chapter Six

Sarie didn't know how long it was before the voice penetrated the blackness that had cloaked her consciousness. The first thing she felt was the pillow of an arm that cradled her neck and the soft stroking of someone's hand across her forehead. She heard a voice, but she could not make out the words for a long while.

"Sarie. Sarie. Sarie," said the voice. She opened one eye slightly, and could see a vague shape looming over her. The voice seemed to be repeating her name over and over again, as if the sound of it were a litany of comfort.

"I'm Sarie," she said thickly.

"Sarie!" the voice changed, the relief in it so strong that Sarie herself was relieved. She was beginning to feel her body again, and it seemed to be all right.

"Who...what...?"

"Shh, darling, don't talk." The hands that stroked her forehead traveled down and pressed gently against her lips. "You're all right. Everything is all right. Thank God, it's all right." She heard the voice lift up and speak softly and rapidly to another person. Then she became aware that there was a lot of activity going on above her head and around her. She strained to make her eyes work.

"Where am I?" As soon as she said it, she realized she was outside, with strong sunlight pouring over her face. She also recognized the voice and the arms of the man who held her. "Vance," she whispered. "What are you doing here?"

His smile wavered into focus. "Good," he said, but his eyes showed strain and concern even as he nodded encouragingly. "You recognize me. That's very good." He spoke again to someone standing above him and the shadowy figure moved off.

"What happened?" Slowly the world was beginning to come together again.

"You rescued some fellow from the building just before the fire wall collapsed," Vance told her. "He was damned lucky you showed up when you did. And you're pretty damned lucky yourself."

Fire Wall? Rescue? Sarie tried to remember what had happened. She vaguely recalled moving toward the door, and then . . . nothing. Just a thick curtain of black confusion. Trying to penetrate it made her head ache even more. But she had to think—had to make herself remember. "I rescued someone?"

"And then needed some rescuing yourself. You were very fortunate that Tom turned up when he did." Vance's voice sounded curiously constricted to Sarie. "Very fortunate indeed."

Suddenly another image forced its way to the surface of her mind—an image of blinding light and heat and of a heavy weight pressing against her. "What about... There was another explosion, though, wasn't there? I remember..."

A hooded expression masked Vance's reply. "Yes," he said briskly. "The metal door blew off its hinges and knocked both of you off your feet. A gas line or something, we think. We're looking into it." He smiled warily. "It's a good thing you were on the right side of that metal door."

Sarie shook her head. "It wasn't a gas line," she said through parched and uncooperative lips. "It was a Jackson device."

Vance looked at her but did not speak.

"Vance." She tugged weakly at his sleeve. "Did you hear me? It was a Jackson device. They both were."

"Both?" His voice was guarded now.

"Yes." It was all coming back to her now—her frantic arrival at the warehouse, Tom's news, her search for... "Tom knows about it. Ask Tom."

"Unfortunately, Tom is in the hospital at the moment."

Sarie struggled to sit up. "Tom!"

"Shh." He patted her back down soothingly. "Don't worry, he'll be all right. He and... He was thrown backward by the explosion and got pretty scraped up. But he'll be fine. I promise you, he's fine. Now just relax. Relax."

His voice had a mesmerizing effect, but Sarie was agitated, fighting to remember. "Don't you believe me, Vance? The fire here was caused by the Jackson device, and then there was a second explosion. It was supposed to..." She stopped and her eyes suddenly opened very wide. The fire was supposed to have trapped Doug—and her, as well, if whoever set it knew she planned to meet with him that morning. A wave of nausea that had nothing to do with her injuries swept over her, and she fell back weakly against Vance's arm.

He looked down at her, and saw the fear in her face. "It's all right, Sarie," he soothed. "Don't try and think about it now. You'll tire yourself out. We'll talk about it later."

Sarie closed her eyes. He was right. She was tired. But the fact that she had narrowly escaped being maimed or killed made rest impossible.

Doug. She had to know about Doug. "How is... What happened to...?"

"The man you rescued has been taken to the hospital. I think he'll be all right, too." Vance's voice sounded curiously harsh.

"But I need to talk to him. I need to know..."

"Sarie, the man's in shock and he's been pretty badly burned along his legs. He won't be in any shape to talk to anyone for several days, you can be sure of that. He's in isolation in the burn unit to guard against infection." It was clear from Vance's tone that there would be no more discussion on the subject.

Sarie was confused by his attitude. Why was he so eager to avoid discussion of Doug? She could not make her brain come up with the answer, and so she let it go. "And what about the other fireman? I didn't get to see who he was. Is he all right?"

"Would you stop worrying about everyone else and think about yourself for a change?" he said bitterly. Then his voice softened as his gaze traveled up and down the body that lay across his lap. "I was the other man, and you can see I'm fine. So are you by the looks of you, thank God." He brushed a stray lock of heavy hair off her neck. "Anything hurt a lot?" he asked tenderly.

Sarie tried to feel her body. "I think I'm all right," she replied slowly. "I'm all here, aren't I?

Vance chuckled. "You're all here. Every beautiful bit of you." Even in her groggy state, Sarie could tell that Vance would have liked to kiss her, but was restraining himself. She would have liked to be kissed but couldn't put the thought into words just yet.

"Nothing seems to hurt. Maybe if I can just..." She tried to get up and was immobilized by a stab of pain behind her eyes. "Ouch!"

"Easy there, darling. You did manage to get quite a conk on the head when you fell. The medic says you're fine, but I think a little rest is called for. You're coming home with me for a while."

Sarie was suddenly afraid, although she could not remember why. He misinterpreted her look of fear and chuckled. "Hey, relax. I just want to make sure you don't have any aftereffects. I'm not going to take advantage of your groggy state, although..." He smiled down at her.

Things were coming back to Sarie now, and she wasn't sure she wanted to be alone with Vance Leland until she had a better idea of what his role was in the whole affair. She didn't know if he had arrived in time to see that the victim had been Doug, but she suspected he knew. What else did he know about the explosion? she wondered. With Doug out of commission, she had a lot of work to do, and she had to do it alone.

"If I'm all right I should get back on the job," she protested, trying once again to get up.

With a firm hand and a steely glint in his eye, Vance restrained her. "You're not going back to work, young lady, and that's final."

Sarie looked around for someone to appeal to, but the rest of the world seemed to be a blur, and she could not make out any faces. ''But I have to make my report,'' she told him lamely.

Vance did not bother to respond to this feeble excuse. Taking her face gently in both hands, he forced her to look directly at him. He spoke in a low voice and she could hear the urgency even through the fog in her throbbing head. ''Sarie, listen to me. I know you don't trust me, but I'm afraid you're going to have to make an effort. Too much depends on it.'' Then, in a lighter voice, he added, ''Besides, I don't care what you say you have to do. I say you need a rest. And I've got pull, remember?'' Smiling, Vance lifted her up and carried her to his car.

Sarie realized that she had no options. Vance would never do anything to hurt her, she thought groggily. This was as good a time as any to get to the bottom of his involvement in the whole affair once and for all. If only her headache would clear up, maybe she would finally be able to get some straight answers out of him. At any rate, it wouldn't hurt to try—and the thought of having him take care of her was suddenly very appealing. After a few more moments of confused debate with herself about the ethics of her situation, Sarie decided that what she really needed was a nap and promptly fell asleep in his arms.

WHEN SHE WOKE UP it was twilight, and she was lying on the biggest bed she had ever seen. The sheets were pure white, crisp and at the same time incredibly soft. The walls of the room were pale gray, and a grouping of abstract paintings on one wall added a brilliant patch of color to the otherwise somber room. Another wall seemed to be all windows, although the fine linen drapes that covered them blocked out any view. It took Sarie a moment to remember where she was, and when she did she sat bold upright.

"Feeling better?" came a voice from the dimness.

Sarie peered into the dusky shadows and made out a shape on an Eames chair in the corner of the room. "Vance?"

Vance came to sit on the edge of the bed. "You sleep like an angel," he whispered, leaning over and stroking her forehead.

Sarie resisted the urge to lie back and give in to his gentle ministrations. "Angels don't have lumps on their foreheads," she replied, rubbing the small egg that had sprouted there. Now that she felt better she was embarrassed about being here, and her thoughts turned to making a quick but graceful exit. In her current state she would probably not do a very good job of cross-examining Vance Leland. She sat up slowly, careful not to wince.

"Is it very bad?" Vance asked anxiously.

"I'm fine," she said, as brightly as she could, and swung her legs over the edge of the bed. *So far,* she thought, *so good.* "I'm sure I can manage to get back to work on my own now." A sudden wave of nausea forced her to stop and she swayed with it as she sat.

"Not so fast, Ace," Vance said, pushing her gently down against the pillows. "You're not ready to budge, that's for sure."

"Vance, I appreciate your concern but . . ."

"No buts. I want you to take it easy until you're sure you're okay. Until *I'm* sure you're okay. There may be no concussion, but you're still pretty shaky and a little green around the gills. Besides, it's after eight o'clock at night. You're off duty anyway. No-where to go but home."

"Home! After eight? My God, I'd better call Tay-lor! He must be frantic!"

"Not to worry. He's at Sarah Jane's. I spoke to both of them and assured them you were in good hands. They're not worried a bit."

Sarie doubted that Sarah Jane wasn't worried, but reflected that if anybody could put her at ease it was Vance Leland. "The Appletons seem to be getting in your way with alarming frequency," she said, at-tempting to make light of her embarrassment.

"I don't find it alarming at all." Vance went through a door and came back with a thick wet wash-cloth. "Here, try this." He applied the cold cloth to Sarie's face, stroking with gentle rhythmic motions that soothed her throbbing head and made the nau-sea slowly recede. In spite of herself, she sighed with relief. "That feel better?"

Sarie's eyes appeared from behind the cloth. "Rel-atively speaking, yes. Now I just feel like a small sta-tion wagon hit me, not a locomotive."

Vance chuckled. "I'm glad to see you're regaining your sense of humor."

My sense of humor, Sarie thought, *and my curios-ity.* "I want to thank you for this morning," she mur-mured demurely.

"Always glad to help a damsel in distress," he said, smiling down at her. "Especially when she's one of the clan."

Sarie bit back a sharp retort. This was no time to be arguing about class consciousness. "I don't know what I would have done without your help," she went on.

Vance narrowed his eyes and cocked his head. "You'd have managed, I'm sure," he said suspiciously. "There were other people around."

"Still, it was nice that you just happened to be there."

His eyes mocked her attempt at innocence. "I'm a sparkie, remember? I always go to fires."

"Even when they're at eight-thirty in the morning?"

"Sure. That's before my workday gets too busy."

Sarie didn't like his flippant attitude. She was sure he was not telling her the truth about his presence at the warehouse. He had been there for a reason—he must have known what to expect. But how? Now that her head was clearing, all the questions were pouring back. She had to take advantage of this opportunity and find out more from Vance—about the Brewery, about his Roxbury investigation notes, about Crane's warehouse and about the Brahmin Trust. But she would have to tread carefully. Vance was not an easy subject to interview. He had his reasons for being cagey, just as Doug Eldridge had. And just as she had.

"It wasn't really the kind of fire that draws sparkies," she went on. "Small, contained blazes, no people to pull out, not a lot of firepower...."

"It seemed to draw Doug Eldridge's interest, didn't it?" he pointed out casually.

Sarie gaped. "You know about Doug Eldridge?" her voice came out in a squeak.

"I know about a lot of things," he said shortly. He leaned toward her, and his eyes sparkled dangerously. "The question is, what do you know about Doug Eldridge?"

Sarie swallowed hard. He kept on catching her off her balance, just when she was beginning to make some headway with him. Or perhaps she wasn't making any headway at all. Perhaps he was just playing a game with her—a deadly game. The fear that had overtaken her so unreasonably while she was lying in Vance's arms returned. If Vance Leland was involved in the Roxbury arson case and all its subsequent horrors, she was playing with fire.

Nevertheless, she decided to brazen it out. After all, she reasoned, she was already here with him in his bedroom. She had nothing to lose by pressing for some more facts—she hoped. "Answering questions with questions—a standard evasive technique." She hoped she looked more cocky than she felt. "It was arson, you know," she added.

"So I've heard," he said dryly.

"A Jackson device," she prodded.

"I've heard that, too." Vance got up and walked to the window. Sarie watched him with a mixture of apprehension and exasperation. He really was impossible! Still, she found herself admiring his lean figure backlit by the twilight outside. He was indeed a handsome man. Too handsome, she reminded herself.

"And I think I know who started it," she announced clearly.

Vance swiveled sharply toward her. "You do? And who is that?"

"His name is Joe Kelly." Sarie knew she was taking a chance by revealing this name. After all, she had no idea who Joe Kelly was, and no evidence that he had planted the Jackson device in Crane's warehouse. But it was worth a shot to see how Vance would react to the name.

Naturally, his response was not at all what she had expected. Instead of surprise or anger, he smiled in apparent relief. "So, you think Joe Kelly's behind it all, do you?"

"You know the name, then?" she asked quickly.

"Of course I do," he snapped. "Joe Kelly's a two-bit local firebug—everybody knows him."

"I didn't."

Vance smirked. "You do now, don't you?" He cocked his head shrewdly.

"And I suppose you know all about his ... current employment, shall we say?"

Sarie took a deep breath. "Of course I do," she said, hoping to drop another bomb. "He told me all about it, you know."

Vance looked at her sharply, clearly not convinced. "He did, did he? Did you talk before or after the explosion?"

Sarie looked up, trying to gauge Vance's mood, but he moved away from the window and she could not see his expression in the pale light. "I know what I need to know," she said, sounding to herself like a character in a second-rate melodrama.

"So you and Mr. Eldridge have become pretty chummy, is that it?"

"We've met before," she replied primly.

"And you got this whole story from him."

"That's right," she said, hoping that her bluff didn't sound as hollow to him as it did to her. Sparring with Vance Leland was more difficult than she had imagined. Her head was beginning to ache again, but she refused to falter.

Vance moved to the foot of the bed. He put his hands on his hips and stood facing her. "Sarie, I hate to break it to you, but if I believed everything Doug Eldridge told me I wouldn't be alive today.''

Sarie stared at him openmouthed and he smiled. "Yes, I know all about Doug Eldridge and Joe Kelly. I've been aware of Doug's . . . defection, shall we call it, for some time. And of course I know all about his ridiculous attempts to rope you into this mess."

"Then you know who he's working for?" In her eagerness, Sarie had revealed that she didn't, and she blushed at having been caught so easily in a lie.

"I didn't say that. Although I do have my suspicions. As," he added soberly, "do you."

Sarie swallowed. He must have known that she suspected him. But if so, why hadn't he attempted to prove to her that he was not implicated? "I don't . . . have all the facts yet," she muttered, and added defensively, "But I have a pretty good idea of what's going on."

Suddenly Vance was all business. "No you don't. You don't have the first idea what's going on. You may think you do, but you're really in so far over your head it's pathetic."

"Don't sell me short, Vance," she retorted, stung by his dismissive attitude. "I know too much for that."

A mocking light came into his eyes. "Oh, you do, do you?"

"That's right." Anger was edging out Sarie's fear. "And I intend to find out the rest."

Vance suddenly threw up his hands in a gesture of acquiescence. "All right, Sarie. You want to talk about it? We'll talk. But first, why don't you take those grubby clothes off and get yourself cleaned up? You can put your things in the washing machine while we have our little tête-à-tête."

Sarie looked down at herself and realized he was right. Her jeans were muddy and her man's pin-striped shirt was definitely the worse for wear. She reached up and felt a thin film of grime across the bridge of her nose, and her hair, she knew, lay in lank strands around her shoulders. *I must look disgusting,* she thought, but a sort of stubborn pride overcame her, and she was determined not to admit that she cared about the way she looked in front of Vance. "It's all right. I don't mind staying in these," she said. She was going to need all the strength she could muster in the next few hours, and she had no energy to waste on vanity.

"It's not all right with me," Vance told her firmly, heading for the door. "I talk better when I'm talking to someone presentable. The shower's through there, and there's a washing machine in the dressing room." He grabbed a thick white robe off a hook on the back of the door and threw it on the bed. "Here. You can wear this until your clothes are dry."

He was gone before she could protest. Sighing, Sarie grabbed the luxurious robe and headed for the white-tiled bathroom. "Presentable, my foot!" she declared hotly to the closed bedroom door. "What do you think this is, a cotillion ball?" But she was glad of the robe's thick protection. Despite her determination to get some answers from Vance, she felt extremely vulnerable alone with him in his apartment. It wasn't so much that she was afraid for her safety, but she knew how easily he seemed to be able to manipulate her senses. She wanted the truth and to get it she would have to retain control.

As a matter of fact, the truth seemed more and more elusive by the moment. Things had become so convoluted and complicated that Sarie was not sure she had a good grasp of those events she did know about, let alone the ones that still remained a mystery. What had begun as a simple arson investigation had become a nightmarish maze of events that defied analysis. Usually Sarie had a good eye for patterns, but so much had happened in the past few days that she was unable to see the forest for the trees.

Of one thing, however, she was certain. More and more, it looked as if Vance Leland was very much involved in whatever was going on. He knew far too much to be just an interested bystander. He had known about Doug right from the very beginning, and he had apparently known about Crane's warehouse, too. He was not about to reveal the contents of his personal notes to anyone, let alone Sarie, and he was a member of the type of blind trust corporation that might have masterminded the Roxbury arsons. He was involved, all right—there was no doubt about that. The question was, how involved? Was he simply bent on conducting his own investigation without anyone's assistance? Was he protecting someone or something? Or was he a perpetrator himself?

Sarie looked at herself critically in the mirror. Intuition was not always dependable. *She* didn't look like someone who would get involved in an arson scandal that touched some of the biggest names in the city, did she? She looked like she should be out playing tennis with the girls. Vance was right: good bones don't lie. She made a face at herself and turned to the huge glass-enclosed shower. Well, Vance Leland had good bones, too, and so did his cronies in the Brahmin Trust, probably. But her intuition had gotten her this far, and she was not about to abandon it now.

Sarie felt her courage return as the throbbing in her head began to fade. Having landed herself in Vance Leland's apartment—in his shower, even!—she was determined to make the most of the opportunity to get at the truth. At the very least, she owed it to herself as a professional fire fighter. She owed it to poor Doug Eldridge, too, to Tom and the other fire fighters. She owed it to the entire city, if it came to that.

But there was something else. If she was perfectly honest with herself, Sarie had to admit that her motive was not strictly altruistic. Her involvement with Vance had progressed beyond any purely professional interest. She was fascinated by him, mesmerized by him, whether or not he was a criminal. She longed to find out what made him tick, what made him such a curious mixture of conventional snobbery and extraordinary mystery. *I'll get to the bottom of Vance Leland* and *the Roxbury fires,* she vowed to herself, turning on the brass taps and letting the steam rise up in her face. She had the feeling that she had better, before one or both of them got to her.

WHEN SHE CAME OUT into the living room, defiantly ignoring the fact that Vance's terry robe hung nearly to her ankles and dripped from her arms like a crazily distorted choir robe, she was surprised to find the glass coffee table set elegantly for two, with china, crystal and what she saw at once to be very good silver.

"What's this?" she inquired, curling up quickly on the pale blue linen couch so that she could pull the robe more completely around her body. "Aunt Minerva Leland's silver service?" She remembered hearing all about the redoubtable Minerva Leland from Sarah Jane.

"Actually, it's Great-Aunt Cecilie's," replied Vance, coming in from the small black-and-white kitchen with a silver tray. "Horace's wife never parted with anything in her life. As a matter of fact, it's my belief that Aunt Minnie is probably buried with her silver service." Sarie laughed at the thought. "I must admit, though," Vance went on, setting the tray on the table and sitting next to her on the oversize couch, "Great-Aunt Cece would turn over in her grave if she saw her silver service being handled by a lady in a bathrobe. Even one who looks so disarming in that attire." His glance took in her thick hair, plastered sleekly back against her small skull, and her shiny face devoid of makeup. "She was very big on dressing for dinner, and you are dressed for... well, not for dinner, shall we say?"

Under his wryly appreciative gaze, Sarie pulled the robe closer at her neck, where it had fallen open. "Great-Aunt Cecilie was right," she said, feeling extremely uncomfortable and exposed all of a sudden. She wished she was in her own clothes. "Maybe I should go put my clothes back on after all." The bravery she felt in the shower deserted her once again, and she decided that she needed all the armor she could muster after all in his elegant presence.

"Don't be silly," he chuckled. "You're not going to let an outdated convention like dressing for dinner stand in your way, are you? That's way too passé for you, my dear. A rebel Appleton shouldn't blanch at dining nude if the situation calls for it."

Sarie knew he was having fun at her expense, and she blushed furiously. "The situation does *not*," she retorted emphatically, and Vance laughed out loud.

"No, I suppose not." He leaned forward and lifted the first of two silver domes that sat on the tray. "Especially not with such elegant fare. Dinner," he added with a flourish, "is served."

Sarie looked at the contents of the dishes and laughed in spite of herself. One held four hot dogs, looking red and overboiled in their buns, and the other held a mountain of potato chips. "Now *that*," she said, chuckling, "would make Cece roll over a few times."

"Sorry, but it was all I could manage on such short notice. I don't usually eat at home. Hope you like hot dogs."

There was something touching about his expression, and about the fact that he had made an effort to prepare the ridiculous meal.

"I love hot dogs," Sarie replied gratefully, and bit into one with real gusto. Hot dogs happened to be a favorite food—something she had been denied during her childhood since they were considered déclassé. She did not care to tell Vance how often she and Taylor indulged in them.

They made short work of all four dogs and the chips, and then Vance produced an excellent Bordeaux for dessert. Sarie was beginning to feel extremely comfortable curled up on his couch, although she was well aware, as they chatted amiably about mutual acquaintances, that they were both waiting to get down to business.

This time, Sarie was determined not to lose her nerve. Finishing her first glass of wine, she put down the Baccarat goblet with finality and wiped her mouth on the linen napkin. "All right, Vance, why don't we talk a little bit about this morning, and all the events that led up to it?''

Vance's eloquent eyebrows lifted. ''What's there to talk about?'' he inquired coolly.

She knew he was playing a game, and he knew she knew it. They looked at each other with knowing little smiles. ''Who's Doug Eldridge, and what was he doing in that warehouse?'' Sarie asked.

Vance shrugged. ''Doug used to work for me, but he doesn't anymore. I no longer have any say—or interest—in his activities. As far as I'm concerned he just happened to be there—worse luck for him. But none of my business.''

She didn't believe that for a second, although she had to admit he was a good liar. ''And you just happened to be there, too, I suppose?''

Vance shook his head. ''Boy, you really have a thing about me going to fires, don't you! Can't a fire buff show up at a fire without arousing suspicion?''

Sarie shook her head. ''Not without arousing mine,'' she told him. The wine was making her both voluble and determined. ''I think you showed up there for a reason. I think you know why Doug was there, too.''

''I could be saying the same thing to you, you know,'' he shot back. ''How did *you* know Doug Eldridge was in the back of that building, Sarie?''

Sarie thought quickly and decided not to reveal the extent of her relationship with Doug. The less Vance knew about what she knew, the more leverage she would have with him. ''A lucky guess,'' she retorted, and then added, ''Your presence couldn't have anything to do with the fact that your friend Edward Crane owns that warehouse, could it?''

Vance looked impatient. "The Brewery was my building, remember? I don't own that warehouse, or Crane Paper." Vance leaned forward and poured them both more wine. "As a matter of fact, Crane himself doesn't own it, either. It was his father's company, and I understand he sold it off a few months ago because it was losing money. I have no idea who owns it now."

"Maybe it's being held in a blind trust," said Sarie, amazed by her own daring. "The Brahmin Trust, perhaps?"

Vance's head snapped up and the wine bottle clinked dangerously against the crystal. "What the hell do you think the Trust has to do with this?"

Sarie spoke very quickly, before she lost her nerve. "Doug told me that he thinks a blind trust owned silent shares in the Roxbury buildings that were torched. Major shares. And no one knew who the members of that trust were. Not even the landlords. Or the insurance companies."

Vance put his wineglass down and seemed to think carefully before speaking. "That's ridiculous, Sarie," he said patiently. "First of all, there's no reason to suspect that a blind trust—even one member of a blind trust—is involved. Second, even if I did think that, there are more than two hundred trusts just like the Brahmin Trust in this city. To find out the names of the members of any of them, all you have to do is get a court order and go to the insurance commissioner's office to look up the records in the confidential files."

"You can?" For some reason, Sarie had envisioned the blind trusts as inviolable secret clubs utterly exempt from the laws that governed normal business transactions.

"Of course you can. The only reason it's called 'blind' is because no names appear on the actual ownership documents, for the usual tax reasons." Sarie didn't know what those usual tax reasons were, but she kept silent. "And the only reason they're called 'trusts' is that the members are supposed to trust each other to handle their individual shares in accordance with the rules." He snorted softly, and Sarie thought he sounded bitter. "My God, there's no great secret to blind trusts. All it takes is a court order and a little legwork to find out what they're doing."

"Legwork that nobody bothered to do during the Roxbury trials, Vance?"

He gave her a guarded look. "The question never came up."

"Do you mean to tell me that it hasn't occurred to anyone that there might be someone behind the whole scheme? Maybe not a blind trust member, but someone who was not apprehended?" She shook her head. "I can't believe that, Vance. And I don't think you believe it, either."

Vance did not reply at once. He drew his fingertips across his brow, and Sarie realized that he was very tired. "There was no reason to think anything of the sort at the time," he said guardedly. "If there had been, of course, I would have had no problem finding the information required." He gave a dry snort of laughter. "One member of the blind trust might not know what the others are doing, but no one can work in absolute secrecy."

"Not even you, Vance?"

His eyes narrowed. "What do you mean, not even me?"

"Obviously you're conducting your own private investigation into the Roxbury fires. What I want to know is why."

"Sarie," he said wearily, "I can't tell you why."

"It's because you have something to hide, isn't it, Vance?"

"What could I possibly have to hide, Sarie? What are you talking about?"

"I'm talking about your personal notes on the Roxbury investigations."

Vance slammed his palm down on the edge of the couch so suddenly that Sarie jumped. "Those notes again! I can't believe..." He shook his head. "Doug Eldridge told you about the notes, too, I suppose?"

Sarie nodded. "He said that's what... He said they would be very revealing."

"Christ, how would he know! He's never set eyes on those notes," Vance muttered, more to himself than to Sarie. Then he looked up shrewdly. "You think Doug was sent to the warehouse to look for those notes, don't you, Sarie?"

Sarie started to deny it and then, seeing his expression, thought better of it. "It's possible," she admitted.

"Did Doug tell you that?"

"He said he had been set up. That someone sent him to the warehouse." She tried not to meet his discerning gaze. "He said there was something in there he wanted to get. Something that would explain everything." She paused and then rushed on. "And I think it was your notes he was talking about."

There was a long silence. "Are you saying you think I had something to do with that explosion, Sarie?" His voice was perilously calm.

Sarie felt her pulse quicken. "No, I'm not saying that at all, Vance."

"Then what are you saying? Just what do you think is happening here, Sarie? Why don't you give me your informed opinion. You do think there's someone involved in the Roxbury arsons who was never apprehended, don't you?"

Sarie swallowed. "Yes," she said as firmly as she could. "That's what I think."

"You have no real evidence for this, but nevertheless, you're pretty convinced, is that right?"

Sarie nodded. "That's right," she murmured.

Vance looked oddly satisfied by this answer, but he went on with his relentless questioning. "Do you think I'm an arsonist, Sarie?"

Sarie nearly choked on her wine. "Of course I don't!" And she thought that at that moment she really didn't think so, despite his vaguely threatening manner.

"Then you think I know who is responsible, and I'm not telling you for some reason? Because I'm trying to protect somebody, perhaps?"

Sarie tried to deny this, too, but she didn't get very far. Things had quickly gotten out of hand. Instead of getting information from Vance, it was she who was being grilled—and she didn't like the feeling at all. "All I'm saying," she said carefully, "is that you know a lot more about this whole thing than you're letting on. And I want to know why."

"I'm not letting on to *you*, you mean," he snapped, suddenly impatient. "That doesn't mean I'm not doing anything about it, you know. It just means I'd like to keep my information quiet for the time being. Surely you'll allow me that, won't you, Sarie?"

"But why? What's your big secret, Vance?"

"What's yours?" he countered at once.

They glared at each other across the couch for several seconds. "Look," Vance said at last with a resigned sigh, "neither of us knows what the other knows about this whole mess or even why we need to pursue it so relentlessly. We both have our suspicions, don't we, Sarie?"

Sarie swallowed hard and nodded.

"Then maybe we should leave it at that for a while longer," he went on. "Until we're really sure, don't you think?"

Sarie knew what he was talking about. Don't accuse me, he was telling her, unless you are certain of what you know. She wasn't sure if it was a challenge or a plea, but she was moved by it nonetheless.

"I'm not sure we can do that," she said slowly.

"I'm not sure we can afford not to," he replied.

"What do you mean, Vance?"

Vance lifted his wineglass to his lips and drank, slowly and deeply. Watching, Sarie became acutely aware of the movement of his long neck and the strong collarbone that disappeared into the Lacoste sport shirt. She knew she was meant to notice all this, but could not bring herself to ignore his powerful attractiveness. She swallowed and waited for him to speak.

He put down the wineglass with equal deliberation, and when he faced her again, his eyes were glittering with some unnameable emotion. "You know," he said slowly, "I've had the feeling ever since I first set eyes on you in Bob Wapshaw's office that you and I were meant to meet. Didn't you think there was something fateful about that afternoon, Sarie?"

"Sure. I almost lost my job that afternoon," she replied lightly, hoping he couldn't see the vein throbbing on the side of her neck.

"Don't be facile, Sarie. It doesn't suit you. You're too honest, and you don't lie well."

"Unlike you, I suppose?" She didn't know what had made her say that. Obviously Vance was making her feel off-balance and defensive.

"I'm probably a better liar than you, yes. In my world, I have to be. But I'm not lying to you when I tell you that I think we were even meant to be facing off like this, Sarie Appleton. Some things are preordained, and this moment is one of them."

Sarie's hand was clammy around the wineglass, and her heartbeat was audible, she was sure. "I wonder if Doug Eldridge knows he's part of a master plan to get you and me together." She laughed nervously, persisting in avoiding his gaze.

"Dammit, Sarie, look at me!" He reached out and took her chin between his thumb and forefinger, and held her face so that she could not look away. "Don't try and laugh this off. You know what I'm talking about," he went on in a surprisingly gentle voice. "You know what I mean about you and me, don't you?"

"I think you're avoiding the issue, Vance. We were talking about . . ."

"No, *you're* avoiding the issue. We were talking about nothing. *This* is what we should be talking about. You and me, Sarie, and why we're together right now. This is serious business—*this* is important."

"I thought we were together because of arson, Vance. That's important, isn't it?"

"Dammit, don't you understand that we belong together?" He looked really angry now, and Sarie felt a frisson of fear. She really didn't know this man at all. She had no idea what his limits were.

"You make it sound like an arranged marriage between two old families," she said with a poor attempt at irony. "That old Brahmin tradition."

"That old Brahmin tradition has much to be said for it," Vance replied, his voice softening again. "After all, we have all that in common, as well."

"As well as what?" Sarie was no longer bantering. She was genuinely confused.

Vance smiled, suddenly, as if all that anger had merely been a ruse. "This," he said, as he gathered her into his arms.

Sarie's first thought was that, if she reached up and put her arms around him, she would be unable to hold her robe—his robe—closed. Then she realized how crazy that was. If she wanted to wrap her arms around him—and she most certainly did—there was no reason in the world for her to be concerned about modesty. That dilemma solved, she was able to give herself over completely to the rapture of his embrace.

Neither of them had any use for preliminaries now. It was as if, but mutual silent consent, they had agreed that they owed themselves this much. Vance slid the robe past her shoulders so that her breasts and ribs were exposed, but he would not let her take it off altogether.

"No, not yet," he whispered huskily when she tried to shrug the thick terry cloth to the floor. "I want to savor your gifts bit by bit." He smiled crookedly. "I don't think I could manage it all at once."

"And I don't think I can wait," Sarie murmured, surprised at the gritty arousal in her voice. She tried to unbutton Vance's crisp shirt, but her fingers were too shaky. Together they managed to remove it. There was a brief moment when they stared at each other, drinking in the smooth voluptuous sight of bare skin straining to be touched. Sarie gave a little sigh of desire, and the pulse in Vance's neck was rocketing against his Adam's apple. Then they flew together, attaching themselves to one another hungrily and with abandon. Sarie felt that she knew Vance's body intimately even as she discovered it. She wrapped her arms around him and remembered the fine, hard muscles of his chest and stomach against her hard nipples, the ribbed edges of his spine under her eager fingers. It was as though his body was a luxury that she would not be denied for a moment longer.

And all the while their lips met in a fury of dedicated passion, searching, grasping, remembering the beautiful pain of contact. Sarie felt herself falling into the depths of his kiss with such a sensation of vertigo that her stomach melted into a liquid center, and she had to hold on more tightly to his back in order to keep from slipping to the floor. She felt light-headed but not fainthearted. She had never been so boldly aware of her own passion. It seemed to her that she had always known Vance's warm, hungry lips, had always felt his keen hard body beneath her fingers and against her loins. She pressed herself closer until she felt the oddly familiar heat and pressure of his hips against hers. Yes, this was what she had always wanted, what she had been longing for with half-remembered desire. He even smelled familiar, a citrusy soap scent undercut by a rich, almost leathery musk. She drank him in thirstily with every sense.

Vance was as enveloped by her. Sarie had used the same soap, but he could not get over how different it was on her, how much sweeter, much younger. Although loathe to leave the hot haven of her mouth, his lips were drawn inescapably to her small shoulders, so frail as they rose from the froth of white terry, that it was hard for him to remember that this woman fought fires, wrestled with heavy hoses, battled fierce heat and danger. She seemed like fine old crystal in his arms. With a guttural rasp of satisfaction, he moved down to the hollow between her collarbone, where he lost himself in the freshness and softness of her skin. He was almost afraid to let himself move lower, thinking that he might lose control altogether if she got any softer, any sweeter.

But then he could not resist the lure of her tiny breasts as they beckoned, fragrant and steamy from the heat of her body and swelling into hot, hard points against his mouth. As he had suspected, the skin on her breasts was unbearably soft, the nipples incredibly dainty even though aroused. He was aware of Sarie's hands stroking the skin on his back, reaching down across his torso as if she could not get close enough to him. The sense that she was as needy as he made him wild with desire; it was all he could do to concentrate on the pleasure exploring those little breasts gave him. He knew the power of restraint, even if she did not.

When he could bear it no longer, he stopped and slipped effortlessly out of his slacks, but still he did not allow her to remove the robe completely. It was like delving into a sweet warm secret, to plunge his hands and face beneath the heavy terry cloth and explore the lean curves of her flanks, the surprising swell of her hips and buttocks below the narrow waist and the rich luxuriance of her long thighs. Vance was a man of much experience, but wrapped in the white robe with Sarie he felt like a young man making love for the first time.

Sarie sensed his rejuvenation and exulted in it. Laughing, she finally shrugged free of the robe and, with a hoarse cry, wrapped herself around him so that their nude bodies met point to point. Vance lifted her against him and, taking hold of her thighs, wrapped her legs around his waist. Welded together, they moved in a graceful dance across the floor to the bedroom. They were not aware of the ghost of the conversation they had never finished, of the smell of chemicals or of the vaporous curtain of smoke that shrouded the room in a secret mist. It was as if they had entered a private world where the only sensation was that of touch, the only commandment that of need.

He lay her down on the huge bed and stood poised over her for a moment, drinking in the taut arch of her body, the powerful arousal in the deceptively small limbs and flanks. He felt exultant already, even before he lowered himself to her. To Sarie, he appeared in the mist like the answer to a prayer she hadn't even known she had spoken. She welcomed him into her loins with an eager moan and a sigh of relief. Once again he began slowly, rocking against her in a slowly accelerating rhythm that was punctuated by breathless kisses and long, silent gazes that seemed to penetrate as deep as his body.

Then, as if finally allowing himself the release he had held at bay for so long, he exploded into a frenzy of passion that brought Sarie up and over the edge of conscious thought. All that existed was his body and hers, in a union that seemed permanent and insoluble. She could not imagine him being outside of her, ever again. She could not think at all—only feel. Had she been able to consider the events that had brought her to this moment, to the climaxes that rose in unexpected wave after wave on the huge bed, she would have concluded that Vance had been right after all. They were destined to be together. And, for the first time in her adult life, Sarie was content to be where she belonged.

Chapter Seven

Sarie awoke to Vance's voice murmuring, she thought, in her ear. Like a cat, she stretched and purred, luxuriating in the greatest physical contentment she ever remembered feeling. The expensive cotton sheets and soft wool blanket made a cozy nest in which she could stretch her bare limbs.

Sarie had been sure they would not sleep a wink—they had been so intent on exploring each other's body, and each other's seemingly endless capacity for pleasure. But somehow, around dawn, she had fallen into a deep dreamless slumber, her body entwined with Vance's in a complicated pattern of latent desire.

Given the efforts of the night, and the small amount of sleep, Sarie was surprised at how rested she felt. She stretched again, hoping to come up against some portion of that body she had come to know and love so well during the past ten hours.

But it was not beside her. She realized that the voice was not murmuring in her ear, but into a telephone a few feet away. She opened one eye and saw Vance's bare back as he sat on the edge of the king-size bed, talking quietly on the phone. Sarie smiled and reached out her fingers, longing to run them up and down the strong silky ridge of his backbone. But she could not quite reach, and before she could roll over to get closer, Vance's words began to sink into her pleasure-drugged brain. She froze on her side and listened.

"I want the truth from you about this mess, Doug," he was saying in a low, tense voice. "No more playing both ends against the middle—you saw where it landed you yesterday." There was a pause while he listened to what Doug had to say. "I know what kind of shape you're in. You're lucky you're not dead, damn you! And believe me, my two-timing friend, you're going to be in a lot worse shape if you don't let me know exactly what happened—with your friends, and with her." He listened again. "Nice of you to ask, seeing as you were to blame for her being there," he snapped. "No, she's not hurt. Just a little . . . a little stunned. And confused, thanks to your half-witted theories. But it could have been worse. And it might get worse. That's what I'm worried about."

Sarie thought she heard the smooth voice soften and catch a bit as he said this, but after another listening pause, Vance went on in the same severe tone.

"Well, of course you've gotten yourself in the middle of a mess!" Vance whispered harshly. "It's been a mess all along, and you've managed to make it even worse, lying down with the other team. Now I've got to untangle a bigger bundle than ever before I'm in the clear. Time is getting short, and my options are running out. Now that she's involved . . . Well, we'll just have to see how far she gets. I'm not worried about her. But if your friends . . . Look, I'm not worried about what they'll do to *you*. They've tried once, and they're not going to pull anything at Mass General. That's why I had you put in a private room. You just lay low in that bed and make sure they keep that guard on your door. And for God's sake, don't talk to anyone. I'm not ready for you to go blurting out your story yet—not until I've straightened things out at my end. I don't care how scared you are—you keep your mouth shut, understand?''

Listening to Vance's cruel tone, Sarie felt a stab of pity for Doug Eldridge, lying in his hospital bed. Vance went on, ''Besides, if you had given it half a thought, you would have figured out that I would never have hidden my notes in that warehouse. I'm not that stupid. Now, the first thing I'll have to do is to check out those ownership papers on record in the insurance commissioner's files and see if the list we're looking for is still there. Obviously that's the key—the only way to prove anything one way or the other, with or without my notes. If we can get that list, we're safe. Then my notes will stand on their own. But if anybody gets their hands on those records before I do, it'll look bad. I need those records, dammit, and I intend to get them, court order or not.''

Although Vance's voice never rose above a low whisper, this last was spoken with brutal determination. Sarie's blood chilled at the sound. Did that cold-blooded voice belong to the same man she had spent the night loving passionately? She heard the receiver click into the cradle and shut her eyes quickly, praying that her pounding heart would not give her away.

Vance sat very still for a moment before turning around, giving Sarie much-needed time to compose her features into what she hoped was a semblance of sleep. Questions were ricocheting around in her mind faster than she could catch them, but she was too upset to face Vance with any of them. She could feel his gaze on her and hoped he did not recognize that she was only faking slumber.

Apparently he did not. "Sweet Sarie," he murmured to himself, and she felt his fingers tangling gently in her hair along the pillow. She could feel his regard warming her skin and struggled with the desire to open her eyes to catch his expression. But she did not dare risk it; he would know instantly that she had overheard his conversation. Instead she lay still, except for the slightest trembling of her hands, which were concealed beneath the blanket, and waited to see what he would do.

After what seemed like hours Vance sighed deeply. Sarie read it as an expression of regret. Then she felt his hips lightly flutter against hers. Unable to bear her own stillness a moment longer, she opened her eyes slowly. But he had already gotten up from the bed, and she was faced again with his naked back, this time retreating into the bathroom.

"Oh, God," she moaned silently as the door to the bathroom clicked shut. "Don't let me have heard what I think I heard. Make this all a big mistake. A terrible stupid mistake." But as she lay there, eyes shut against the sudden urge to weep, Sarie knew there was no mistake.

She was still too shocked to make sense of the phone conversation or to even try and connect it with the events of the past few days. Somehow Vance's personal notes contained information that might link him—or someone else—to the Roxbury fires. Those notes were crucial—and so were the insurance records that would corroborate them. But what did they prove—Vance's innocence? Or his guilt?

Either way, Sarie knew that she could hide her dismay from Vance, and so she stayed where she was. When he came back into the room, fully dressed, she was feigning deep sleep.

"A real sweet sleeper, aren't you?" he whispered with fond amusement. She could smell the spicy tang of his after-shave, hear the faint rustle of his crisp suit as he bent to brush his lips against her hair again. "Sleep on, my angel. You're going to need the rest."

Mercifully, he was gone in a moment. Sarie heard the heavy door of the apartment shut behind him and lay there for another moment or two to collect herself before opening her eyes. Daylight was streaming in through the curtains, but it was gray light, not sunlight. "Good," Sarie muttered bitterly. "I don't think I could face a gorgeous spring day." All the pleasure she had felt on waking was gone, irretrievably lost amid the echoing sound of the soft, stern words she had overheard.

Sarie got up, wrapping the sheet around her naked body, and tiptoed into the living room to make sure Vance had gone. There was no one there, and now, safely alone, she felt a stab of regret. "I should have confronted him," she said angrily as she dropped the sheet and stalked to the bathroom. "I should have told him I knew he was up to something and made him tell me what the hell was going on."

The unfamiliar oath was satisfying, so she tried another. "Damn, damn, damn!" Sarie turned on the bathroom light and was confronted with a note stuck under the beveled edge of the mirror. All her bravado left her in an instant, and she sat down unsteadily on the commode to read it.

" 'My darling,' " she read aloud. " 'I couldn't bear to interrupt your sweet slumber, even though the urge to make love to you again was great. You are everything I imagined you would be and more. Have a good day at work. All my everything, V.' "

She tried to summon another oath, but, to her great surprise, two fat tears rolled down her cheeks instead. After what she had overheard on the phone, she knew that the note was as insincere as last night's lovemaking. She was clearly being used—for what purpose she was not yet sure, but it didn't much matter. What mattered was that the special night of love had not been special at all to Vance Leland. It hurt to know that what had been so magical for her had merely been a game for Vance.

Determined not to let her emotions get the better of her, Sarie turned on the shower as hot as she could stand it and stood beneath the harsh massage jet, willing her courage back. "How dare he?" she demanded of the blank white tiles. "What kind of idiot does he think I am? How dare he think I could fall into his trap, fall prey to his charms?"

But Sarie knew she had done just that, and even the hot water could not reduce the chill she felt in her heart. The nagging doubts poured in on her, needling her awake more effectively than the shower spray. She was now certain that Vance was very much involved in whatever foul play had led to the Brewery fire and the explosion in Crane's warehouse—that he knew a lot more about both than he was telling the authorities, much less her. Furthermore, he knew that Doug had been looking for his notes at the warehouse and that someone else wanted them very badly. And for some reason he was determined that those notes—and the ınsurance records he had mentioned—were not to see the light of day.

She was still shivering as she dried herself with one of Vance's thick towels. But why all the secrecy? What was there of such importance in those notes that Vance had felt the need to keep them hidden for so many months? What information did he have access to that would be devastating to someone if it were to become public and who was that someone? As far as Sarie could tell, there were only two options. Vance's innocence now seemed like an elusive dream that remained just beyond her grasp, regardless of how badly she wanted to believe in it. It was more likely that Vance was very much involved in a scandal of major proportions. He might be covering up for someone close to him, a member of his own social circle—a member of the Brahmin Trust, perhaps? Sarie thought about Vance's Uncle Horace; Parkman, the upright commissioner of insurance; and Fred Hapgood sitting in Vance's office that morning. It seemed incredible that any of them could be capable let alone responsible. Edward Crane—now that was a bit more likely. After all, he had owned the warehouse Doug had been sent to. But Edward Crane had looked foolish and incompetent, and Vance had told her that he no longer owned Crane Paper.

The list of possible villains was dwindling, leaving Sarie to face the unwanted question—could it have been Vance himself?

This possibility was unbearable to contemplate. "No," she said, toweling herself briskly as if to rub the notion from her mind. "I might have been wrong about him, but I couldn't possibly have been *that* wrong.'' She studied her drawn face in the mirror but could find no conviction behind her words.

Despite her disillusionment, Sarie still could not shake the sense that Vance was right—that they were, in some strange way, soul mates, fated to be together. Last night, the surprising certainty that this was true had been a source of elation. This morning, it only deepened her gloom. Until she knew what had really happened in the Roxbury fires, she could not be sure about Vance Leland. And she had to be absolutely sure.

As she got ready to leave the apartment, she looked around with a wistful glance, aware of the sad possibility that she would not be going back there again. Just as she was about to shut the door behind her, the phone rang. For a moment she paused, debating with herself whether to answer it or not. It took only an instant for her to decide that she had no business answering Vance's phone, but, in that moment, his telephone answering machine clicked on, making her decision irrelevant.

Still, she could not resist sticking around a moment longer to hear the message. "555-8693," came Vance's businesslike voice over the machine. "I can't make it to the phone, but if you'll leave a message I'll get back to you." Then there was a short buzz, and a click. Sarie sighed and started to close the door again.

But the sound of the other voice made her stop at once. It was such an unexpected voice, so different from Vance's smooth, distinctive Brahmin vowels, that she was surprised to hear it coming from his machine. The voice was rough, raspy and heavy with the broad "a" of East Boston. Sarie was used to that kind of voice at work, but in this urbane, plush environment, it was so out of place that she paused to listen to what it had to say.

"Leland? Joe Kelly here. You know who I am, and I know who you are, so I won't bother explaining. I know you're there listening—you rich people just don't like to pick up your own phones, do ya? Well, then, listen good. Your friend got a little surprise yesterday when he went to look for those notes of yours, didn't he? Too bad he didn't find what he was looking for, but then I guess you're not surprised—after all, you know where they are, and we don't." There was a nasty chuckle. "Of course, we can get our hands on some records that you might find interesting, too. So I think maybe it's time we got together and tried to work something out to our mutual satisfaction, eh? Mr.... My employer seems to agree. Why don't we meet out at your old carriage house in, say, about an hour? Then maybe we can settle this thing before too many more people get hurt. After all, you can only fight fire with fire for so long." He cackled viciously. "If we don't get cooperation, we'll just have to drag out the heavy artillery. And your pretty little fire fighter might get caught in the line of fire again."

There was another click and then a loud buzz, but Sarie didn't hear either. For a good two minutes she stood like a statue with her hand still on the door, half in, half out of Vance's marbled entry foyer. Suddenly she was seized with the desire to escape from the apartment as fast as she could, and she rushed down twelve flights of stairs in the emergency stairwell, unable to wait for the elevator.

Out on the street, Sarie walked for several blocks before she realized that she was walking in circles. She still could not believe what she had heard. Obviously

Doug Eldridge had been sent to the warehouse by Joe Kelly and had been told he would find Vance's private notes hidden there. But Sarie knew Doug had not intended to give them to Joe Kelly and his employer as they expected. Instead he had planned to use them to buy his own safety and freedom. Joe, however, had second-guessed him—he already knew Vance's notes were not hidden in the Crane warehouse, and sending him there had only been a ruse to get Doug—and maybe herself, too—there for the explosion. But it was clear that Joe and his boss wanted to get their hands on those notes as much as Doug had. That meant, she reasoned bleakly, that Joe and his boss had been responsible for the Brewery fire—possibly as a warning to Vance or possibly because they had suspected that he had stored his precious notes there.

This changed things dramatically and reminded Sarie that there had always been an outside, antagonistic element in the equation—Doug's nameless employer, the man who gave Joe Kelly his orders. Was *he* responsible for the fires, and if so, did Vance know it? Maybe Vance's notes contained information implicating him, and that was why it was so important to Joe Kelly that he get his hands on them.

But if Vance knew his notes were so important, why hide them? Did they contain information that would imperil Vance or someone he was trying to protect? Why not go straight to the authorities and get the court order to open the confidential insurance files? What was in those files that both Joe Kelly and Vance thought so crucial? Would that information validate Vance's notes, or was there something that would show them to be falsified?

So many questions—too many, Sarie decided. And besides, they all paled before the big one: what was the heavy artillery that Joe had mentioned with such sinister relish, and how soon would it be before Sarie became the target?

She had to do something—anything—to uncover the truth. It was too late to be cautious—she was already in danger. It was no longer a matter of the city's safety or her own. She was too deeply involved with Vance to back out now, even if she had wanted to. Even more than her duty as a fire fighter, she had a duty to herself—to find out once and for all who, and what, he really was.

The decision was no longer hers. Destiny had brought her to a world of dangerous criminals, and she was afraid she might be falling in love with one of them.

The question was how to go about finding answers. She did not know where to begin and so she let her mind go blank, hoping her intuition would take over, as it so often had in the past. She had stopped walking in circles, but it took her a while before she realized where she was headed. Despite all rational impulses to the contrary, she was headed toward Jamaica Plain. Toward the carriage house that held Vance's magnanimous gift to the city.

And an interview with Joe Kelly.

Chapter Eight

The carriage house was quiet when Sarie got there, full of that peculiar silence that attended old things. She had a moment of panic—what if Vance had picked up the message and showed up for the meeting with Joe, as well? How would she explain her presence? But there seemed to be no one around, and as she let herself in, Sarie wondered if perhaps she hadn't imagined the whole thing.

She hadn't. Sitting at the desk in the old tack room was a man with a shock of salt-and-pepper hair and a red-tinged mustache. He was small and wiry, and wore a shabby suit in a hideous plaid. He did not look up when Sarie approached.

That's him? she thought. *That's the man Vance Leland is up against?* It didn't seem like an even match, but she knew better than to underestimate either of them. Besides, she reminded herself, Joe Kelly was not the real problem. There was someone else—some nameless person whose anonymity made him an even more sinister player than Joe Kelly.

"Who the hell are you?" The man had seen her and was on his feet in a flash, an ugly snarl on his lips.

Even though she had mentally prepared herself, Sarie jumped. "I...uh...I'm..." She steeled herself and thought quickly. "Vance sent me."

The snarl developed into a sneer. "Hah! The hell he did."

Sarie took a deep breath and tried to make her voice sound cocky. "I was with him when you called. On the answering machine. You said you wanted to fight fire with fire, didn't you, Joe? Well, I'm here about the notes—and I know all about fires."

Her attempt to sound threatening was unsuccessful, but Joe looked at her with sharp interest. "How'd you know about them?"

"I told you. Vance sent me. We've talked."

"Well, *I* don't talk to hired help—especially female hired help. Where's Vance?"

"He's at the hospital. Visiting Doug Eldridge, thanks to you." Sarie looked at her unprepossessing opponent and decided to play a hunch. "Anyway, you're hired help yourself, aren't you, Joe? I don't see why I should bother with you, either."

This remark hit home. Joe hoisted his pants and snorted belligerently. "Look, lady. I'm not here to play onesies. Your boss is making life very difficult for my boss, and we're tired of showing muscle. We want his notes."

"Why? There's nothing in them that could interest you or your boss, is there?" She paused dramatically. "Unless, of course, there's something in those records your boss doesn't want the world to know about. Something that could prove his link to the Roxbury arson ring, perhaps?"

Joe's eyes narrowed. "That's for us to decide."

Sarie thought she detected a note of nervousness in his voice and knew she was on the right track. She made an attempt to shrug casually. "Not if Vance doesn't want you to, it isn't. After all, he has the notes."

Joe took a threatening step forward. "Hey, sweetheart, you know something? I don't like your attitude one bit. You're as snooty as your boss Leland. You two are cut from the same uppity rich-folk cloth."

Sarie's rueful grimace was genuine. "You might say we are, Joe. You might say that."

"Well, I don't care what fancy family you come from, lady. All I care about is those notes. We want them—and we're getting very impatient."

Sarie suddenly felt weary and defeated. She was getting in way over her head, and she was confused and frightened. Hidden notes, records at the insurance commissioner's office—she wished she had not come. "We know you want the notes, Joe." She sighed. "You've made that perfectly clear."

"No, lady, I don't think we have. If we had, your buddy Vance Leland would be here with them in his hands, begging us to lay off." The ugly snarl returned to his thin lips. "Apparently we're still not making ourselves clear to your boy. So maybe you'd better tell him that next time we won't bother with penny-ante stuff."

"I don't call planting Jackson devices all over town penny-ante," she retorted angrily.

"You don't, eh? Well, just you wait—if we don't get those records, you'll see some real blazes. The kind of stuff the BFD can't lift a finger against—even with Mr. Sparkie Leland on their team."

He started to leave, but Sarie blocked his path, noticing with some relief that he was not much taller than she was and that, if she had to, she could probably defend herself against him. "Listen," she said, hoping she sounded conspiratorial. "Let's stop pretending, shall we, Joe? Maybe we could make a deal to our mutual satisfaction. I want to know about the insurance records, and you want the notes, right?" Sarie tried not to sound breathless as she made her brazen proposition. "So why don't you just tell me what's in those insurance records, and I'll tell you what's in the notes. It could save us all a lot of trouble."

Joe chuckled and leered. "Hey, lady, you're a class act, you know that? I don't know where Vance found you, but he hit the jackpot." He wet his lips. "I'll bet you two have some real hot meetings, don't you? Lots of body talk, maybe?"

Sarie tried to ignore this remark, even though it made her color violently. "What do you say, Joe?" she inquired ingratiatingly. "You let me know about those insurance records, and I'll tell you what you want to know about Vance's notes."

The sneer returned. "I say forget it, honey. You think I'm gonna let you off the hook so easy? No way. I bet you don't know a thing about those notes. Why should I trust you? After all, I don't trust Vance Leland as far as I can throw him—not after what he's been up to." His eyes glittered coldly. "And you shouldn't, either, if you know what's good for you."

"What do you mean, let him off the hook?" Sarie was suddenly scared again. "What do you think he's been up to?"

A shrewd glint lit up Joe's pale brown eyes. "You think Vance Leland's a hero? You think his hands are clean? Hey, baby, wake up and face the music. Your terrific Mr. High-and-Mighty is in this thing pretty deep. So deep he wants out as bad as we do. So no buy-offs. We want his notes, and we want *him*. Understand?'' He jabbed her chest with an ugly finger. "Not his latest roll in the hay."

And before she could say another word, he was gone.

Sarie did not want to stay at the carriage house. She didn't know where Vance had gone when he left the apartment; if he had gotten Joe's message, he might show up at any moment. Aside from wanting to avoid the awkwardness of having to explain her presence, Sarie was still not ready to face him. Not until she had proven to herself once and for all that he was or was not behind the Roxbury arson ring.

But where to go from there? What could she do to try and find the solution before Vance—or Joe Kelly and his boss—arrived at a solution of their own? Technically, Sarie was back on active duty, but the idea of returning to the station house was unthinkable, even though she knew she was putting herself in considerable jeopardy with the chief by not making an appearance. Losing her job was no longer important to her. She was like a woman possessed, and nothing mattered except getting to the bottom of the mystery. Now. Today. She would either prove Vance's innocence to herself and let herself love him, or she would prove his guilt and make herself stop. In either case, she *had* to know.

The next logical step was, of course, to find Vance's notes. Sarie knew that they must hold some of the answers she was looking for. Vance must have known all along that the arson ring had been more extensive than everyone else thought. He would naturally have wanted to keep that information private if he was protecting someone else—or himself.

But then she thought about Joe Kelly and knew there had to be other possibilities. Suppose Vance *had* come across information implicating someone else— someone he was not trying to protect but whose guilt he could not prove? Had his notes been withheld because his investigation was incomplete? If Joe Kelly worked for the man who had really been behind the arsons, then he was someone who was so powerful in the city that even Vance had been unable to touch him. If Vance knew about this person, had evidence, however slim, then Vance was in as much danger as Sarie.

Odd as it seemed, Sarie ardently hoped that was the case. But her hopes were fading fast. The pendulum of her intuition was swinging too wildly for her to trust it. She needed hard, cold facts, not willful supposition. She needed to find those notes, to find out if he knew who was behind the arsons—or if he was trying to keep others from knowing. She cursed herself for not having thought about searching his apartment while she was there. If she could just get her hands on his notes...

Or the insurance records. Clearly they were as important to Vance—and to Joe Kelly's employer as the notes; maybe more so, since they would contain hard evidence. But what sort of evidence? Sarie wasn't sure she would recognize the damning evidence in those records even if she could get into the confidential files. It probably had something to do with ownership of the burned buildings. Ownership seemed to be at the root of the mystery. Whoever had been behind the Roxbury arsons had arranged the fires for monetary gain—hoping to make a profit on the insurance pay-off without anybody knowing about it. That pointed to a blind trust, although not necessarily to the Brahmin Trust. Sarie thought again about the men sitting around the long cherry conference table. Vance and his uncle, E. T. Crane, Clifford Parkman, the insurance commissioner—could any of those staid and upright men be so cold-blooded, so chillingly competent at ruining so many lives? Sarie could not believe it of them any more than she could believe it of Vance, but she knew she had to consider the possibility. Any one of them might have been buying shares in the Roxbury buildings and—according to Vance's own admission—no one would be the wiser. But was that really true? Implicating his partners would be a sure way to get himself off the hook, especially if none of them had known he was involved in the first place.

Vance had discounted Doug's blind-trust theory as untenable, but he had seemed pretty determined to get hold of those records, which meant he knew they contained some interesting material. She did not know what they would prove, but the proof was in there, somewhere—proof that would either support or deny whatever it was he had in his notes. If she could not get her hands on Vance's notes, the insurance records would have to do. She knew Vance was planning to get hold of that confidential material. How could she beat him to it?

Clearly Vance had the advantage. He knew what he was looking for and how to get it. He was used to purchasing information using money or power as legal tender. After all, he had been able to get information during the original investigation that no one else had been able to get. Sarie forced herself to put aside the possibility that Vance had had access to the information from the inside—that he had actually been a party to the crime himself. She had to act fast and could not afford to be paralyzed by doubt. Although she suspected that he had only been using her as a pawn in his deadly game, she could not deny her feelings for him. In spite of all she thought she knew about the man, she was undeniably bound to him, and that was the most frightening thought of all. She would not have a moment's peace until she knew, one way or the other, exactly what Vance Leland had to do with the Roxbury arson ring and the Brewery fire. Her own future depended upon what she found.

So. The insurance records were her next target. She would have to look for some unknown list of names—some way to put together the bits and pieces of supposition that were all she had to go on so far. But how could she get to those confidential files?

Sarie felt a wave of despair wash over her. What could she do without money and power? For the first time in years she found herself wishing she still had access to the Appleton influence. Without it, as Sarah Jane was fond of pointing out, one was forced to fall back on one's own wits.

Wits. That was it. Tobey Witt. He may not be a mover and shaker in the city, but in his own way Sarie figured he had some pretty impressive connections. You couldn't work in the records department of a mammoth city agency for twenty years without knowing some other records department officials. Sarie could only pray that he would be willing to help her out again. She picked up the phone and dialed the station house, asking to be connected with the records department.

"Tobey? Hi, it's Sarie Appleton."

"You again? What's wrong, not enough information in those records for your boy?"

"As a matter of fact, Tobey, you're right."

"That's ridiculous," said Tobey, sounding offended. "Those records are exhaustive."

"Oh, I know. I know they're excellent. But I was looking... I mean, Taylor was hoping..." Sarie bit her lip. She was not a very good liar. "We were wondering if you could help us out just a little bit more."

Tobey was getting suspicious. "Hey, Sarie, how old's your kid? Nine? Ten? What's a ten-year-old doing writing a congressional report on an arson scandal?"

"I told you, he..."

"I know what you told me. I just don't believe it."

Sarie sighed. It was no use. "Okay, Tobey, you're right. This is something...some private work I'm doing on the side."

"Investigative work?"

"Yes. You know...for some...interested parties." *That much was true,* she thought grimly. "You know how hard it is for a single woman to make ends meet on a fire fighter's salary?" she added with a dismal attempt at a laugh.

But Tobey seemed to rise to the bait. "Yeah, yeah, I know. So you're doing a little digging on the side and you want my help, is that it?"

Sarie concocted an extemporaneous story for his benefit. "I'm working for some people who want to make sure they collected the right amount—got enough from the insurance companies. So I need to know how I can get in to those insurance commissioner's records." She squinted her eyes tightly shut against any possible outburst from the other end of the line, but none came. "I figured you'd be a good person to give me the name of a connection in the records department over at city hall."

"You wanna get into the confidential files, is that it?"

"That's right."

"You know it's not kosher, don't you?"

"I know."

"And you still want to do it?"

"That's right, Tobey. I have to do it. For my clients."

Tobey still sounded doubtful. "It'll cost you, you know."

"I'll make it worth your while, Tobey."

"Not me, you goon. I would never charge you for my help." He sounded disgusted. "But the guy I know down there...he's not quite so altruistic. He'll need his palm greased."

"That's okay, I...my clients will pick up the tab."

"All right. His name is Fred Lightman. I'll call him and tell him to expect you tonight."

"Tonight?" Sarie was panicked. "Can't I go over there right now?" She had to get there before Vance did.

"Of course not! Those records are confidential for a reason, Sarie. They can only be opened by a court order or—some other higher authority."

"What do you mean, some other higher authority?" *Was there another way to get at that information?*

Tobey smirked. "I meant bribery, of course. Money or power will buy your way in, and that's about it."

"I know what you mean," she said dryly. Vance Leland had plenty of both. She just had to hope she was first. "Well, Tobey, thanks a million. I really appreciate your help."

"Don't mention it. Definitely don't mention it. And remember, Sarie, be careful. What you're doing is illegal!"

Tobey, Sarie thought grimly, *you don't know the half of it.*

Chapter Nine

Fred Lightman, records librarian for the office of the insurance commissioner, was everything that Tobey Witt said he would be—except that his "fee" was considerably higher than Sarie had expected.

"I can't understand why anybody would want me to go to all the trouble of unearthing those old documents," he complained as he led Sarie down aisle after aisle filled with microfiche files. "I mean, isn't that case dead history for the fire department?"

Sarie had told Fred only that she was with the BFD and doing some research on the Roxbury arson investigation. She assumed he would not ask any questions, especially since it would be difficult for her to explain why she was conducting departmental business at six o'clock in the evening. But Fred, despite the fact that he was breaking the law by allowing her access to the confidential files without official sanction, acted as if it were perfectly normal for her to be there. Sarie decided to play along with his casual attitude, even though her heart was well up into her throat.

"It's mostly routine," she said lightly. "You know how bureaucracies can be—everything has to be done in triplicate."

"Don't I know it," he replied gloomily. He stopped suddenly and began thumbing through the stacks that were labeled in a code that was illegible to Sarie.

"By the way," she asked as he led her to the microfiche reader, "has anyone else been around asking for these records today?"

Fred glared at her. "Of course not! I don't make a habit of this, you know."

"I'm sorry," Sarie murmured, hiding her relief. So she had gotten there in time. Now, if she could only find what she wanted . . .

"You realize," Fred was saying, "that this means I'll have to stay here while you work. I can't have you in here alone, you know. Mr. Parkman wouldn't like it one bit."

Sarie smile. "I'll make it worth your while, I promise."

Fred's "while" had been expensive, Sarie now reflected as she huddled over the machine. She had started with the insurance reports on the burned buildings, even though condensed versions of them had been included in the court records. The complete versions were pages long, but Sarie had hoped that the full reports might give her a clue. She had been peering at them on the tiny view screen for over two hours already, though, and nothing out of the ordinary caught her eye. Obviously there was no list of blind-trust holding companies neatly recorded on the titles. If there had been, she reflected glumly, there would have been no mystery to begin with.

But if she could not find any names in those files, she was at a loss as to where else to find them. She turned to the original deeds on the buildings in question, but again, she was unsuccessful. By law, she discovered, only one name—that of the majority owner—had to be listed on the original title. The names of the eight men who had been arrested appeared in the proper place on all the deeds she looked at. There wasn't even a way to determine whether or not those ownerships were complete or whether there had been other investors.

Sarie rubbed her eyes and turned away from the screen to give them a rest. She felt weary and defeated. No wonder it had been so hard to find out who else might have had anything to gain in the original investigation. Without reason to suspect that everything was not as it seemed, the information seemed to be all there, and the names of the men responsible quite obvious. Too obvious, she saw now, but she understood that there would have been no way to see that back then.

It was clear to her that even the accused themselves had not known of the master hand that had fashioned the web that caught them. Each of the owners of the burned buildings held title to their property individually—none of them shared ownership with the others. And since each of them had majority control of his own building, the question of how they had raised the money to buy those buildings in the first place had obviously never come up, either in court or among themselves. Besides, reasoned Sarie, if they had gotten the money to buy their properties from a blind trust, even the owners might not know the identity of the person directly responsible for those investments. They had been bound together only by their arson scheme, and only the member or members of the blind trust would have known that there was a common thread binding them all together.

Sarie had to admit it was a masterful scheme, but she still wasn't sure she understood how the mastermind had pulled it off. How had he planted the seed of this atrocious plan in the minds of eight men without revealing himself? How had he made those men believe that the plan to burn the buildings and collect the insurance was of their own devising? Whoever was responsible had the power to manipulate all those people as if they were so many wooden marionettes, utterly without regard for their futures. He must have known that they would eventually take the blame for his plan. And he had been right. All of the owners had been tried and convicted of their crimes without ever having suspected that they were not solely responsible.

And what about Ira Jackson and company? Had the mastermind been responsible for planting the idea that he brought in from Detroit, as well? Surely that was beyond the bounds of even that sort of power and influence. And yet, it made sense, in a terrible sort of way. Ira Jackson had no ties to Boston, and therefore would not be likely to finger anyone other than the men who had hired him—the owners themselves. And, like them, he and his fellow arsonists were serving their sentences in Concord State Prison, never knowing how they had been manipulated and played against one another for maximum effect and profit. Sarie shuddered at the power and influence the man—or men— had had to wield to pull off such a coup. She knew of only a few people in the city who might have been able to manage it, and Vance Leland was one of them.

Sarie's head ached from reading the small print. She remembered Vance's phone conversation with Doug and Joe Kelly's insistence that the insurance records were crucial, and she convinced herself to go on. Whatever they wanted from the insurance records was not in the files she had read so far. It must be somewhere else. But where?

Sarie flipped through the microfiche records again distractedly. There had to be another way to look at the information—some way to find out the names of the blind-trust investor or investors who had put up the money for those buildings in the first place. She picked out another file at random from the pile Fred had dumped before her on the table. This one just had lists of all the deeds and titles, cross-referenced to the more complete listings she had just looked at. After the deed and title listings there was a block-by-block breakdown of the buildings in each neighborhood, dividing the streets up into numbered parcels. The list included the building plans for each structure within the parcel. Sarie had had some experience with building plans in her training as a fire fighter, since they were sometimes used to pinpoint the source of a blaze after the fact. Idly, and without much hope, she found the page that included some of the buildings that had been burned. There was not much chance she would find anything new here.

Page 487-B listed blocks K and L in parcel 28 of the city of Boston, as of June, 1950. At the top of the page was a jumble of architectural plans, diagrams and mechanical drawings for each building. At the bottom, on the right-hand side of the page, was a list of those buildings in geographical order, according to the plot plan described at the top of the page. Then, on the left, was a condensed version of the information pertinent to the insurance records of each—who owned the building, how much had been paid for it, its current valuation, who held the deed, previous owners...a whole arsenal of facts and figures presented in list form without any explanation.

Sarie didn't bother deciphering the whole thing. Half of the buildings on that page had not even been affected by the Roxbury blazes. "Why isn't there anything here?" she asked herself plaintively. "All I want is something—anything—to pin my hopes on. Just a name, one little name. It doesn't seem too much to ask, does it?"

And then, suddenly, there it was. At first Sarie didn't believe her eyes. She thought her strong desire had made her see something that wasn't there. But no, it was real, all right. On page 487-B, amid the intricate confusion of diagrams, lists and figures for block number K16, parcel 28, a set of initials appeared, once, twice and then with increasing regularity as she homed in on the other streets that had had buildings affected by the fires.

"Brh.T." There it was, without preamble or clarification. Just Brh.T., and then a figure after it—obviously the amount of money invested. The figure differed in each case. Sometimes it was $50,000, sometimes only $10,000. But the initials remained the same on every building she looked at. It also appeared on some of the buildings that had not burned, but it was always there when she looked for it.

Brh.T.—Brahmin Trust.

Sarie repeated the name silently over and over again. Her heart seemed to be beating out the name. All her worst fears had been realized, and yet all she could do was sit there and chant the name like a litany of defeat. Brahmin Trust.

Yet her heart refused to believe what her brain had just digested. Perhaps the initials stood for something else. After all, as Vance had said, there were hundreds of blind trusts in the city—it was one of the favored ways for rich people to make money without having other rich people know how hard they worked to get it. Maybe "Brh.T." stood for another blind trust—one in which Vance Leland had no interest at all. Maybe someone in the Trust was responsible but Vance didn't know about it. She thought about all the members who never showed up for meetings, who worked in absolute secrecy. Could it have been one of them? Or someone . . . more familiar? She had to find out for sure.

"Fred, could you get me one more file?"

Fred, who had been sitting in the outer office, reading a computer magazine and eating potato chips, sighed heavily. "It's already after eight o'clock," he said petulantly. "I've got to get my dinner sometime, you know."

"I'll give you a bonus," Sarie prompted. "And I'll take you out to dinner when we're done."

"All right." He rose ponderously to his feet. "What do you want this time?"

"Do you have a list of all the land-holding trusts established in the city in the past thirty years? Blind trusts?"

Fred stared at her. "What on earth do you want that for?"

Sarie shook her head. "I just need it, Fred," she said firmly. "Now, does such a list exist?"

He looked dubious. "Sure, it must, somewhere."

"And would it also list the members of those trusts?"

"Probably. But it's probably old and out-of-date. Those blind trusts don't change, even when members die. They just stay the same forever. Most of them aren't even operative anymore. Besides," he added, "that information is classified."

"So is this," Sarie reminded him severely. Now that she was so close, she wasn't going to let Fred's cold feet keep her from her objective. "We're already breaking the law, Fred. What does it matter if we break it a little further?"

He looked extremely uncomfortable. "I don't know," he began.

Sarie stood up. "Maybe I should look for them myself," she said, looking at the stacks of records behind her.

Fred blanched visibly. "No! Nobody can touch those files except me!"

Sarie had been counting on that reaction. It was exactly what Tobey Witt would have said. "Well, then, would you look and see if you have them?"

Fred pressed his thick lips together, appeared to ponder the question miserably for a while and then gave in with a sigh. "They're in here somewhere," he admitted reluctantly, "but they're not on microfilm, I can assure you. The old bound ledgers are way back in the stacks." He cocked his head craftily and waited for Sarie to respond to this information.

Now it was Sarie's turn to sigh. "You'll get paid for your efforts," she said crossly.

With a greedy grin of satisfaction, Fred lumbered off and soon returned with a huge leather-bound book. "This stuff is as old as the hills," he told her, slamming it on the table in a cloud of dust. "And it's probably all out-of-date anyway, I'm warning you."

"That's okay," said Sarie, opening the heavy cover. "I have a feeling the information I'm looking for hasn't changed in generations. I'll take my chances." She waited pointedly until Fred took the hint and left the room.

Sarie grew more and more excited as she leafed through the alphabetical listings in the heavy tome. At last, she was going to be able to answer some of the questions that had been haunting her for so long. If Brh.T was indeed the Brahmin Trust, there would be an indication of that under the listing. Each of the other trusts had their own initial code, probably so that the names would remain as confidential as possible. Sarie couldn't help thinking mutinous thoughts about the kind of people who would lust after money, property and power and not want anybody to know how much of it they had. It was typical of the Boston Brahmin, she thought bitterly. Appletons were probably listed in there somewhere too. But Appletons were not what she was looking for. "Bakersfield, Beaton, Boylston…" She read aloud, and then stopped. From Boylston at the bottom of the page, the list skipped all the way to Creedon Trust at the top of the next. Where was Brahmin? Sarie looked at the page numbers and her heart leaped into her throat.

One page was missing. Sliced neatly with a razor, so carefully as to be almost invisible. Someone had taken the list with the names of the members of Brahmin Trust. And the cut looked fresh and clean.

She looked up at Fred. "Fred, I thought you said no one else has been in here today looking for any information about the Roxbury arsons?"

Fred started guiltily. "No one was!" he whined.

"I don't believe you," Sarie told him.

He colored but shook his head vehemently. "I'm telling you, no one was in here to ask about the Roxbury fires."

Sarie took a deep breath to control her fury. "All right, Fred. Was someone in here today asking for some other kind of information? Information like this, perhaps?" She indicated the ledger with a sweep of her hand.

Fred's skin was blotchy with discomfort, and he kept looking nervously from Sarie to the ledger to the door, as if hoping that help would appear to rescue him. "Well," he drawled in a high-pitched voice, "I really can't say."

"What do you mean, you can't say?" Her anger was getting the better of her. "Did a man come in here and pay you to look through this ledger? Is that why you were so reluctant to let me see it?"

"Hey, I don't need to take this from you," Fred complained bitterly. "I get paid well to do my job, and so I do it, no questions asked."

"You mean you get bribed well to do your job," Sarie snapped.

"I'm not telling you anything," Fred retorted primly. "I don't have to tell you a thing."

Sarie looked at him disgustedly. "Of course you don't. Whoever was here before me paid you better than I ever could to keep your mouth shut. Who was it? Was it Vance Leland? Joe Kelly? Or someone else?"

Fred went white as a sheet and pursed his lips tightly. "I refuse to reveal the name of my client," he said with as much dignity as he could muster. "Mr. Parkman would never allow me to do that."

Sarie realized she would not get the name out of
him. If the insurance commissioner had given special
instructions, then it was clear what she was up against.
And, she decided, it didn't really matter. She didn't
care who had the list anymore. Now she was sure that
the Brahmin Trust, one or several of its members, had
been responsible for the Roxbury fires and everything
that had happened afterward. And there was no way
Vance couldn't have known about it. The fact that he
had gotten to the records proved that. Obviously that
meant that he was involved, as she had feared all
along.

A cold, blind fury possessed her. She would not allow herself to feel the pain that the revelation of
Vance's involvement would cause her—a revelation
that once and for all dashed her hopes about the man.
Now she only cared to find out whether Vance had
acted alone or in concert with the other members of
the trust. And there was only one way left to find that
out. She would have to face him and ask him herself.

Sarie would have walked out of the office without
paying Fred, if he had not stopped her and demanded
his due. Moving like a somnambulist, Sarie took out
some cash, handed it to the eager Fred and left the
deserted building, walking out into the surprisingly
warm spring twilight.

It all made sense to her now—perfect, terrible sense.
Vance had known all along that a member of the
trust—himself or a colleague—had been behind the
Roxbury arson ring.

Sarie suspected Edward Crane, but it didn't much
matter. By undertaking the investigation himself,
Vance had been able to protect the trust—and himself—from public scrutiny. He had been able to ma-

nipulate the evidence that did appear so that no one ever guessed who the real beneficiaries of the fires would be. The Brahmin Trust might not have been able to collect on the insurance money, which had to be returned once the arsons were discovered, but they still owned interests in all that valuable property—and it was only a matter of time before they could manipulate things so that profitable buildings were erected on the sites of those burned-out shells. And no one would ever be the wiser.

Sarie walked sightlessly across town, not knowing or caring where she went. There were still questions unanswered, but she thought she could fill in the blanks. Who, for instance, had started the Brewery fire? Had it been just a copycat crime after all? Or had it been part of an elaborate ruse to draw attention away from the guilty party? Only when Sarie had tried to push for a full-scale investigation had Vance begun to get nervous about his notes, which probably contained records of the Brahmin Trust's private transactions in the matter and therefore had to be suppressed.

But who was the man Joe Kelly and Doug worked for? That, too, was fairly easy to explain. Probably someone else had begun to suspect that all was not as it had seemed—most likely a member of the underworld who had heard hints to that effect from the street. Whoever he was, someone was pressuring Vance, probably with threats of blackmail about what he knew. And Vance was out to make sure that there was nothing to blackmail him with.

If Vance had gotten the page from the ledger, he was safe, but if Joe Kelly had gotten his hands on it, he was in danger. In any case, Sarie told herself bleakly, it no

longer mattered to her. He was guilty, she was sure—
of protecting his own interests, or those of the Brahmin Trust. Sarie suddenly remembered what Joe had
said about Vance: his hands weren't clean, either. She
remembered those same hands stroking her body into
a raging flame of desire and shuddered. The hot tears
stinging her eyes only made her more angry—at
Vance, and at herself.

She walked on, blinded to the festive lights strung
around the waterfront area. It was the first real spring
night, and a lot of people were strolling in a celebratory mood. But Sarie was too filled with pain to notice the sweet-scented air or the laughing couples she
passed on her way to Vance's. She had allowed too
many opportunities for the truth to slip away, had allowed herself to be drawn into the potent magic circle
of Vance's charm and his seeming desire for her. She
had fallen victim to her own feelings for him, allowing herself to believe that Vance was right—they *did*
belong together in some mysterious, powerful way.
And now she had to face him with the fact of his own
guilt. Face him and bear the consequences herself. She
had no other choice.

The doorman rang up ahead and announced her, so
Sarie expected to be greeted at the door when she
stepped off the elevator on the twelfth floor. But, although the door to his apartment was ajar, Vance was
nowhere to be seen. Sarie paused in the foyer, fighting the urge to bolt. Then she heard a voice floating
down the hallway and followed it to the bedroom
door. It was Joe Kelly's voice. Sarie felt her heart leap
into her throat. If Vance was talking to Joe, then she
was in greater danger than she thought. Still, she could
not turn and walk away. She forced herself to go on.

But Vance was alone. Sarie realized that Joe's voice was saying something very familiar. Vance was listening to his recording machine, to the message Sarie had heard that morning. She felt relief flood through her that disappeared as soon as she looked at Vance's face.

But Vance didn't seem to notice her dismay. He turned as she appeared and gave her a big welcoming smile. "Hi, darling! Come on in. I'll just be a second." He turned back to the machine, and she heard the rest of Joe's message. His face was stern and unforgiving, and she was struck again by Vance's amazing ability to change his moods with chameleonlike rapidity. She reminded herself bleakly that the welcoming smile had not been sincere—it was the imperious profile she now saw that represented the real Vance Leland.

"That damned..." he began, as he switched off the machine, turning to face Sarie. His face cleared immediately and lit up with an incandescent smile. "I'm so glad to see you!" he said, getting up and coming over to wrap his arms around her. "This is such a pleasant surprise!"

If Vance had greeted her any other way, Sarie might have kept control of her temper. But his insistence on keeping up an elaborate charade of caring was too much for her to bear. With unexpected violence she pulled away from him, pushing against his chest so hard that Vance had to take a few steps back to keep from stumbling.

"How dare you!" she raged, her voice quavering as much as her body. "How dare you act as though nothing is wrong! As if you really care!"

The confusion that crossed Vance's face looked real, but Sarie knew what a good actor he was. Even in her anger she was aware of an urge to run into his arms and bury herself in the warm protection they offered. "Don't!" she cried, putting her hand out to ward him off as he took a step forward. "I can't bear this game another minute! Stay away from me, please!"

"Sarie, what's wrong with you?" He seemed genuinely upset.

"It's no use, Vance," she replied miserably. "I already know."

"Know what?" he asked. "For God's sake, Sarie, do you mind telling me what this is all about?"

"I just came from the insurance commissioner's records stacks," she said, trying to keep her voice from trembling with tears.

"You what?" He seemed really shocked.

"Unfortunately, you had already been there, so I didn't get what I wanted."

He looked at her as if she was crazy. "Who told you I was there?"

"Oh, don't worry," she said bitterly, "Fred kept your secret. But the missing page told me all I had to know."

"Missing page?"

"That's right. The one with the information linking the Roxbury fires to Brh.T." She could not keep herself from trembling as she stood before him.

A cloud of fury passed over his expression. "God, so he got there before me!" He looked narrowly at Sarie. "Are you sure that page is missing?" he inquired.

"It's missing, all right," she snapped. "But it doesn't matter. I already know about Brahmin Trust." Sarie tried to gauge Vance's reaction to her statement, but her eyes were too filled with tears to be able to see clearly. She felt as though the room were filling with mist, and she was having trouble breathing. "Which one of them is it, Vance? Is it Ed Crane? Your uncle? Or is it really you?"

He shook his head sadly. "I'm afraid it's not what you think, Sarie," he began, but she could not bear to hear his denial in the face of what she knew to be true.

"Don't tell me that!" she screamed. "Don't tell me you don't know that someone in the Brahmin Trust was behind the Roxbury arsons and that you've purposely covered it up to protect the trust—to protect yourself."

"I have to tell you that," he said with admirable calm, "because it's true."

"But I know better, Vance. Don't lie to me. I can't bear any more lies!"

His voice was maddeningly gentle. "Then why don't you let me tell you the truth?"

"I don't want to hear your truth!" she cried, and then, aware of the hysteria in her voice, made an effort to calm down. "Are you going to stand there and tell me that you didn't go into the insurance files and rip out the page that listed the Brahmin Trust?" It was still hard to breathe, even though she was trying to slow down her racing pulse.

"That's exactly what I'm trying to tell you," he replied, and it seemed to her that he was breathing shallowly, too. "But I think I know who did."

"Are you going to try and blame it on Joe Kelly again?" she said. "How do I know Kelly isn't working for you, too?"

"That's absurd. How could he possibly—" Vance broke off and sniffed the air. "What's that?"

"What's what?" Sarie felt the mists of rage swimming before her, and she was having trouble seeing clearly. Her balance seemed to be affected, as well.

"That smell? Smells like . . ."

At last Sarie became aware that the choking sensation in her throat was not caused by her own pain but by a curious acrid smell. She pulled away from Vance and looked around the room, sniffing and coughing. Suddenly she was grasped by a terror so strong that everything else receded.

"There's a bomb planted in here!" she managed to choke. "I can smell the tetrachloride!"

Vance's eyes reflected her own panic. "I know that! But where's it coming from?" They both looked around wildly.

"It's coming from under the bed!" Sarie cried after what seemed like hours, and they both dived down at the same time.

They were just in time. Vance's arms were longer, so he pulled out the long narrow tube of metal and wire, from which a plume of thin white smoke was issuing.

Sarie recognized it immediately. "Quick! Pull the detonator thread out of the casing!"

Vance looked at her in confusion and Sarie grabbed the device out of his hand, wrenching the wire free with a mighty effort. There was a small pop and another billow of smoke, this one larger than the first and even more acrid. Choking and spluttering, the two of them stumbled out of the bedroom into the living room.

Vance slammed the door shut behind them and then ran to the windows, opening the sliding doors to let in the cool spring night. They both leaned against the doorjamb and gasped huge draughts of the clean salt-tinged air. Their eyes were watering, and they were both shaking.

"A...a Jackson device?" asked Vance when he was able to talk.

Sarie nodded and coughed. "We caught it just as it was releasing the chemical explosive. Another moment and the fuse would have detonated." She looked at him and shivered. "It would have destroyed that entire room."

"And us with it." With a low groan Vance lunged toward her and gathered her into his arms. "My God, my God," he muttered against her hair, "To think I almost lost you."

Sarie pulled away and stared at him, trying to assimilate what had just happened. She had been about to accuse Vance of being behind the Roxbury fires. But now someone had just tried to blow him up. Having gone to such lengths to convince herself of his guilt, her mind refused to digest this new bit of information.

"But I—I don't understand," she spluttered. She felt as if the world had just tipped its lid and tumbled her out into a strange new place.

"No, from what you've been trying to tell me, I didn't think you did," he said with a sad little smile.

Sarie shook her head confusedly. "But I thought...I was sure—" She broke off. Why would Vance stage an explosion in his own home?

He was watching her closely, and his voice revealed his concern. "I knew you were jumping to the wrong conclusions, but I couldn't seem to stop you."

"But why..." She and Vance were still both breathing hard with fear and shock. But the force of what she was beginning to understand literally took her breath away. It was suddenly very clear to her. Vance knew all about the Roxbury fires, but he couldn't have been the mastermind behind them. Whoever *that* was had just tried to kill him. Looking at his pale face, at the real concern in his brilliant eyes as he watched her, she was suddenly more sure of that than she had ever been of his guilt. Vance was innocent of the crime, and he was clearly not protecting the real culprit. For now, the identity of the mastermind didn't matter. The man she loved was innocent.

With this certainty, the accumulated emotional strain of the past few days suddenly caught up to her and Sarie began to weep uncontrollably. Vance seemed to have expected this. For a long time he stood with her by the open door, and then he led her gently to the couch, where he sat down and took her onto his lap as if she were a small child.

"I thought . . . I was sure . . ."

"Hush, hush," he said soothingly. "I know, darling. I know, and I understand. It's all right. It's all right."

But Sarie could not be consoled. Now that it was clear that Vance could not have been responsible, she could not believe that she had even begun to suspect him of any wrongdoing. This was the man she loved— how could she have thought he was capable of hurting anyone? She was filled with remorse, shaken with fear and above all, overcome by great waves of relief.

Sarie pulled out of his warming embrace and tried to talk. She had to tell him how she felt. "Vance, I want to . . . I need to . . ." It was important to her that she confess her suspicions to him, explain her actions.

But Vance only smiled and shook his head. "Darling Sarie, please don't. You and I belong together, don't we?"

Sarie nodded, hiccuping slightly.

"And we've never needed words to tell each other what must be said." He cupped his hands around her chin and drank in her tear-stained face as if it was the most beautiful thing in the world.

"Now, why don't you just show me what you wanted to say?" he finished with a smile.

"But the explosion." Sarie gestured weakly toward the bedroom door. "We should... We have to... I need to know what really happened! I need to know who was behind all this. Was it a member of the Trust after all? Or someone else?"

Vance sighed. "You'll know soon enough, I'm afraid. I can't keep trying to protect you from the truth any longer—seeing as I've been singularly unsuccessful at it." He stroked her cheeks with his thumbs, looking at her with a mixture of love and wonder. "God, when I think what I risked—" He broke off with a grimace.

Despite her relief, Sarie knew they had to talk about what had happened. "We don't have much time," she reminded him halfheartedly. "If Joe has that list..."

Vance shook his head again. "Not now, my love. The list won't matter for a while. And besides, we have something much more important to think about. Something much more wonderful."

"But Vance, someone just tried to kill you—to kill us!"

He chuckled softly. "Well, at least we'll be safe until they realize they've failed, won't we? Until they see signs of life from in here, we can be relatively sure that the world will not blow up again while we tell each other what needs to be said.''

Hiccups subsiding at last, Sarie smiled and nodded. Then she gently removed his hands from her face and placed them around the back of her neck. And, taking his neck in her small hands, slowly pulled his lips onto hers. With her mouth, and her hands, and her whole body, she told Vance what she wanted to say—that she loved him and that she knew they belonged together.

IT WASN'T UNTIL the next morning that they got around to discussing what had happened. They had fallen into a deep slumber on the wide couch after Vance had ventured into the bedroom and rescued a light blanket and two pillows that had not been ruined with the awful smell of chemical explosive.

They had not stayed up all night making love as they had the previous night, but they had remained locked together in passionate attachment even as they slept. It was as if, having finally acknowledged the depth of their need for each other, their bodies could not bear to detach, even in sleep.

Now, over cups of coffee, they both knew, without saying so, that the time had come to discuss the business at hand. The smell from the bedroom was a pungent reminder that something had to be done.

''Tell me,'' Vance asked her gently, ''how did you know to look in the insurance records?''

''I overheard you talking to Doug the other morning,'' she confessed.

''And Joe Kelly? How did you know about him?''

''I . . . I had a little meeting with him.''

"Of course! The message on the phone machine!" recalled Vance, slapping his hand to his forehead. "I should have realized you might have heard it before you left this morning. Tell me what happened."

Sarie recounted her conversation with Joe.

"I can't believe you actually tried to do business with him," Vance said, chuckling dryly, when she had finished. "He's a pretty tough customer, you know."

"I can take care of myself," Sarie reminded him.

"Apparently so," he said, and reached out to stroke her cheek. "Although if I have anything to do with it, you won't be gallivanting around like that anymore."

"Don't be silly, Vance."

"I'm not being silly," he said sternly. "I'm being deadly serious. Sarie, you could have gotten into a lot of trouble going there to meet him alone."

"I had no choice," she told him simply. "I had to find out what was going on. Vance, who does Joe work for?" Sarie asked. It was time to find out the truth. "Who wants those records so badly?"

Vance shrugged lightly, but did not meet her eyes. "That's what I'm not sure of yet, Sarie. I have my suspicions, but nothing solid yet."

She did not believe him. "What are your suspicions, then?"

But Vance ignored the question. "Joe Kelly is a local two-bit arsonist who was overlooked for the job when the Roxbury landlords called in Ira Jackson from Detroit. He was pretty peeved about the whole affair and, at one point during my investigation, was pretty eager to sell me information. I began to wonder who his source was, and that's when I started looking into the records and turned up Brahmin Trust."

"You mean, you didn't know that members of your own corporation were involved?"

"I told you, we don't meet that often, and every member has autonomy and is empowered to act on the trust's behalf. If any member wants a transaction to stay private, all he has to do is not report it to the corporation at the meeting." He looked bitter. "The whole thing is founded on the noble notion of trust, you see."

"But if it was all so secret, how did you begin to suspect who was behind it? It could have been any of them. It could have been one of the members you never even see!"

"Well, I was pretty sure it was someone I knew— someone who had been to meetings, just to keep an eye on things and make sure we didn't stumble onto his secret. So I went through my list. The only man I could be sure it wasn't was Uncle Horace," he said with a short laugh. "He may be a rascal and a curmudgeon, but he's not a criminal. But you're right, it could have been any of the others. That's what made it so terrible for me. To know that one of my colleagues had brazenly used the trust to perpetrate such a horror. It went against everything I had ever believed about my world."

"I think I understand what you mean," she said softly.

He smiled at her. "I thought you might," he murmured. "But of course that was why I had to proceed with my investigation so carefully and secretly. I do have the family honor to protect."

"Then the Brewery fire was started to warn you off when Joe Kelly and his boss realized you were beginning to have your suspicions."

"Right. I guess they thought I would get scared enough to leave it alone. After all, as far as everybody else in this city is concerned, the case is closed. Of course, when they realized I wasn't going to stop investigating, they went after my notes, figuring they probably contained damning evidence just like the insurance records did."

"That's where Doug came in, right?"

"Right. When Joe and…his boss approached Doug and made him an offer he couldn't refuse, it was with an eye to getting him to lead them to my notes. Of course they couldn't have known that Doug knew nothing and was only pretending to know in order to get their cash."

"But what happened to make Doug come to me? Why did he get so scared?"

"Probably because they realized that he was no use to them anymore," he replied tightly. "They knew he wouldn't dare come back to me, and that he couldn't risk going to the authorities."

Sarie sighed. "Now he'll have to, though, won't he? Poor Doug."

Vance nodded. "When it's time, I think I can arrange a deal in return for his giving evidence against his employers."

"But what about the list Joe took from Fred's ledger?" Sarie asked. "If you knew it contained the information you needed, why didn't you get it sooner?"

"I wasn't sure until recently," he told her, "and I had to overcome a certain amount of reluctance about my suspicions, as you can imagine." He cast her a sidelong glance. "As a matter of fact, I was waiting for a court order to come through today to grant me

access to those files," he said. "Some people believe
in going through legal channels, you know."

Sarie blushed. "I didn't think I had the time," she
admitted. "But now that the page is gone, how can
you prove anything?"

He pursed his lips grimly. "That's one of the ends
I've got to tie up."

At last Sarie could bear it no longer. "Vance, you
have to tell me—who do you think it is?" Sarie had
her own suspicions, but she wanted to hear from
Vance first.

He looked at her for a long time. "I can see why you
might have your doubts about me, Sarie. I'm sorry for
keeping you in the dark all this time. I know you've
been as worried as I have, but I felt I had to protect
you from danger."

"And now?"

"I'm sorry, Sarie, but I can't tell you, not just yet.
I need to be a little more certain—to have just a little
more proof." He reached out and pulled her against
him. "Won't you trust me just a little longer?"

"It doesn't look like I have a choice," she said,
sighing, and snuggled against his bare chest. "At least
you could tell me where those famous notes are. You
do really have them, don't you?"

"Of course I do. Even a big shot like me has to have
some written proof. I have records, all right."

"Where are they?"

He grinned suddenly. "Didn't you guess? I keep
them in the old carriage house museum. Inside that
1930 Hercules your son is so in love with."

Chapter Ten

"You've got to be kidding! You mean...?"

Vance chuckled. "Yup. When he started up the pumps that day, I was thinking my stars it was the Cyclorama he was fooling around with. If it had been the Hercules, he might have found my stash or sprayed it, ruining it forever." He shook his head. "That boy is a marvel, the way he can figure things out."

"Yeah, a marvel of a pain, sometimes." Sarie was filled with a sudden longing for her son. It was a good thing Sarah Jane was around to take up the slack. It seemed as if years had passed since Sarie had seen Taylor. Certainly a lot had happened since she saw him off to school two mornings ago.

Vance read her thoughts again. He smiled and brushed back her hair fondly. "He's going to have a lot of new things to get used to, isn't he?"

"What do you mean?" Sarie asked, knowing perfectly well what he meant.

"Us, of course. You and I—and him—being together. It's going to be a new life for all of us."

Sarie was filled with a surge of joy, which she did her best to temper with reality. "Vance, I..."

"Hush." He put his fingers against her lips. "I won't hear a word of it."

Sarie removed his hand. "But you have to hear it, because it's what I'm thinking."

He sighed and sat back. "Okay, what are you thinking? As if I didn't know."

She wrinkled her nose at him. "I'm thinking that I don't want this...us...to move too fast. After all, we haven't known each other for long...."

"Please, Sarie, spare me the conventional platitudes. They don't suit your rebel soul any more than they suit mine."

Sarie ignored him. "And besides, we haven't exactly been together under the most normal circumstances."

Vance's eyebrows ricocheted upward. "And I thought I was the conservative, conventional member of this duet!" He leaned forward, his eyes sparkling with intensity. "I told you this the first time I met you, Sarah Elizabeth Appleton, and it still holds true. You and I were meant to be together, as surely as if we had been pledged at birth."

Sarie laughed. "Vance, you sound positively medieval!"

But he was serious. "Some of the old ways weren't bad, Sarie." He took her face and held it so that their eyes were only inches apart. "Can you really look at me and tell me you don't know what our future is together?"

Sarie gazed into the cobalt depths of his eyes and knew she could not. She shook her head, and they smiled silently in mutual commitment.

"Of course," Vance said at last, sitting back again, clearly satisfied, "this all depends on our getting out of our current situation without getting blown to bits."

He said this so matter-of-factly that Sarie had to giggle. "Oh, I completely agree." Relief and new-found love had combined to make her feel light-headed and giddy. "After all, what good are we to each other in lots of little parts?"

Vance made a face. "You have a gruesome mind, you know that? It must be from hanging around with those fire fighter friends of yours."

"And don't forget Joe Kelly."

"No," he replied, standing up. "I do not intend to forget Joe Kelly." His voice was hard and determined.

"What are we going to do about him?"

"We?" He looked down at her skeptically.

"Yes, we. Us. You and me." Sarie stood up next to him and looked up defiantly into his eyes. "Don't start protecting me now, Vance. We belong together, remember?"

He grabbed her for a brief hug. "I remember. How could I forget?"

Sarie pulled lose. "Okay. So what are our plans?"

"I think it's about time I went to beard the lion in his den," he said after a moment's thought. "I don't have all the hard evidence I'd like, but I think if I face him as one Brahmin to another I may be able to get somewhere with him."

"With who?" Sarie tried to make the question sound casual. *Come on,* she prayed silently, *share it with me, Vance. Tell me I'm right with my guess.*

"Ah, no, Sarie. I'll go only so far with this equal-involvement bit. I'm afraid I simply won't tell you who I think it is until I've checked it out for myself."

"Who are you protecting now, Vance?" she asked hotly.

But Vance would not be moved by her display. "You. And the rest of the members of the Brahmin Trust. We have to concede to some conventions, Sarie. We can't just go in there blasting away like Bonnie and Clyde." Seeing the determined set of her face, his softened. "But not to worry. I have an assignment for you, too."

"What?"

"I want you to go over to the carriage house and get my notes. The museum is slated to open soon, and I want those things out of there before some other curious nine-year-old blows my cover." His brow furrowed. "Besides, I don't want Joe Kelly to get his hands on them first."

"Okay. I'll get right over there." Sarie turned away but Vance's hand stopped her.

"Where do you think you're going, young lady?" he demanded sternly.

"To the carriage house, of course."

"Dressed in a toga?"

Sarie followed his gaze and remembered that she was only wearing a fine white cotton sheet. She looked up and giggled. "Not exactly de rigueur for a day of crime busting, is it?"

"Not exactly," he replied dryly. In his most imperious Brahmin voice he went on, "I suggest we repair to the sleeping chamber and don our smoke-infested duds before we bust any heads, don't you agree, my pet?'' He spun around smartly toward the bedroom door and offered her his crooked elbow with a crisp flourish.

Sarie fell in step with him and nodded sedately. "Why of course, my dear," she returned in the same regal tone. "I couldn't agree with you more." She slipped her arm through his. "Shall we?"

"But, of course," said Vance as they made their way in stately splendor to the bedroom. "Why ever not?"

SARIE WAS SURE she knew which member of the Trust was responsible for the crimes. "It has to be Edward Crane," she muttered to herself as she unlocked the door to the carriage house and slipped inside. "He knew that warehouse, even though he didn't own it any longer. Why else would Doug Eldridge have believed that the papers might be hidden in there unless Crane had been able to convince him of it?" Crane must have been angry over losing the family business and decided to make his own fortune in his own way. She just knew it was Edward Crane.

Not that it mattered. Everything would be explained to her in good time, as soon as Vance confronted him with what he knew. Sarie wondered briefly how Vance was going to prove his accusations if the accused had already destroyed the insurance list. But she figured that Vance's notes had to have enough evidence in them after all. Besides, she was confident enough of her new love not to let it bother her too much. Right now, she had a job to do. She had to get those notes. She couldn't *wait* to get those notes.

Whoever had taken over her job as curator of the museum had clearly been a lot more efficient than she had. Even in the darkness Sarie could see that the place was spotless and in perfect order. The cleanup crew had apparently done more than just clean up the effects of Taylor's flood. Everything was in place for the opening. Next to each machine, on a small wrought-iron stand, was a plaque describing the machine and its history. A pile of thin pamphlets stood on tables by the door and around the room. Spotlights, dark now, had been trained neatly on each piece in the collection, and a series of enlarged photographs of old fire fighters lined the main room. Yards and yards of bunting were neatly looped around the perimeter, obviously in anticipation of the upcoming opening celebration. It was hard to believe that so much had been accomplished in such a short time.

"I'm impressed," she said, nodding and pursing her lips as she looked around. "But I'm sure glad *I* didn't have to do all this."

There was a tiny stream of light coming in from the high barred windows so Sarie did not turn on the spots. Besides, Vance had given her explicit directions for finding the documents in the Hercules, and she knew exactly where to go and what to do. She was eager to read the documents and fit in the last pieces of the puzzle. Vance had asked her not to get in touch with the officials at the fire department or the police until he had completed his business. Sarie had no intention of going anywhere near Chief Wapshaw's domain and would respect Vance's decision to wait before calling the police. She looked forward to returning to his apartment with her booty, as she had arranged with Vance to do, and settling in there until he joined her.

The Hercules had been given a place of honor in the center of the smaller tack room, with three spotlights strategically placed so that they would highlight its intricate chrome-work and elegant lines. Sarie remembered Taylor tangled up in the hosing and smiled.

"Hello, old thing," Sarie said, stroking the sleek sides of the wagon.

"Hello yourself."

Sarie recognized the voice instantly and froze. At the same moment the spotlights went on, flooding her in a sharp white bath of light. The rest of the room was in darkness, and she couldn't see a thing outside her own circle of brightness.

"Joe?"

"None other," replied the voice, sounding oddly disembodied.

"Where are you?" She tried to make her voice sound strong, although her knees were weak with fright. "What are you doing here?"

"I should be asking you that," replied the voice. "Looks like your boss has you doing all the dirty work, doesn't he?"

"What do you want?" Sarie repeated. Fear made her voice sharp and hard. She heard a movement close by on her left, and she spun her head around in that direction. Slowly she began to make out the shape of a man walking toward her.

Joe paused on the edge of the circle of light and sneered. "What d'ya think, little lady? I want what you want, of course." The sneer turned ugly. "What you came for."

Sarie was sure Joe would be able to tell she was lying but she tried to be as convincing as she could. "I...just came to check on the museum for the opening."

"Right. And I'm just here to admire the scenery." Joe took another step so that he was more clearly in view. Sarie did not like what she saw. He stood on tiptoe and made a show of peering over her shoulder. "Like that little number you're standing next to," he went on in a voice dripping with false innocence. "What's the name of that machine?"

"It's a Hercules wagon." Sarie removed her hand from the side of the engine. "Circa 1930," she added as if he really cared to know.

Joe nodded, pursing his lips in a parody of appreciation. "Ain't that something, now." He began to move slowly around the machine, keeping his body half in, half out of the perimeter of light so that Sarie had to squint to keep her eyes on him. "Well, that's really something. *Reaaally* something." He rubbed his scrubby beard with the nail-bitten fingers of one hand, and Sarie felt her stomach turn over with fear and revulsion. She shifted her weight involuntarily, and Joe was instantly alert.

"Now, I wouldn't go making any sudden moves, Sarie," he hissed. His other hand was stuffed into the pocket of his polyester sports jacket, and he moved it menacingly without revealing its contents. "You don't want the patrons to get nervous, now, do you?"

Sarie had been frightened, but now she began to feel the icy chill of terror. "How did you know my name?" she croaked.

Joe smiled out of one side of his mouth. "I made it my business to find out. I've been looking after you ever since you left here. You've been doing some interesting things, haven't you? Visiting the commissioner's office, visiting your buddy Vance, doing your little antiarson bit—''

"So it was *you* who planted that Jackson device!"

Joe ignored this accusation. "Why, you're a regular one-woman SWAT team, aren't you. 'Course, you didn't get what you wanted, and you won't get it here, either. Still, you've made a lot of trouble for my boss and me.''

"Who's your boss?" she asked automatically.

Joe ignored her question. "We knew you were a fire fighter with the BFD and that you were in charge of that little Brewery fire we set to give your buddy Vance a scare. We knew you and Mr. Hotshot Leland were more than just pals—'' he leered dangerously and Sarie gasped in spite of herself "—but we didn't expect you to hook up with the ill-favored Mr. Eldridge, and we certainly didn't expect you and your fancy friend to keep up this private little inquisition.''

"Just what *did* you expect us to do?" Sarie inquired, deciding she had nothing to lose. "Overlook the fact that you committed all those Roxbury arsons, Joe?''

"Not me," he replied too quickly. "My boss.''

Sarie seized the opportunity of this slight hint to press her point home. "But you are involved, aren't you? You may not have been responsible for those first fires, but you're in this mess up to your neck now, aren't you, Joe?''

His face darkened. "They didn't want me for the big-time games," he said bitterly. "They thought they'd do better to bring in big guns from Detroit.''

His face was curled into an ugly snarl of revenge. "The local torches just weren't good enough, they said. Well, look where it got 'em. Behind bars."

"And where do you think it's going to get you, Joe?"

He barked a short laugh. "Me? Hell, honey, I'm gonna go scot-free. You know why? Because I work for the big guy now. Not just the penny-ante jerks who think they can make a killing by torching a tenement. No, I've joined the big leagues." He was bragging now, and Sarie stayed quiet, hoping he would reveal something as he swaggered. "After the Roxbury fires, see, I figured out that everything wasn't cleaned up like your boss said it was in his published report. I had heard on the street that there was someone behind the whole scam—some Mr. Big who hadn't even been touched by the arrests. So I says to myself, 'Joe, you got eyes and ears, use 'em!' Sooner or later someone's gonna wanna pay you for using 'em. And I was right. Someone did." He snorted. "I just never figured it would be someone so big."

"Someone from Brahmin Trust hired you to set the Brewery fire and the explosion in Crane's warehouse, right?"

"Not bad, not bad." Joe looked at her with new appreciation. "So you know about Brahmin Trust. I'm not surprised, considering your boyfriend's practically a member."

"And he knows who your boss is, Joe," Sarie said, hoping she sounded as sure of herself as Vance had.

"Yeah, right. He may know, but he'll never blow the whistle on them. The old boys always protect each other. Don't you know that, Sarie?"

"Vance is on his way right now, to confront him, to tell him that he's going to turn him in."

Joe paled for a moment and then sneered. "Yeah, sure, that's what he told you, maybe. But you don't really think he'll rat on his buddy, do you? It's a manner of honor among those guys. Nobody knows about all the dirt they do among themselves—they keep it quiet." He cocked his head. "Of course, you're not a part of that scene, are you? And there's no telling if your boyfriend plans to pull you in on his protection plan, is there?"

"There is no protection plan," Sarie snapped.

"'Course there is. And, being a woman, you couldn't buy into the code of silence even if you wanted to, even if you are an Appleton. You're just as much of a peon as me, you know. How do you know Vance isn't over there with Mr. . . . with my boss right now, trying to figure out how to hide the evidence?" He leered at her nastily. "How do you know he didn't send you here knowing you'd meet up with me?"

This ugly suggestion only stung for a moment before Sarie rejected it. "I know Vance better than that," she said defensively. "He's too honest."

"Honest? Hah! That's a laugh!" He uttered a mirthless bark. "But ya know, it doesn't matter, does it? Because he sent you here to get his notes, didn't he? Without those notes, he's got nothing on anybody. I don't care what kind of showdown he's planning—he's sunk without them." He took a menacing step closer to her. "And if I get my hands on them before he does, then the whole subject will just have to be dropped, regardless of Mr. Leland's famous honesty."

"Don't be silly, Joe," Sarie snapped. "I can just tell the police that you . . ." She was stopped by the glittering menace in his small eyes.

"You can't tell them anything if you're not around to talk," he said quietly. "Can you?"

If she had any doubts before, Sarie knew now why Joe had followed her. His boss already had the list that had been pulled out of the old insurance ledger—that took care of any possibility of a connection between him and the Roxbury buildings. Now all they needed were Vance's notes, and there would be no trace of the crime. Joe and his boss, whoever he was, needed those notes. And they would let nothing—or no one—stand in their way.

"Okay, kiddo," he said, putting out his hand. "No more fooling around. Let's have them—now."

"Have what?" Sarie asked, desperately trying to buy herself a moment to think.

But Joe had reached the end of his patience. "*You* know what!" he shouted so loudly that Sarie jumped. "The notes! I want them now!"

"I don't have any notes, Joe," she said, her voice shaking. "I don't know what you're talking about."

Joe took three steps so that he was very close to Sarie, and she got a bitter foretaste of the physical danger she was in. Joe was not tall, but he was built solidly, and she could tell that he was strong. He was so close that she could see the enlarged pores beneath his stubble and the hard glitter of his dark bright eyes.

"I wouldn't play that game if I were you," he whispered with an almost sensuous smile. "It will only make things worse for you if you do."

Sarie tried to swallow but her mouth was bone-dry. "What are you going to do to me?" she asked.

He shrugged slightly. "Same thing we tried to do last night," he sneered. "Although we expected you two to be so busy in bed that you'd never notice the Jackson device."

Sarie felt faint and had to struggle to keep from slumping against the fire wagon. "If you had killed us, you wouldn't have been able to find out where Vance's notes are."

Again the lazy smile. "If we'd killed you, we wouldn't have needed them. We've got the list, remember? No one'd ever think to go through those old ledgers, and even if they did they'd just assume the page was torn out years ago. The matter ends with us, don't you see, Miss Appleton? With you two out of the way the notes would have become irrelevant. They could lie rotting in this old museum for a thousand years and no one would be the wiser."

Sarie began to retort that they would never have gotten away with that when it occurred to her that Joe did not know exactly where the papers were hidden. He apparently had not realized they were so close by, buried in the body of the Hercules.

She thought quickly. If she could get Joe away from the Hercules, then she could concentrate on getting away from him. The notes would be safe for the moment—certainly a lot safer than she was. But how? He was standing directly in front of her, and the menace in his pose was clear and immediate. If she moved to run away he would have no trouble grabbing her. There was no way she could hit him.

Or was there? Sarie suddenly had a clear image of her son, Taylor, fighting helplessly with a strong arc of water from the old Cyclorama. She had been so surprised at the power in the old hose line and at the strength of the water pressure. It had been strong enough to reach practically all the way across the room. Would the Hercules shoot as strong a stream of water as the Cyclorama? Strong enough, perhaps, to send a grown man sprawling?

Sarie's hand was only inches away from the nozzle of the hose and right by the confusing array of old brass levers and pulleys. She kept her eyes trained on Joe while she desperately tried to remember which lever Vance had shown Taylor to pull to unleash the stream. She knew she would only have one chance to move, and in that moment she would have to throw the lever and yank the hose off its bracket in order to train it on Joe. Her fire-fighting experience would stand her in good stead for the latter job, but what if she couldn't find the right lever?

"Come on, sweetheart," Joe drawled, still holding out his hand. "I can't wait forever."

"I . . . um . . ." Sarie tried to look frightened and indecisive, knowing that her wide eyes and blanched complexion were pretty convincing. "I'm trying to think."

This made Joe angry. "Don't give me that bull!" he snapped ferociously. "You know exactly where the damn things are. Now let's have them!"

But Sarie had been counting on his anger to keep his attention from wandering to her busy right hand. She had found what she thought was the right lever.

Please, she prayed silently, *make this the one Tay used.*
And then she shoved it down.

For a moment nothing happened, except that Joe
noticed the sudden gesture and turned to look at her
hand. "What the...?"

Then the water hit him. Sarie remembered her fire-
fighting training, particularly the instructions on how
not to knock down a fellow fire fighter with a hose.
Immediately she trained the water on a vulnerable part
of Joe's body—his face. He gasped and opened his
mouth to swear, but that was a mistake, because the
full force of the water nearly drowned him where he
stood.

It was enough to knock him down, though, and this
is what Sarie had hoped for. She did not wait around
to inflict any more damage, but, dropping the hose,
bolted for the front door.

She had forgotten that the main room was in darkness. Having been blinded by the strong spotlight, she
stumbled against the Cyclone, banging her knee
sharply against the grillwork. Her leg crumpled beneath her and she fell with a cry.

Despite the pain, she got up right away, but now she
could hear Joe close behind her. His wet footsteps
squished menacingly close by, and only the fact that
he, too, was blinded saved her from being caught at
once. Sarie scrambled around the back of the Cyclone, hoping that her labored breathing wouldn't give
her away.

But Joe had gone straight for the light switch, and
suddenly the room was flooded with light. She could
see him, dripping from head to toe, standing smugly

by the door with one hand still on the switch, blocking her last hope of exit.

"Well, well, well," he said with a smile as she walked slowly around the side of the machine. "That was a refreshing little interlude." The smile disappeared. "Now maybe we can get back to business."

Sarie knew there was no use in trying to escape or to hold him off any longer. "I'll show you where the papers are," she said, and turned toward the tack room.

"No."

"No?" She turned around, surprised.

Joe had looked menacing before, but it was nothing compared to the dark sneer that transfigured his expression now. "I don't need the papers now," he said quietly. "I'll just finish up with step two and be done with it." And, without moving from where he stood, he withdrew from his jacket pocket a familiar-looking little device.

Sarie screamed and covered her face with her hands.

"Looks familiar, doesn't it?" Joe asked. "Of course, I would have preferred to use my own particular brand of torching device, but I'm supposed to be retired from the field of arson, so this will have to do. Besides, my boss seems to have developed a fondness for these things." He approached Sarie and, grabbing her roughly by the arm, dragged her back to the tack room. "And I must admit there is a certain amount of poetic justice in using the Jackson device one last time, isn't there?"

"Joe," Sarie began, but she recognized that he was too far gone in his murderous state to listen to reason.

"Joe, Joe," he mimicked, and then brutally thrust her against the Hercules. "Don't Joe me," he spat.

"It's too late for that. It didn't work at Vance's place, and now there won't be any mistakes."

He turned off the water and, using the thick hose, tied Sarie to the machine, strapping her painfully to the chrome-work. "I'll give you the papers now," she pleaded.

"I don't want the papers now," he said, working busily. "It occurred to me that if the papers are destroyed in a fire, your boss won't have any evidence to use against us, even if he does decide to play the knight in shining armor." He stopped for a moment and leered. "And if you're destroyed along with them, we can easily make it look like you got torched by Mr. Vance Leland himself. After all, this is his museum, isn't it? Sort of the two-birds-with-one-stone idea." He laughed sickeningly.

"You won't get away with it, Joe. People know where I am. They know about Vance's investigation."

"Who knows? Doug Eldridge? He'll keep his mouth shut. He's too scared to tell the police anything, and anyway, who'd believe him?"

"He's planning to turn state's evidence," she said desperately.

"Who says? Your buddy Vance? Forget it. Doug'll go to the highest bidder—he always has. And that'll be Mr. Parkman, I can assure you."

"Parkman?"

Joe paused, realizing that he had let the name slip, and then shrugged carelessly. "Ah, what the hell, it don't matter now what you know, does it?"

In her shock, Sarie momentarily forgot her fear. "Your boss is Clifford Parkman, the insurance commissioner?"

Joe looked almost proud. "You bet, honey. Howd'ya think he knew to get a hold of those records listing his name as a member of the Brahmin Trust? His records librarian is a greedy man, too, in case you hadn't noticed. It didn't take much for him to look the other way while I got that list—not after his boss made sure he was handsomely paid for his silence."

"Parkman." Sarie let out her breath in a slow wave of recognition. Of course. Why hadn't she thought of that before?

Now that Joe had told her, he seemed eager that she know all the details. "And howd'ya think he knew about the Roxbury buildings and the kind of payoff he'd be looking at if the property values in that neighborhood went up nice and slow, so nobody'd guess he was responsible for it. He's been buying up property through that Trust he's a member of, so no one would be the wiser. He even bought out some of his cronies, although they didn't know it was him." He sneered. "God bless the blind trust, is what Mr. Parkman says."

"How did you get hooked up with him?" Sarie heard her voice through a thick padding of shock.

"It was sort of a match made in heaven, know what I mean? After the Roxbury fires I felt pretty lousy, seeing as nobody thought to use a nice local boy like me for the torch job. So I decided to find out who did the hiring and tell 'em a thing or two. Lo and behold, as I begin to ask around on the street, it turns out the guys who owned the buildings might not be at the top of the ladder, so to speak.''

"And you figured out that it was Parkman?'' A kind of dull ache had settled over Sarie's brain. It was hard to believe that this two-bit crook had succeeded where the efforts of an entire city—and Vance Leland—had failed.

Joe chuckled. "Damn right I did,'' he said, sounding proud. "Well, actually we found each other. Seems the commissioner had gotten wind that Leland was on his tail and decided to scare him a little with the Brewery fire. Since his Detroit man was behind bars, he was looking for another torch. That's where I came into the picture. 'Course, he tried to keep a low profile, like he had before. He got someone else to contact me on his behalf. But I'm not as dumb as those landlords he had all strung up like puppets, dancing away for him. Not me. All I had to do was put two and two together—plus a little pressure on Parkman's fellow, of course—and I came up with the answer.''

"Who was Parkman's man?''

Another sinister laugh. "The guy you rescued, little lady. Doug Eldridge, of course. He was ticked off because generous Vance Leland hadn't paid him enough for his undercover work on the Roxbury fires. I guess Leland figured it was a public service. But guys like Doug Eldridge and me, we can't afford public service. We have to deal in cold hard cash.'' The grin turned into a grimace. "'Course, then old Doug tried to double-cross us, so we had to put the fear of the Lord into him. I doubt he'll try that little game again.''

"But Parkman is only a partner in Brahmin Trust. All the profits of the Trust are shared. How much could he stand to gain even if his plan worked?"

"He's been buying out his partners slowly over the past years anyway. Bought Crane Paper and the warehouse from Edward Crane when the paper business went belly-up, and got hold of a lot of other buildings, too. Most of those guys don't even know what they own. Slowly the Trust has come under his control, so that he gets a majority of the profits. Works good, because no one even looks at their principal, and he just uses it to reinvest." He snorted derisively. "Hell, no one even knows who's alive and who's dead in that group. They all just go on meeting every six months, being real careful not to ask any dangerous questions like who's doing what with the money. Talk about blind loyalty—hah! Blind dumb, if you ask me!"

Sarie was suddenly unable to listen to another word. "You wouldn't understand," she muttered, as if she did. All she wanted was for him to stop talking, stop making those nattering sounds while her world was coming to an end.

"No, I guess not. I guess you rich folks just don't make any sense to poor slobs like me, huh?" He took a few steps closer to Sarie and waved the Jackson device menacingly in her face. "Not that it matters much to you now, does it, princess?"

In the presence of such danger, Sarie found herself falling back on patterns of thought and behavior that had been ingrained since birth. She felt disgust and pity for Joe Kelly, and an imperious urge to explain the situation to him in her terms. "You know you'll be caught if you try to hurt me, Joe," she told him. "If you let me go and turn yourself in, I'm sure we can arrange..."

Joe snapped the device so close to her head that Sarie screamed. "You can arrange? *You* can arrange? Hah! That's rich! Listen, you Beacon Hill brat, I work for Clifford Parkman, remember? He's one of the most powerful men in the city—even more powerful than your social-butterfly boyfriend. If I torch you along with the records, it's gonna be Leland's word against Parkman's—and who do you think is gonna come out ahead? If anything does come to light, it'll look like old Vance himself has been the villain all along. Especially with a dead body in his little museum. One match and you're both cooked!"

Joe's maniacal rage brought the full horror of her situation back to Sarie, and she began to shake. It was quite possible that Joe was right—she was going to die in the museum along with the evidence Vance would need to condemn Parkman and exonerate himself. Joe must have seen her courage failing, and he moved in for the kill.

"Not so brave now, are we, princess?" He pulled a lighter out of his pocket and flicked it on. "All I have to do is light this and skedaddle, and you're history, kiddo. Nobody influential to take care of you now." He waved the lighter in front of the wick of the Jackson device. Sarie turned her head away so that she would not have to look. She thought about Taylor and Sarah Jane, the people she loved most in the world. Then she added Vance to the list. Vance....

Joe seemed to have picked up on her thoughts. "Where's your rich friend when you need him most, huh?"

Suddenly there was a flash of motion. Sarie, sure it was the bomb exploding, shut her eyes and screamed loud and long. Her whole body vibrated with the sound, and she waited for the blast to reach her, wondering if things always moved in such slow motion when one was about to die. Then she realized that the flash was not the bomb, but Joe's lighter falling to the ground as he was torn off his feet from behind. By the time the sound of her own scream had faded to an echo, she could hear the strangulated sounds of Joe's, muffled by the thick impact of fist against flesh.

The whole thing took less than a second, although it was much longer before it sunk into Sarie's fear-numbed brain. Then a figure stood over Joe's prostrate body, slapping his hands together as if to rid them of an unbearable filth.

"I'm right where I'm supposed to be, bozo," said Vance. "Taking care of business."

Chapter Eleven

Half an hour later Sarie was still firmly wrapped in
Vance's arms. She would not have moved from that
warm circle of protection even if he had allowed her
to, which he most certainly would not. But the tears
and shaking had subsided, and once the police arrived, she began to feel calm enough to talk about the
ordeal she had just survived.

"Boy, you really knocked him out, didn't you?" she
murmured, watching distastefully as two policemen
dragged off the half-conscious body of Joe Kelly. They
were sitting on the running board of the Hercules in
the side room, listening to the hubbub of activity that
swirled around them and yet only aware of each other.

"I didn't intend to hit him quite that hard," Vance
replied, shaking his head. "But when I saw him
threaten you..." He kissed the top of her hair and
squeezed her even more tightly. "I guess I just went a
little bit crazy."

Sarie snuggled closer. "I'm glad you went crazy,"
she whispered. "Although I hope you realize that at-
tacking a man holding a cigarette lighter and a Jack-

son device is an extremely hazardous thing to do. As a sparkie you should know that, Vance."

Vance chuckled, relieved that Sarie was recovering her dry sense of humor so quickly. "So, arrest me!" he retorted, giving her a quick squeeze.

"If that's what I have to do to keep you right here beside me, then I will. I'll make a citizen's arrest."

"I just hope I'm getting a life sentence."

They looked gently into each other's eyes. This was not a time for kisses, which were silently promised for later. After a moment Sarie asked the question that had been on her mind ever since Vance's timely appearance.

"Vance, how did you know to come here? I mean, if you hadn't arrived when you did . . ." She shuddered again.

"Hush. Don't think about that. I did arrive, didn't I?" He made a comforting sound in the back of his throat and Sarie leaned closer against the vibrating purr.

"It was almost like magic, your showing up when you did," she murmured dreamily.

"It wasn't magic. It was sheer luck." Vance's voice betrayed his relief. "After you left the apartment I called Cliff and made an appointment to see him right away."

Sarie lifted her head, surprised. "So you did know it was Parkman after all!"

Vance smiled. "I told you we both had our suspicions. Who were you betting on—after you decided it wasn't me, I mean?"

"That's not fair, Vance!"

"Why not?" He was amused at her discomfort. "You did suspect me, didn't you? And you had every right to, I suppose. But tell the truth, who were you betting on?"

"Well, it could have been any of them," Sarie pointed out, "and I still don't know the names of any of the members except the ones I met at your office that morning. But I have to admit," she murmured in some embarrassment, "I did think it was Ed Crane."

"That wasn't a bad guess at all," Vance told her. "As a matter of fact, I had my doubts about Ed, too, especially after the fire in his warehouse. But I knew he no longer owned the building and that he was having some tough times financially, even though he would never have admitted it in a Brahmin Trust meeting." He sniffed derisively. "I have a feeling the Trust isn't going to operate in the old secret ways from now on."

"Sounds like it'll be an improvement."

"It will if I have anything to say about it. Anyway, when I talked to Ed, he mentioned that he was having some tax trouble and that someone had been buying out all his property interests almost before he put them on the market. He was really worried about it."

"And that's when you started thinking it might be Parkman?"

"Right. After all, who else but the insurance commissioner would have known about property going up for sale because of tax problems? He had easy access to the insurance ledgers and would know exactly which records to pull in order to make the blind trust investors in the Roxbury buildings untraceable." He paused, and his eyes narrowed bitterly. "Besides, Cliff

Parkman is the only member of the Trust who has the ability to manipulate so many people. He's the only one I could imagine conducting business with people like Joe Kelly—the other members wouldn't know where to begin to talk to a thug like that. Parkman has always had a killer instinct when it comes to business—that's how he rose to such a powerful position in the city. I just never expected him to have the instincts of a real killer, as well.''

"You still haven't told me how you found me here, Vance," Sarie pointed out.

"That's because you've been asking too many questions again—as usual." He gave her a kiss and a squeeze. "But it was sheer luck, as I said. I called Parkman's office, and he seemed pretty intent on putting me off for an hour or two, even though he didn't know for sure why I wanted to see him. So I figured that he must have been waiting for word from Joe Kelly on something. And then it struck me that Kelly must have been tailing me or else he wouldn't have known when to plant the Jackson device in my apartment. And if he was tailing me, he could be tailing you, too—which I most definitely didn't want.''

"Because I was going to get the records, right?"

"No, you goose, because I didn't want him anywhere near you, period." He looked at her and shook his head. "I swear, Sarie, sometimes your penchant for dangerous living makes me very nervous.''

He sounded so worried that Sarie laughed. "Not to worry, Vance," she said, patting his cheek. "We'll work something out so you're not always wondering if I'm in a jam."

"You're damn lucky I was wondering this time. I raced down to my car just in time to see Kelly take off after you."

Sarie stared. "You mean . . . you were following us ever since then?"

"That's right."

"But why didn't you come in sooner?"

He shrugged. "I wanted to see what would happen."

Sarie jumped to her feet so fast that Vance was nearly knocked over. Her recent brush with death still left its mark on her nerves. "Do you mean to tell me that you were out there all the time?" she shrieked.

"Calm down, calm down." Vance tried to pull her down beside him, but she yanked her hand away.

"I could have been killed, and you wanted to see what would happen?"

He raised his eyebrows. "You told me not to try and protect you, didn't you?"

Sarie gaped at him for a full minute before recognizing the ludicrous nature of the situation. She started to smile in spite of herself. "Hoist by my own petard, is that it?"

He pulled her back down beside him. "Not really. I'm about as accomplished at tailing people as Doug Eldridge. I got hung up in traffic and got here just in time to hear the threats." He gathered her face between his hands. "Forgive me?"

She kissed him. "Forgiven."

They stared into each other's eyes for a few happy moments. "Now what happens?" Sarie murmured.

"You mean to us?" he whispered against her lips.

"No. To Parkman. To Joe Kelly. And to Doug."

Vance took a deep breath and pulled away from her. "Doug is still in the hospital, although I called last night and they said he was out of isolation and doing fine. Joe Kelly will probably be laid up for some time too, until it's time for him to go to jail, at least. But it's Parkman we have to tackle now. And that's the hard part." He shook his head bitterly. "Uncle Horace is going to take this hard. He's known Cliff all his life. *I've* known him all my life. My God," he burst out, "how could I have been so blind? So stupid?"

Sarie looked at him sympathetically. "It hurts you to think that someone you thought you knew so well might have tried to have you hurt, doesn't it?"

He shook his head. "Not me. You." His lips went white with compressed fury. "I could kill him for what he tried to do to you."

"You once told me that things aren't always what they seem, Vance. Well, that's true about people, too. I should know."

He looked at her and smiled weakly. "I know you do, darling. But this is more than a case of mistaken class identity. This man is an attempted murderer, Sarie!"

"Maybe not. Maybe the fires at the Brewery and the warehouse and your apartment weren't Parkman's idea," Sarie pointed out. "Maybe he just left Joe to take care of all the details, and Joe was the one responsible for all the bombs. After all, Joe does have a record as an arsonist. Maybe Parkman just wanted the records without the violence." But she didn't believe her own words for a second.

Neither did Vance. "Joe may have done the deeds, but you can be sure Parkman was behind them. That's the way he operates. Plant the seed and then sit back and let the other guys do your dirty work. As far as I'm concerned, he's guiltier than the men he hired. He's a monster.'' He stared up at the high barred windows, and Sarie saw pain as well as rage in his expression. "God, I wish I wasn't so sure of that."

"Why don't we go find out for certain?" she whispered.

He looked at her, swallowed and nodded. They both stood up and went into the main room. As soon as he saw them emerge from the tack room, a police sergeant came over and, for the fourth time in an hour, Vance and Sarie had to go over their stories again. By the time they had finished the rest of the men had gone, and the carriage house looked as if nothing untoward had ever happened to it.

"I don't suppose we're going to want to come back here for a long time," Vance said as they stood in the doorway, his arms still draped protectively across her shoulder.

"Don't you have to come for the opening?" she asked him.

"Not if it means leaving your side I won't."

Sarie was feeling safe enough to smile and shake her head. "Vance, it's over. You don't have to worry about me any more, remember?"

"I intend to worry about you for the rest of my life," he replied firmly, and kissed her. "Besides," he added softly. "We still have one more thing to do before we leave this place."

Sarie felt her heart turn over. "What's that?"

He grinned. "We have to get my famous notes."

Together they went back into the tack room. The Hercules stood there in careless splendor, untouched by the upheaval that had gone on around it. Vance went up to the hose chute strapped to the side and lifted one of the chrome bolts that held it in place. There was a slot behind the plate, and by inserting his fingers inside, he managed to pull out a thin manila envelope. This he held up triumphantly for Sarie to see.

"It doesn't look like much," she commented, "to have caused all this ruckus."

Vance looked at her and chuckled. "Want to know the biggest laugh of all? It isn't much." He opened the envelope and inspected the contents to make sure it was all there. "It was just that Parkman was afraid it might contain damning evidence."

Sarie was surprised. "You mean there's nothing conclusive in your notes after all?"

Vance shrugged apologetically. "Not a thing. To tell you the truth, it's all speculation and conjecture. Oh, there was some talk on the streets that all the guys involved hadn't been caught, and I wrote that down, along with my own suspicions about the Brahmin Trust. But there's nothing here that would stand up in court for a minute." He held out the handwritten sheets. "Here, look for yourself. Nothing but the suspicious ramblings of an overly curious sparkie."

"Whew!" Sarie looked at the sheaf of papers and let out her breath slowly. "And to think that I almost got . . ." She shuddered.

"Don't even think it," Vance said soothingly. "It's over now."

Sarie smiled weakly. "That's true. Besides, if Parkman hadn't been afraid of these notes, we never would have been able to connect him with Joe Kelly or the Brewery fire. It doesn't really matter what's in them—they've served their purpose."

"And now they're going to do one more little thing—make one Mr. Clifford A. Parkman extremely nervous." Vance pocketed the documents.

"I'm a little nervous myself," Sarie admitted as they left the carriage house.

"I know you are, sweetheart. I am, too, to tell you the truth. But don't worry. The police will be there waiting in the outer office while we go in and do our little number with the commissioner."

"Why can't they come in with us?" she asked nervously.

"They'll be there, don't worry. But I've asked them to hold off for a few moments while we go in and speak to him privately.

"Why?" Sarie looked at Vance's stern profile. "You don't owe him any courtesies, Vance, not after what he's done."

Vance's expression hardened. "I know that. That's not why I'm doing it this way. I want to go face-to-face and one-on-one with that man, Sarie. I want him to tell me why he did what he did. I want him to try and give me an explanation for his treachery." His face softened. "And yes, I do feel I owe it to him."

"For God's sake, Vance, why?" Sarie spluttered.

But Vance just shook his head. "I know you don't understand it, Sarie, but that's the way it is. I've got to give him a chance to confess to a member of the

Trust before I turn him over to the rest of the world. I'm sorry, but you'll just have to accept that.''

Sarie nodded. In a way, she did understand. Even after all these years of rejecting her heritage, she was beginning to understand that she was still an Appleton. Silently she squeezed his hand, and he gave her a grateful smile. Then they got into his BMW and drove back through Boston to State Street and the office of the City Insurance Commission. Sarie had been there the night before, but Clifford Parkman's offices were nothing like the bleary institutional decor of the records office. His outer reception room was lushly carpeted and paneled in rich dark wood, and his secretary sat at a desk much like the one in Vance's office.

Sarie would have made a joke about this fact, but she was too nervous to say much of anything. The secretary looked at Vance respectfully but couldn't seem to figure out what Sarie, rumpled and disheveled in yesterday's clothes, could possibly be doing with such a distinguished visitor. In a surprisingly level voice, Vance asked to be announced, and the secretary said they could go right in.

The inner office was even more impressive—filled with carefully chosen antiques and an Oriental rug that Sarie knew must be priceless. Clifford Parkman, a small but impeccable gentleman with a receding hairline and owlish eyes, sat behind a small Chippendale desk. If he was surprised to see Vance with Sarie in tow, he did not register it.

''Vance, my boy!'' he said, and started to get out of the chair. ''What a pleasant surprise!''

''Don't get up, Cliff,'' said Vance, his expression equally unrevealing. ''We'll sit.'' He led Sarie to a leather settee and took a seat beside her without saying another word.

Parkman pressed the fingertips of his manicured hands together in front of his lips. "Are you going to introduce me to your friend, Vance?" he asked unctuously.

Sarie and Vance were both aware that Parkman must have known exactly who she was and why she was there. But he was apparently going to play the role of innocent, and Vance decided to play along for a moment, "This is Sarah Appleton, Cliff. Sarie, this is Clifford A. Parkman. You met briefly at my office, during the last Trust meeting, remember?"

"I do indeed," said Parkman with an infuriatingly sincere welcoming smile. "Pleased to meet you again, Miss Appleton."

The formality of the introduction was incongruous, given the situation, but both Sarie and Parkman, well versed in such social amenities, exchanged polite smiles and murmurs of greeting without even thinking about how fraudulent the niceties were in the situation.

It was time to press their point home. "Sarie is a member of the Boston Fire Department, Cliff," Vance went on after a small pause. "In fact, she's a lieutenant, third grade."

Parkman smiled politely, although he was clearly not impressed. "Really? How interesting!"

Sarie had heard this same disdainful response so often that she automatically opened her mouth to retort, but Vance squeezed her hand slightly to stop her.

"I thought you'd find it interesting, Cliff," he went on smoothly. "Especially since you've had such close dealings with them of late."

For the first time since they came in, Clifford Parkman appeared to pale slightly. "The BFD? I thought that was your department. Aren't you a fire buff, or something like that, Vance? I'm sure you know more about them than I do."

Vance chose to ignore this. "Or should I say, you've managed to steer clear of dealings with them of late?"

Now Parkman's pallor was tinged with an unhealthy-looking red flush. "I'm afraid I don't understand."

Vance turned to Sarie and nodded. "Okay, Sarie. I think you deserve the honors on this one. Why don't you tell Mr. Parkman what we're talking about?"

Sarie looked at Vance, who nodded encouragingly, and then turned back to Parkman. "Mr. Parkman, we know about the Roxbury fires. We know that you were responsible for organizing the landlords and influencing their decision to torch those buildings. We know you hired Joe Kelly. You started the Brewery fire, too, when you began to suspect that Vance knew the case wasn't closed."

Parkman looked from Sarie to Vance and back again. His eyelids drooped slightly, and his fingers were now knitted together so tightly that the knuckles were white. But his voice did not change. "And how do you know all this, may I ask?"

"That's easy," said Vance, and he pulled out the folded sheaf of notes from his breast pocket.

Parkman stared at them for several moments and slowly leaned forward in his chair, as if to rise. Then, suddenly, he sat back heavily. The flush disappeared, leaving him looking ghostly and sick, and for a moment Sarie thought he was going to faint. But, after taking several deep breaths, he began to speak.

"I see."

"We know about the fire in the warehouse, too, Cliff," Vance added.

"Ah. And I suppose Mr. Eldridge is only too willing to turn state's evidence, is that it?"

Vance nodded. "That's right. He's agreed to tell us what he knows about you and Mr. Kelly. He's willing to take a jail sentence if necessary, although I suspect his attorney will be able to negotiate a reduced sentence since Doug is willing to help."

"I don't much doubt it," said Parkman evenly. "But I'm afraid he doesn't know much."

"Enough, I'm sure," Vance said dryly. The two men were facing each other across the room, and Sarie could feel the tension between them even though both their voices maintained that maddening cool. She wished Parkman would fall apart or Vance would shout. But neither man gave an inch.

"I didn't give Mr. Eldridge enough credit," Parkman said softly. "I expected that he would go to any lengths to avoid taking an accessory to arson rap, what with his previous record. But I should have known, when he began to get so nervous about you, Vance, that he was ready to double-cross us."

"Is that why you sent him to the warehouse?" Sarie inquired. "Because you wanted him out of the way?"

"Please, Miss Appleton, give me some credit!" The tone of voice was slightly supercilious. "I would never knowingly or willingly send a man to his death. I'm afraid that was Mr. Kelly getting overzealous. He told Doug that the records were hidden in Edward Crane's warehouse and that I wanted them. Naturally Doug, having decided to switch horses in midstream, went after them himself, hoping to return them to Vance before we got our hands on them. If Doug had known the warehouse no longer belonged to Ed Crane, perhaps he would have been more wary. Perhaps he would have figured out that there was no way those notes would be there." He spread his palms upward. "All I wanted to do was scare the man a bit, make him realize that he had better keep his mouth shut if he wanted to play in the big time. The bomb was Mr. Kelly's idea, not mine."

"I don't believe you, Cliff," Vance said coldly.

"That doesn't matter much, does it, Vance?" Parkman said. "After all, the burden of proof rests on you; and I've made quite sure there's no way I can be connected directly to those crimes—even by Mr. Kelly's testimony."

"It's not that easy to escape blame, Mr. Parkman," Sarie pointed out when Vance did not reply to this audacious comment. "People may not have been killed in the Roxbury fires, but they were hurt, and many of them lost their homes, their lives, irreplaceable parts of themselves." Sarie was angry now, and her voice rose. "And what about the bomb in Vance's apartment? And the device Joe had in his pocket just now at the carriage house?"

Parkman half rose out of his chair. "That little fool!" His voice rose for the first time. "He had no authority to use force on you!" He looked really an-

gry, but Sarie wasn't sure if he was genuinely out-
raged or merely pretending.

Not that it mattered. "You can't lie down with dogs
and expect to get up smelling like a rose, Mr. Parkman," she pointed out forcefully. "Besides, you still
have Roxbury to account for. The Roxbury fires are
what started this whole mess. And you can't blame
Roxbury on Joe Kelly, can you?"

"That was not my doing, either," Parkman said,
but there was a slight tremor in his voice, and Sarie
knew he was beginning to realize he was trapped.
"The men who owned those buildings made their own
decisions as to when and where and how. You'll never
prove I had anything to do with it. I just realized that
there was a profit to be made on the site—a profit,"
he added, turning to Vance, "that the Brahmin Trust
sorely needed."

"And so you managed to convince them that they
were making their own decisions, didn't you, Cliff?"
Vance said, speaking for the first time. Sarie could
hear the rage in his voice, although it was much more
effectively controlled than hers. "I'll bet you were very
good at making them think they were acting on their
own initiative. I'll bet they never knew what hit them.
Even when the trial came up it never occurred to any
of them that you had actually masterminded the whole
thing." He stopped for a moment to get control of
himself and then went on. "I've seen you operate,
Clifford. It's well within your skills to pull off something like that. I just never imagined you'd be capable of it."

Clifford Parkman opened and shut his mouth several times before speaking. He seemed to be having a

lot of trouble saying what he wanted to say. "Vance," he managed to croak at last, "I don't suppose..."

Vance shook his head. "Don't even consider it, Clifford."

"Your uncle and I have been friends for a long time," Parkman pointed out, in a last-ditch attempt to win Vance's sympathies. "I'm sure he'd understand that I had to do something—it was for the good of the Trust, don't you see?"

"Don't give me that line, Parkman. You of all people should know that I don't believe it for a minute. It was for the good of Clifford Parkman and no one else. That's why you were buying up everybody's shares—Crane's, and I don't know who else's. The bigger the share of Brahmin Trust in your hands, the more power you could wield, and that's what you wanted even more than money, isn't it, Clifford? Power."

Parkman was now clearly desperate. "Vance, please. Think of my family. My position in the city. Think of the reputation of the Trust!"

Vance's voice and eyes hardened. "You should have thought of that yourself, Cliff. There's no question of us keeping this quiet, Clifford. You're on your own now. You've betrayed the Trust—you've betrayed us all." He paused. "I've spoken to my uncle about this. Horace wants it this way, too."

This seemed to crush Parkman more completely than anything else that had been said so far. Sarie watched in horrified fascination as the man slowly crumpled, his face falling onto his hands and his body racked by great silent sobs of defeat.

Vance had the decency to wait until Parkman had collected himself. Then, rising, he said quietly, "The police will be waiting outside. I've asked them to send plainclothesmen, Clifford, so there won't be any... fuss.'' Sarie looked at Vance, surprised that he would allow this concession to appearances at such a time.

Parkman rose like a zombie. ''Thank you, Vance. I appreciate it.'' There was no irony in his voice, and she realized he really was grateful for Vance's thoughtfulness. He steadied himself for a moment by holding on to the edge of the Chippendale desk. Then he gave them both a pale smile. ''I'm ready now.''

There were two plainclothes policemen sitting on the tufted leather settee in the reception area. They rose when they saw the little group emerge and moved across the room to either side of Parkman. While the receptionist looked on in mute surprise, they fell into step beside him, flanking him as he walked away. Watching, Sarie couldn't help noticing his regal carriage and proud profile. People like Clifford Parkman, she reflected, really did think of themselves as being in a separate class from the rest of the world. She looked at Vance, and recognized the regret in his expression as he, too, silently watched his old friend being led away. She touched his arm gently.

''He's not above the law, Vance,'' she murmured softly.

Vance sighed. ''I know. I know.'' He put his arm around Sarie. ''Let's go, shall we?'' They turned to the double doors and Vance uttered a soft oath. ''Oh, no! Reporters!''

Sarie followed his gaze and noticed the group of eager faces peering through the glazed partitions. ''What'll we do?'' she asked.

Vance sighed and shrugged. "We'll have to face the music sometime," he told her, and then grinned wryly. "After all, we're heroes, you know."

"I don't feel like a hero," she muttered, and, looking down at her grubby clothes, added, "I don't look like a hero, either."

Vance chuckled. "You look fine to me. What do you feel like?"

She smiled shyly. "Like being with you—alone."

He nodded, and she saw the sensual light of desire heat his blue-gray gaze. "Me, too. But first we'd better get rid of the hordes, shall we? Then we can be alone. I promise."

And, holding her hand, he led her out into the crowded hall. "Let me talk," he whispered, and she nodded silently, only too happy to let Vance take control of the situation.

"Mr. Leland, Mr. Leland!" the nearest reporter shouted. "What made you first suspect Mr. Parkman?"

"Actually, it was my Uncle Horace," replied Vance. "He came to me last winter and said he had noticed odd things happening with the Brahmin Trust holdings. At first they seemed to be dwindling, and then there was a lot of unexplained activity in the portfolio. Since each member has autonomy within the Trust, he didn't know who was responsible. After the Roxbury fires, it never occurred to my uncle or to me that Mr. Parkman might be involved."

"So when did you make that connection?" asked another.

Vance smiled. "Trial and error, I'm afraid." He squeezed Sarie's hand. "And a little help from some friends."

"Like Doug Eldridge, maybe?" came a third voice.

"Doug has turned out to be a friend, yes," Vance said, and Sarie realized how much more adept he was than she at fielding this type of barrage.

"How did you first get involved with him?" the man pressed on.

"Doug is a sparkie, just like me," Vance replied. "I'd met him at several fires, and we got to talking. He seemed like a natural person for me to turn to when I decided to investigate, because he had spent so much of his life right here on the streets of Boston. I figured that if anybody could help me find out what the word was on those streets, it was Doug." Vance frowned. "Of course, I had no idea he would be persuaded by an offer of cash to work against me. But I'm glad to say that Doug's conscience proved as durable as I had hoped it would, and his testimony will be essential to our case."

"How does it feel to know that all those men were sent to jail on your evidence last time, Mr. Leland, when it wasn't their fault at all?"

Vance turned his most withering gaze to the reporter who asked this question. "Not their fault? Those men are just as guilty as Cliff Parkman. He may have planted the seed in their minds, but they carried it through. They all deserve what they got," he said severely, and then finished in a softer voice. "I'm only sorry I couldn't have seen all the truth sooner. It would have caused a lot of people a lot less pain."

"And what about you, Lieutenant Appleton?" came a woman's voice from the back of the crowd. "What made you suspect that the Brewery fire was tied to the Roxbury arsons?"

"It was just a feeling at first. I knew there had to be a connection because of the way the Brewery fire was set. And I knew that there had to be someone still at large who was involved, although I had no idea who and didn't know where to begin looking. Mostly I was just feeling my way until I had something solid to go on."

"That's ridiculous," said Vance, and he put his arm around her again. "Miss Appleton was responsible for getting to the bottom of this mess," he told the group in his best public-speaking voice. "She was the only member of the fire department to recognize that there was a connection, and she pursued it in spite of the resistance she got from everyone—including me. I might add that I was a suspect, too, for a while, and with good reason. I had hoped to keep her out of danger by not telling her of my own suspicions." He squeezed her tightly. "Of course, that was before I realized she's perfectly capable of taking care of herself."

They looked at one another fondly, and the reporters began scribbling madly. "Ah," said one, "it appears as if you two have solved more than the Roxbury arson case." The reporter grinned and waved her pencil at their happy smiles. "Is this information for public consumption?" she inquired.

"No," said Sarie.

"Yes," said Vance at the same time. "I want the world to know how I feel about Miss Appleton. I love her, and I hope she loves me, too." And then, without a word of warning, he bent down and planted his lips firmly over hers, ignoring the flashbulbs that went off like a mad fireworks display around them.

FOUR WEEKS LATER, Sarie and Vance stood in a small, elegantly furnished office high atop the Federal Building, looking out at the brilliant June sunshine flooding the inner harbor. Despite the bustle of activity throughout the city at their feet, there was an air of serenity and peace this high up, making the hubbub below seem as if it were happening a million miles rather than twenty-six floors away.

For four weeks they had been deep in the middle of that hubbub. The entire city had reacted with astonishment and relief when the truth about the insurance commissioner came out, and Sarie and Vance had been at the epicenter of the huge wave of publicity that surrounded Clifford Parkman's trial. Aside from the endless hours spent talking with authorities and testifying, they had been subject to the unquenchable curiosity of the public, which had gleefully pounced on their obvious affection for each other and made it into a media event.

"Society fire fighters in love," claimed one paper.

"Boston couple find answers and each other," declared another.

Vance and Sarie were worn out by the constant glare of publicity. Now that the excitement of the case was behind them, they longed to have the privacy in which to explore their newfound love. They still had much to learn about each other, and the process was difficult under the hot glare of public scrutiny. Even Chief

Wapshaw, who had done a remarkable about-face where Sarie was concerned, revealed a rather endearing streak of romanticism. "I knew it," he had said, hovering around Sarie like a huge horsefly while she tried to go about her job at the station house. "I just knew you two were meant for each other. Tell me, when did you first know?"

"About the connection between the Brewery fire and the Roxbury arsons?" Sarie had asked.

"No! About you and Vance. When did you know you were in love?"

Sarie had gaped at him in astonishment for a moment and then laughed. "I guess we'll have to give you credit for bringing us together, chief, won't we?" He had seemed only too pleased to take the blame.

Now, standing with her arm around Vance's waist and looking out at the seamless blue sky, Sarie smiled and answered the question again. "I knew all along," she murmured. "Right from the beginning, I think I knew."

"Knew what, my love?" Vance stroked the thick nap of the bone-colored satin dress she wore, marveling at the way it brought out the pale sheen of Sarie's skin.

She turned to him and smiled. "Knew that I loved you. I think I knew right from the start."

His elegant eyebrows arched wryly. "Even while you were accusing me of arson and mayhem? That's a strange way of declaring one's love, don't you think?"

Sarie giggled. "I didn't know it was love then. I just knew there was some connection."

Vance took her hand and twined it in his. "Oh, there was a connection, all right." He looked back over his shoulder, where a justice of the peace stood waiting for them with a benign smile. "And my old friend Judge Sutton will help us make it permanent." He kissed the sprig of freesia in her hair and then stood back to inspect her. "You look lovely," he breathed.

Sarie smiled. "So do you."

"Are you sure you want to do it this way, Sarie?" he asked for the umpteenth time. "I'm perfectly willing to go ahead and have a big wedding. You know, church, maids of honor, the works. Just say the word."

"I've already said it a thousand times, Vance," she remonstrated gently. "After all we've been through, the last thing I want is a big to-do. The sooner we're married, the sooner the public will let us live our lives in peace."

"They'll all be livid, you know—Sarah Jane, Taylor and even Horace."

Sarie nodded. "I know. But they would never have allowed us to do it this way, so it's better they don't know until it's over."

"You're right, of course. Whatever you say. Just don't expect me to protect you from the wrath of those three when they do find out. I know Horace'll make Joe Kelly look like Mr. Nice Guy."

Sarie grinned. "So will S.J. and Tay. But never mind, darling—we'll protect each other."

He stroked her soft skin. "Always."

After a moment he turned to Spencer Sutton, who stood waiting with amiable patience. "Okay, Spencer. We're ready."

Judge Sutton nodded and began the ceremony, which lasted less than twenty minutes. When it was over, Sarie and Vance Leland rode the elevator down to their waiting car, speechless with joy.

Vance's BMW wasn't parked where it should have been on the curb. Instead there was a huge gray limousine in its place. Vance and Sarie stood blinking in the sunlight for a few seconds until the door opened and an authoritative voice boomed out.

"So, you think you can pull one over on us, do you?" It was Horace Leland at his crusty and demanding best. With him were Sarah Jane and Taylor, both dressed in their stiff Sunday clothes and managing to look both delighted and annoyed.

"Shame on you, young lady," said Sarah Jane, a twinkle in her eye belying the seriousness of her voice. "How could you get married and not invite us?"

"Yeah, Mom," piped Taylor. "I wasn't at your last wedding—the least you could'a done was invite me to this one."

Sarie opened her mouth to explain, but Horace would hear nothing of it. "Don't bother, Mrs. Leland," he said briskly, pulling her toward the car with a gnarled hand. "Just come along with us and pay your penance."

"What are you talking about, Horace?" demanded Vance, who nevertheless allowed himself to be pulled toward the limo by an eager Taylor.

"I'm talking about your reception dinner, of course," snapped Horace. "It's all arranged with Joseph at the Ritz, isn't it, Sarah Jane?"

"Yes, Horace," agreed Sarah Jane, smiling so fondly at him that Sarie suspected another budding relationship between Leland and Appleton.

Vance noticed it, too, and laughed. "Why, you two rascals! You've been sneaking around behind our backs arranging this, haven't you? You've known about our secret plan for weeks!"

"Who's been sneaking around behind whose back?" demand Horace. "Now come on, Vance. I'm paying for this limo by the hour."

They arrived at the Ritz at the same time as a platoon of fire trucks. At first Sarie thought there might be a fire, until she saw the entire department waving at them from their perches.

"What on earth?" gasped Sarah Jane. Even Horace was dumbfounded at this sight.

"Who the devil is responsible for this travesty? I wanted a small celebration, not a circus!"

"I called them," announced Taylor, sounding not at all contrite. "I figured if there was gonna be a party there might as well be a good one." He leaned his head out the window and waved gleefully at Tom, who was perched atop engine number 10. "Okay, boys, let her rip!"

And, while all the other inhabitants of the car watched in amazement, seven huge fire trucks released streams of water high into the air in a watery salute to the newlyweds.

Vance shook his head, shaking with laughter. "You seem to have a real flare with water, don't you, Taylor, old boy?"

"You don't mind, do you, Vance?"

"Are you kidding?" Vance ruffled his hair fondly. "I think it's the best idea anyone's had all day." He looked meaningfully at Sarie. "Well, maybe the second-best."

Taylor didn't notice the private sparks that flew between his mother and new stepfather. "Are you mad, Ma?" he inquired anxiously. "I don't want you to be mad on your wedding day, even if you did try and sneak it past me."

Sarie leaned back on the suede upholstery and sighed contentedly. Although she had taken great pains to keep her wedding a secret, all of a sudden she didn't mind the commotion one bit. She had her family around her, and she felt celebratory and light-headed. She took her son's hand and squeezed it. "Of course I'm not mad," she said, smiling at Taylor, who was watching her eagerly. "It was a lovely thought, Tay, and I'm glad you did it." She turned to Vance. "You don't mind, do you, darling?"

Vance grinned at her and looked around at his uncle's disapproving expression. "I think it's about time we all did something a little unconventional." Then, without warning, Vance jumped out of the car. Before anyone could stop him, he strode out into the middle of the street and approached the fire trucks. With three deliberate steps, he placed himself squarely beneath a heavy shower of water, and within seconds his immaculate light gray suit was drenched. "I think it's the best wedding present we could have gotten," he shouted from beneath his waterfall. "Come on, Sarie, Taylor, Sarah Jane. Let's show Boston that the Brahmins can have some fun, too!"

It didn't take Sarie long to join him beneath the canopy of water, and Taylor scrambled out as soon as he saw that no one was mad at him. It took Sarah Jane and Horace another moment or two, but they rose to the occasion with their usual aplomb. "Well, my dear," said Horace with a raspy sigh, "I guess we've been outdone. Shall we join the younger generation?"

"I'd be proud to, Horace," she said, and the five of them gathered beneath a cascade of water and sun while Vance and Sarie exchanged a glistening, silent vow.

ATTRACTIVE, SPACE SAVING BOOK RACK

Display your most prized novels on this handsome and sturdy book rack. The hand-rubbed walnut finish will blend into your library decor with quiet elegance, providing a practical organizer for your favorite hard-or soft-covered books.

Only $9.95

Approximately 16" x 8" when assembled

Assembles in seconds!

To order, rush your name, address and zip code, along with a check or money order for $10.70* ($9.95 plus 75¢ postage and handling) payable to *Harlequin Reader Service*:

Harlequin Reader Service
Book Rack Offer
901 Fuhrmann Blvd.
P.O. Box 1325
Buffalo, NY 14269-1325

Offer not available in Canada.

BKR-1R

*New York residents add appropriate sales tax.

Janet Dailey

Americana

A romantic tour of America with
Janet Dailey!

Enjoy two releases each month from this
collection of your favorite previously
published Janet Dailey titles, presented
alphabetically state by state.

Available NOW wherever paperback books
are sold.

JDA-B-1

HARLEQUIN HISTORICAL

Explore love with Harlequin in the Middle
Ages, the Renaissance, in the Regency, the
Victorian and other eras.

Relive within these books the endless ages of
romance, set against authentic historical
backgrounds. Two new historical love stories
published each month.

Available now wherever paperback books are sold.

AT LAST YOU CAN FIND
TRUE ROMANCE ON TELEVISION!

PRESENTING THE SHOWTIME●

S E R I E S

Full-scale romance movies, taken from your favorite Harlequin novels. Beautifully photographed on location, it's romance the way you've always dreamed. Exclusively on Showtime cable TV!

HARLEQUIN ON SHOWTIME
COMING ATTRACTIONS:

CLOUD WALTZING. Based on the Tory Cates novel, starring Kathleen Beller.

ONLY ON SHOWTIME

This winter, look for an **Exclusives Explosion** on Showtime!

- **Exclusive Movies**–Down And Out In Beverly Hills, Gung Ho, Fool For Love.
- **Exclusive Music Events**–Motown On Showtime.
- **Exclusive Comedy Series**–Brothers, It's Garry Shandling's Show and, of course . . .

HARLEQUIN ON SHOWTIME – THE ONLY
PLACE ON TV TO FIND TRUE ROMANCE!

CALL YOUR CABLE COMPANY TODAY TO ORDER SHOWTIME

HMVA-1

Take 4 best-selling
love stories FREE
Plus get a FREE surprise gift!

Special Limited-Time Offer

Mail to   **Harlequin Reader Service®**

In the U.S.   In Canada
901 Fuhrmann Blvd.   P.O. Box 609
P.O. Box 1394   Fort Erie, Ontario
Buffalo, N.Y. 14240-1394   L2A 5X3

YES!   Please send me 4 free Harlequin Romance® novels
and my free surprise gift. Then send me 6 brand-new novels every
month as they come off the presses. Bill me at the low price of
$1.66 each*—a 15% saving off the retail price. There are no
shipping, handling or other hidden costs. There is no minimum
number of books I must purchase. I can always return a shipment
and cancel at any time. Even if I never buy another book from
Harlequin, the 4 free novels and the surprise gift are mine to keep
forever.   116 BPR BP7S

*$1.75 in Canada plus 69¢ postage and handling per shipment.

_____
Name   (PLEASE PRINT)

_____
Address   Apt. No.

_____
City   State/Prov.   Zip/Postal Code

This offer is limited to one order per household and not valid to present
subscribers. Price is subject to change.   HR-SUB-1A